Rogue Lawman:
Border Snakes

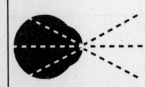

ROGUE LAWMAN: BORDER SNAKES

PETER BRANDVOLD

WHEELER PUBLISHING
A part of Gale, Cengage Learning

GALE
CENGAGE Learning

Detroit • New York • San Francisco • New Haven, Conn • Waterville, Maine • London

Copyright © 2010 by Peter Brandvold.
Wheeler Publishing, a part of Gale, Cengage Learning.

Wheeler Publishing Large Print Western.
The text of this Large Print edition is unabridged.
Other aspects of the book may vary from the original edition.
Set in 16 pt. Plantin.

LIBRARY OF CONGRESS CATALOGING-IN-PUBLICATION DATA

Brandvold, Peter.
  [Border snakes]
  Rogue lawman—border snakes / By Peter Brandvold.
    p. cm. — (Wheeler Publishing large print western)
  ISBN-13: 978-1-4104-2627-7 (alk. paper)
  ISBN-10: 1-4104-2627-0 (alk. paper)
  1. Hawk, Gideon (Fictitious character)—Fiction. 2. Large type
books. I. Title.
PS3552.R3236B63 2010
813'.54—dc22   2010003114

Published in 2010 by arrangement with The Berkley Publishing Group, a member of Penguin Group (USA) Inc.

For my sis, Stacey,
who inspired Saradee

1.
EXECUTIONER'S SONG

The man known as the Rogue Lawman thumbed open the loading gate of his big Russian horse pistol and shoved a bullet into the chamber that he normally kept empty beneath the hammer. He closed the loading gate and spun the cylinder, the clicks sounding like a low, distant scream beneath the howling wind.

Sliding the Russian into the cross-draw holster sitting high on his left hip, and angled so that the gun's grips nudged his belly, he stared ahead over the twitching ears of his grulla. The town he'd been heading for these past three days lay ahead — unpainted frame buildings and adobe-brick hovels situated among dun boulders between two rocky ridges slumped like long-dead, mineralized dinosaurs.

Blowing dust and tumbleweeds sheathed the town in a tawny gauze. No one appeared on the broad street between the twin rows of shabby buildings and stock corrals. Not even a horse was out — at least, none that Gideon Hawk could see from this distance of fifty yards. There was the caterwauling of shingle chains and the lower, more distant and intermittent clapping of an unlatched door against its frame.

A man's howl of unbound revelry reached Hawk's ears. It rose for just a moment above the howling of the wind, the screech of the rusty chains, and the clatter of the door. And then it died, leaving only the wind again, mewling over the spinelike northern ridge like the devil's demon dogs loosed from hell on a mission of bloody mischief.

Hawk tipped the brim of his black, flat-brimmed hat down low over his eyes, turned up the collar of his sheepskin coat against the chill, autumn gale, and toed the grulla forward. His head swiveled on his shoulders, eyes working back and forth across the trail, as sheds and small stables began moving up around him. He passed a sign along the trail — nothing more than two small planks nailed to a short post with the name MESILLA burned into the wood with a running iron.

Beyond the signpost the trail widened into the town's main thoroughfare.

The grulla's steady clomps were drowned

by the wind and the screeching chains. Dust, seeds, straw, and small bits of manure pelted Hawk like small-gauge buckshot. He winced against it, making out the business buildings around him, a few with high false fronts, several without. Many of the dwellings were simple frame affairs constructed of whipsawed planks that either had never been painted or had been stripped of their paint long ago by the searing, high-altitude sun of southwestern Colorado.

Among them, one building stuck out like a red dress in a funeral procession.

It was from this building that more whoops and cries of revelry came, along with the faint tinkling of a rapidly played piano. And it was toward this building — large and red and with a broad front porch sitting up high on stilts — that Hawk had started to angle when he saw a man with a rifle step out of an alley mouth on the right side of the street.

The man turned toward Hawk, froze as Hawk rode toward him, then stepped straight backward, turned, and disappeared down the alley between two shabby buildings.

Hawk angled the grulla toward the alley mouth and caught a glimpse of the rifleman just as the man slipped around the rear corner of the drugstore on Hawk's right. Hawk's jade-green eyes stared out from leathery sockets set deep in a ruggedly carved, high-cheekboned face.

It was the face of an Indian; in fact, Hawk's father had been a Ute war chief. His mother, the daughter of Norwegian immigrants. The cold eyes blinked once, and then Hawk gave a wry snort, swung his right boot over the saddle horn, and dropped smoothly out of the saddle, landing flat-footed — an oddly graceful move for a man of Hawk's large size and breadth of shoulder.

He took long strides through the alley strewn with windblown trash.

As he rounded the drugstore's rear corner, he drew the big Russian from its cross-draw holster and ratcheted back the hammer. The wind was howling too loudly back here for the man ahead of him — the man facing in the opposite direction, crouched over his rifle as he stole along the rear of the drugstore to the opposite side — to hear the ominous click.

Hawk's voice froze him. "Willie Dumas?"

The man, who was small and wiry, dressed in a shabby canvas duster and checked wool trousers, their cuffs stuffed into high-topped boots, turned around slowly. His young, whiskered cheeks lost their color, and his colorless eyes glinted fearfully when they'd taken the measure of the big, black-hatted man before him, whose face personified thunder.

"Who the hell are you?"

Hawk set his lips as he raised the Russian, dropping his chin slightly and canting his head as he aimed down the barrel. "Your executioner."

The Russian roared.

The .44-caliber round plunked through Willie Dumas's forehead, and drove the young killer straight back off his heels.

For a moment he teetered like a windmill in a high mountain gale, eyes crossing, arms thrown out to his sides. He released his rifle. A second after it hit the ground, Willie Dumas hit the ground, as well, one leg curled beneath the other.

His boots twitched and his eyes danced and his hands opened and closed as though clutching at the last remnants of his life.

Without so much as a second glance at the brigand, Hawk stepped over the near-lifeless body, turned the drugstore's far corner, and walked up the gap between the drugstore and a shabby two-story brick building to the main street. At the mouth of the gap, he stared at the big, red building on the other side of the street and up a ways, sitting alone on a weed-choked lot behind two broad front galleries — one on the first story, another on the second.

The piano could no longer be heard from inside. Just as Hawk noted this, a pistol popped behind the building's walls. A girl shrieked. A few seconds later, a man laughed and another woman yelled, her voice pitched in admonishment.

Hawk glanced to his left.

The grulla stood where he'd left it, ground-tied. The well-trained mount had moved only far enough to face downwind, and its tail blew up between its legs in the steady, sand-swirling gale.

Staring at the red building, part adobe brick and part wood, and which large letters painted across the front identified as A THOUSAND DELIGHTS SALOON AND SPORTING PARLOR, Hawk whistled. The grulla trotted over to him.

Hawk took his eyes off the sporting parlor only long enough to shuck his sixteen-shot Henry repeating rifle from his saddle scabbard. He levered a cartridge into the rifle's firing chamber, off-cocked the hammer, and set the rifle atop his right shoulder, his black-gloved hand wrapped around the neck of the rifle's stock.

Taking his customary long, confident strides, black hat tipped low, Hawk angled across the street to the sporting parlor. He mounted the front steps, crossed the broad front porch, and pushed through one of the two stout wooden doors adorned with brass knockers in the shapes of naked women.

As he stepped inside, a pretty brunette in a long, red dress was admonishing a man sitting on a brocade sofa with a little, scantily clad blonde for discharging firearms on the premises. The man — bearded, wearing a checked shirt, and with a battered Stetson tipped back off his forehead — was telling the woman she ought not to have rats on her premises if she didn't "want men discharging guns at 'em." The pistol in his hand was still smoking.

The argument died unresolved as all eyes in the room, including those of the arguers, turned toward the newcomer just now shutting the door on the cold wind.

Hawk let his eyes rake the room quickly, taking in the ornate furnishings, which included varnished tables, richly upholstered chairs and fainting couches with here and there a flimsy privacy screen and heavy, elegant drapes hung across shadowy alcoves. There were potted palms and ferns hanging from ceiling beams.

A fire popped in a large hearth in the room's right wall, smoke billowing when the wind gusted down the chimney. A long, mahogany bar with a mirrored back bar ran across the room's rear, beneath a second-story balcony and flanked by a carpeted staircase. In the bright light of lanterns, candles, and leaping flames, the glasses pyramided on the bar and stacked on the shelves behind it gleamed like jewels.

A man stood behind the bar, filling three shot glasses while a girl with a serving tray waited. The girl had turned to glance over a bare shoulder at Hawk. The bartender regarded him from beneath bushy black brows.

The piano had stopped when Hawk had walked in.

Now he strode toward the bar, following a path between the tables, his rifle on a shoulder and his boots clomping loudly upon the scarred puncheons. The piano player — a lean old gent in a top hat — began playing again, with less vigor than before. Most of the heads in the room swiveled to follow Hawk to the bar.

There were seven men visible, he half-consciously counted. Four were playing cards at a table while the other three were scattered about the room. All were with

14

women. They all bore the faces of human wolves. Several Hawk recognized from wanted dodgers.

As the serving girl removed her tray from the bar top and shambled off to the table at which the cardplayers sat in sudden, moody silence, Hawk laid his rifle on the bar and said, "Bourbon."

The barman likely doubled as a bouncer. He was nearly as tall and broad-shouldered as Hawk. His left brow and his nose were badly scarred. As he reached under the bar for a bottle, Hawk said, "I'll take the good stuff — not what you've been serving these border snakes. Been a long trail."

The bartender arched a brow at the pretty brunette who'd been reading the riot act to the man who'd discharged his pistol. In the back bar mirror, Hawk saw the woman dip her dimpled chin. The barman lifted a labeled bottle from beneath the bar, swept a glass off the pyramid to his left, and filled it.

Hawk tossed a half eagle on the bar. "Leave the bottle."

The piano spoke a little louder, and voices sounded behind Hawk as a couple of conversations resumed. He could see in the mirror that the four cardplayers had continued their game, albeit haltingly and continuing to cast skeptical glances toward the rangy, rifle-packing newcomer at the bar.

Hawk threw back half his drink. A girl who had been sitting alone and looking bored near the fireplace got up and strolled over to him, resting one elbow atop the bar. She was a willowy honey blonde with pale blue eyes and a sharp nose, wearing a dress of pink taffeta. What there was of it. Her white shoulders were bare, as was most of her cleavage. A black choker encircled her thin neck.

"Need someone to talk to, stranger?" She had a nice voice, vaguely accented.

"Get away from him, Clara!" a man grumbled behind Hawk.

Boots thudded on the brothel's wood floor.

Hawk had already watched in the back bar mirror the hard case who'd discharged his weapon rise from the fainting couch where he'd been sitting between a black girl and a redhead. Now the man, his thumbs hooked behind his cartridge belt, sauntered up to the bar, gimlet eyes on Hawk.

"Why should I?" Clara said. "You already got you a girl, Laramie. Two of 'em!"

"I said, git!" Laramie snarled, grabbing the girl's arm and swinging her back away from the bar. Clara glared at the hard case

16

but retreated to her chair near the fire.

The pretty brunette, whom Hawk assumed ran the place, watched Hawk and Laramie from the shadows near a ceiling joist, frowning cautiously.

Laramie, standing in the same position as that of the girl a moment ago, one elbow resting on the bar, looked at Hawk. The Rogue Lawman lifted his shot glass and tossed back the rest of his drink.

"Who are you, mister?" Laramie asked slowly.

He was lean and saturnine, with a black hat and a short, coyote-hide jacket. He wore two pistols on his lean hips, and the handle of another in a shoulder rig peeked out from behind a flap of his open jacket. He had a small, hand-rolled quirley wedged between the first two fingers of his left hand, and the smoke from the cigarette curled up between him and Hawk.

Hawk refilled his shot glass. "You ask too many questions, friend."

"That's the only one I've asked."

"That's one too many."

Laramie's eyes flickered faintly. A corner of his mouth quirked up as he glanced at the men behind him.

At the same time, the piano player stopped playing, lifting his old, clawlike hands from the keys and turning around to face the bar, sensing the menace as he scowled dreadfully behind his steel-framed spectacles.

2.
BEWARE THE PREACHER'S PIG

"Come on, friend," Laramie prodded Hawk, feigning a grin. "There's no secrets in A Thousand Delights. We'll tell you who we are, if you tell us who you are. Now, that's fair, ain't it?"

Hawk sipped his second whiskey shot. He nodded thoughtfully, set the shot glass back down on the bar, then turned to Laramie.

"Well, since you asked so damn nice, and since I know who you are, Blaxton, and since I know who all your men are — most of 'em, anyway — I reckon it's only fair that I tell you that I tracked you over from Trinidad, after your third bank robbery in as many days, and that I'm here to kill every last one of you yellow-livered privy rats. Just as dead as I killed your picket, Willie Dumas, in an alley across the street."

Laramie Blaxton's grin faded. His face darkened, an eye narrowed, and an incredulous cast entered his gaze. "You . . . you

19

think you're gonna kill *all* of us?"

"That's right," Hawk said matter-of-factly.

A hush fell over the room. It was like a held breath. Laramie Blaxton leaned against the bar and stared up at Hawk, who was a good four inches taller than the outlaw leader. Suddenly, recognition slackened the muscles in the outlaw's raptor-like face.

"Well, Gideon Henry-goddamned-Hawk," he said in bemused awe and genuine surprise. "Fellas," he said to the room while keeping his eyes on Hawk, "look who we been so honored to have shadowin' our trail. The Rogue Lawman his ownself!"

The wolflike faces stared at Hawk, expressionless.

The four poker players were holding their cards tensely. One chomped down hard on the fat stogy wedged in a corner of his mouth. The pretty brunette who ran the place stood stiffly where she'd been standing before, her wide brown eyes wary, skeptical. She didn't realize it, but she saved Hawk's life when she lifted her gaze toward the balcony over the bar.

Hawk grabbed the Henry off the bar top and, thumbing back the hammer, took two quick strides past Blaxton. He'd only taken one, however, before a rifle barked above the bar.

The bullet cut the air just off Hawk's left shoulder and made a wet cracking sound as it tore through the crown of Blaxton's hat. The outlaw leader didn't make a sound as his head bobbed suddenly, violently, and he staggered forward, arms hanging slack at his sides.

A girl in the room screamed. An outlaw shouted.

Hawk looked up, pressing the stock of his Henry against his right shoulder and raising the barrel. The man who'd just killed Blaxton stood in balbriggans and socks atop the balcony, a battered sombrero on his head, looking down with a shocked expression at the result of his errant shot. His rifle barrel dangled over the rail, smoke dribbling from its octagonal maw.

Hawk planted a bead on the outlaw's wrinkled, sunburned forehead, and just as the man jerked his eyes toward the Henry's barrel, Hawk squeezed the trigger. A ragged, quarter-sized hole appeared just above and a little left of the man's exasperated eyes.

The man screamed as his head jerked back. His knees buckled. As he fell, he began pulling his rifle back behind the rail. The stock got caught, and he released it.

The rifle tumbled straight down and smashed against the bar top. The man himself slumped back against the balcony's spooled rail as though he figured he'd just sit there and collect his thoughts for a while.

"Good God almighty!" the bartender bellowed, backing against the shelves of the back bar and holding his hands up around his head as if to shield himself from bullets.

As the echo of Hawk's blast chased itself around the building's adobe-brick walls, Hawk levered a fresh cartridge into the Henry's firing chamber and pivoted toward the room behind him.

Less than five seconds had elapsed since Hawk had seen the pretty brunette's eyes lift toward the balcony, but all seven of the hard cases in the saloon hall were on the move. The poker table looked as though a stick of dynamite had been detonated beneath it; as the four players leapt to their feet, the table shot straight up in the air, and the four whores that had been hovering close to the gamblers flew back from around the men in a blur of swirling hair and dancing dresses, their screams rising shrilly.

Bottles and glasses crashed to the floor.

"Git that son of a bitch!" one of the gamblers shouted, lifting a baby LeMat in one hand and a brass-chased Colt Navy in the other.

Calmly, without expression, as though he were merely plinking cans off fence posts,

22

Hawk drew a bead on him and shattered his breastbone.

Screaming as the bullet exited his body under his left arm and shattered a bracket lamp on the post beside him, the man fired both pistols into the still-jouncing table. As the man stumbled backward, leaking blood badly, Hawk smoothly ejected the spent cartridge from his Henry's chamber, seated fresh, and lined his sights up on another cardplayer just as his target triggered a black-barreled Colt, the slug of which curled the air off Hawk's left cheek and crashed into the mirror behind him.

K-chow!

Hawk's finely tuned and regularly cleaned and oiled Henry leapt in the Rogue Lawman's hands. In his haste, however, he hadn't gotten a clear picture of his jerking target, and the slug hammered off the man's Colt, ripped through the face of the man standing three feet to the hard case's right, and tore into the ceiling with an angry bark.

Both men screamed.

The one with the damaged gun dropped the weapon like molten iron while the one with gaping holes in both cheeks staggered back two herky-jerky steps, eyes wide as saucers, and swung his Sheriff's model Colt toward Hawk, who shot him a second time

— this time on purpose and this time for keeps.

But not before the man's own slug sliced a burning line across one of Hawk's right-side ribs. It was a sting like that of an angry wasp.

Hawk's narrowly focused mind only vaguely registered the nip. He was too busy levering and firing, levering and firing, seeing smoke puffs from the pistols aimed at him, hearing the barks and the screeches of the bullets careening around him and thumping into the bar or the back bar mirror or annihilating the pyramid of neatly stacked shot glasses to his right.

Like a man possessed, he dispatched one outlaw after another as he stood before the bar, sidewise to the room, boots spread a little more than shoulder-width apart. Only his pivoting hips and his hands moved, sliding the rifle this way and that in his arms.

In the roughly twelve seconds it took him to cut each of the gun wolves down and to set them howling like banshees over a fresh kill — those that did not die instantly, that was — Hawk never blinked. If anyone were watching his face — and no one was, as everyone in the room was either shooting or dying or lying facedown on the floor with her arms over her head, wailing — he or she might have seen the right side of Hawk's long mouth quirk with a faintly amused, bemused, exhilarated grin.

Hawk levered a fresh round but froze his trigger finger as he aimed the Henry's long, octagonal barrel through the wafting powder smoke. He looked for movement but saw nothing but the smoke itself.

A funereal silence fell over the room. A silence so heavy that only the snapping of the fire in the hearth penetrated with an eerie, stubborn indifference.

After a few stretched seconds, the silence was compromised by a man's grunt.

Then a groan.

Hawk spied movement through the shifting smoke cloud, somewhere behind an overturned chair and a small table, near a still-standing palm. A head took shape in the weirdly lighted smoke. It shifted this way and that as a man tried to gain his feet.

Hawk drew a bead on the head — just a pale oval beneath a line of black hair. He fired, the Henry speaking again loudly. The bullet plunked into one of the front doors with a sharp, wooden thud.

The head still moved. Hawk fired again.

"Ohh!" the man said, stumbling backward and hitting the floor with a hollow boom.

Hawk didn't bother ejecting the spent

cartridge. He lowered the Henry and, having unconsciously counted his shots and knowing he'd capped all sixteen as well as the one he'd had in the breech at the start of the dance, set the long gun on the bar.

He pulled his silver-plated Russian from the cross-draw holster on his left hip. He slipped his long-barreled, horn-gripped Colt Army from his second holster thonged on his right thigh. Thumbing both hammers back, he strode slowly forward, swinging the guns around, looking for movement out of any of the quarry he'd dispatched.

The whores lay groaning or wailing. All but the pretty brunette, that was. She sat with her back to the ceiling joist she'd been standing in front of earlier.

She had her knees up, her hands on them. Her fine-boned cheeks were pale and her sherry-brown eyes were dark as she studied Hawk in pensive silence. Anger and exasperation were in those eyes, both emotions tempered by hushed amazement.

Six of the outlaws were down and unmoving and, judging by the amount of blood they were spilling, were pounding on hell's gates. The seventh, however, staggered to a half crouch just as Hawk reached the front of the room.

"Murderin' *devil!*" the man roared as he

lifted a snub-nosed revolver in his left fist, his long, brown hair hanging over his face like a tattered screen.

Hawk killed him easily with a round from his Colt. The man wailed again and triggered his empty pistol at the floor, the ping of the hammer ringing like a cracked bell, and flew backward through a window. When the scream of the breaking glass had died, it was replaced by the howling of the wind outside.

Beneath the wind, Hawk heard the scrape of a boot somewhere above the brothel's main saloon hall. Holding both smoking revolvers barrel up, and keeping the brunt of his attention on the balcony obscured by gun smoke above the bullet-riddled bar, he made his way to the back of the room.

The barman inched his head above the bar top. He had glass in his hair. His eyes were dark.

"What in tarnation?" he said in hushed awe, sliding his incredulous gaze from Hawk to the smoky room.

Hawk started up the narrow stairs, taking one slow step at a time, his own spurs ringing softly on the thick, red carpet. When he was halfway to the top, a face took shape in the shadows ahead. A rifle barrel glinted in the room's wan light. The rifleman bolted forward, to the edge of the stairs, bellowing maniacally and angling the rifle down toward Hawk.

The Rogue Lawman extended both revolvers at the same time.

Both guns spoke simultaneously, punching twin holes into the rifleman's bare chest. Smoke and flames geysered from the rifle's maw, the bullet clipping the railing to Hawk's left.

The rifle dropped to the floor and slid down the stairs as the shooter, clad in only lye-yellowed underwear bottoms, fell to his knees. He gave Hawk a blank stare, then, lids slowly closing over his eyes, he sagged forward, turned a somersault, and continued turning them until he'd piled up atop his rifle at the bottom of the stairs.

Hawk stared up at the balcony.

Spying no movement among the smoky shadows shunted this way and that by wan candlelight from somewhere down a dingy hall, he continued climbing the steps. Slowly, he continued across the balcony into a hall that smelled of sex, smoke, and spilled liquor. He set his boots down carefully, but still the floorboards creaked faintly beneath the musty carpet runner.

Rough-timbered doors stood closed on either side of the hall, the walls of which were constructed of low-grade pine planks. When he was halfway between the stairs and the hall's end, a door opened suddenly at the end of the hall on the left.

Hawk crouched, extending both pistols.

A figure bolted out the open door and across the hall so quickly, disappearing in a blur down an intersecting hall, that Hawk had no time to get a shot off. Hearing boots clomping away from him, he bolted forward, then slowed when he reached the open door from which the man had fled.

Sour air emanated from the dim, cluttered room. Just beyond the open door, a slender Indian girl sat at the edge of a rumpled bed, long hair hanging straight down the sides of her dark-eyed face. She was naked but did nothing to cover herself. Her breasts were small and pear-shaped, with dark brown nipples. As Hawk peered into the room, looking for other gunmen, the girl shook her hair from her eyes and lifted a long, black cheroot to her lips.

The cheroot's coal glowed as she took a long drag and leaned back on one out-stretched arm, regarding Hawk without expression.

Hawk swung away from her, quickly trod the ten feet to a dark, rickety back stairs, and ran down three steps at a time. At the bottom of the steps, an unlatched outside door banged against the building's outside wall in the moaning wind. Hawk bolted through it and slid both cocked pistols around in front of him.

Straight out from the brothel's back door, a man ran toward the brown, rocky ridge rising in the south. He wore baggy denims and a battered Stetson, and his cartridge belt was draped over his left shoulder. The flaps of his unbuttoned shirt blew behind him in the wind.

Beneath the wind, Hawk could hear the soft trills of his hammering spurs.

Hawk fired two quick shots. Dust puffed around the man's scissoring boots. He leapt with a start, but Hawk didn't think he'd hit him.

He lunged forward, running, his own spurs lifting a raucous clatter.

Ahead of the running man lay a rickety-looking brick shack, with a wooden stable off the left side. The stable was enclosed by a dilapidated board fence around which sage and scrub willows grew thick. A sign was nailed to the front of the fence, but Hawk couldn't read it from this distance.

The fleeing outlaw slowed his pace near the shack, then slithered through the fence, losing his hat in the process. As the hat bounced and tumbled away with the sand and tumbleweeds and flying trash on the chill wind, the cutthroat drew his head back inside the fence, then stuck a pistol out between the slats.

Smoke puffed from the gun's barrel.

It was followed a quarter second later by a hollow crack that was quickly snuffed by the wind. The bullet chewed into the ground several feet from Hawk's pounding boots.

Hawk stopped and raised both his pistols. He was about to squeeze the triggers when a bizarre squeal rose from the behind the fence.

There was the almost inaudible drumming of fast-moving hooves, and then the shooter loosed a scream that tightened the skin between Hawk's shoulders. He held fire, staring over the barrels of his leveled guns and into the pen from which the screams of the man now rose with the shrill, savage mewls of an enraged pig.

Hawk could see little from this distance and angle. But between the slats of the fence he caught glimpses of frenzied movement and occasional splashes of dull color — the man's white shirt, blue denim trousers, and the pig's pink, mottled-black hide with a little curl of tail rising up from its broad ass.

Hawk strode forward.

The pig's frenzied squeals steadily grew louder while those of the man dwindled, became higher, thinner, more pleading and intermittent.

By the time Hawk got up to the fence, the man's cries had died entirely, and Hawk saw why. The pig had him down on his back, unmoving, the man's arms flung above his shoulders.

His torso was drenched in blood. The pig's head, also painted scarlet, thrashed violently from side to side as it dug into the man's belly with its broad, square snout and snapping teeth.

Hawk depressed his gun hammers as he lowered both weapons. He stepped back to read the sign hanging from the fence's top rail by a rusty nail — just a two-foot-by-one-foot scrap of hand-painted lumber: BEWARE THE PREACHER'S PIG.

Hawk holstered his weapons and peered once more into the pen. The pig was still busily slashing and tearing at the bloody corpse, jerking and dragging the body around violently.

Hawk turned, pulled his hat down tight, and started back to the brothel, squinting against the swirling, wind-churned grit. "Should've learned how to read, friend."

3.
MRS. PARKER

Hawk strode around the front of the building to take a gander at the town in the wake of the dustup in A Thousand Delights.

From the high front porch, he saw his horse standing where he'd left it, facing downwind. A couple of boys in wool coats and cloth caps were milling around the front of the brothel, eyeing with morbid fascination the dead man lying in a pile of bloodsplashed broken glass near Hawk's boots. Hawk flipped them each a quarter to stable, feed, and curry his horse, as well as to fetch his saddlebags, and they ran delightedly down the street, shoving the quarters into the pockets of their patched, wash-worn trousers.

They were the only people he could see in the windblown dust, but as he turned to reenter the brothel, he glimpsed movement farther down the street and stopped for a closer look.

Three men were moving toward him out of the dust haze. They all carried rifles. They all wore long coats, hats pulled down low on their foreheads. As they came closer, glancing at the lone horse on the side of the street and which the two boys were approaching now, one reaching for the reins, the other the bridle, Hawk saw badges glinting dully on their coat lapels.

He smiled and went into the brothel.

The pretty brunette stood near the door, looking around. The only other person in the room now — living person, that was — was the bartender kneeling beside one of the bloody, staring corpses. He was grunting and bunching his lips as he wrenched a ring off a lifeless middle finger.

Hawk closed the door and started past the woman. Girl or woman — it was hard to tell. She seemed neither old nor young though obviously older than the sporting girls Hawk had seen earlier. Her figure was full, almost fleshy in the hips. Her eyes were dark with faint red lights in them, and her face was heart-shaped, the nose small and straight, the lips long and plump. Her skin bore no age wrinkles that Hawk could see, not even around her eyes. It was the bold directness of the eyes themselves that betrayed her maturity.

"You did a wonderful job here, mister," she said with an ever-so-slight Southern accent. "And who do you think's going to clean up this mess and pay for the damage?"

Hawk stopped in front of her but glanced at the bartender. "The apron has the right idea. The Stony Hills Bunch are wealthy men — if you can catch them early enough after a robbery. Let them pay for it." Hawk pulled a wallet from an inside pocket of his fleece-lined buckskin mackinaw and peeled off five hundred-dollar bills. "But just so there's no hard feelin's. . . ."

He stuffed the bills down into the deep, warm cleavage revealed by her bloodred whalebone corset. Her eyes sparkled, and color rose in her cheeks.

She parted her lips slightly as if to speak, but said nothing as Hawk turned away from her and strode down the long room, stepping around overturned chairs and tables and over a couple of bodies. He scooped his empty rifle off the table he'd laid it on and set it on his shoulder.

Amazingly, his whiskey bottle was the only thing around the bar that hadn't been hit in the firestorm. He grabbed the bottle and his glass, picked up a chair, set it before a table that had only two bullet holes in it, and sat down. Sitting back in his chair, he tripped the Henry's loading tube free of the stock and filled it with shells from his cartridge belt.

When he had sixteen in the tube, he racked one into the chamber, off-cocked the hammer, then shoved one more cartridge into the tube before sliding the tube back up into the stock. Setting the rifle on the table before him, Hawk popped the cork from the whiskey bottle and splashed whiskey into his shot glass.

He looked up when the door squawked open and three men filed in — the three lawmen he'd seen heading toward the brothel. The brunette was picking up a chair, but now she turned to the door with a cool, ironic expression on her pretty, heart-shaped face.

"Why, Sheriff Wiley — what a surprise. The shooting's over, but you can help me clean up, if you like."

The man who'd first walked in the door and who now stood at the front of the room, roughly flanked by the other two men, looked across the carnage toward Hawk but spoke out the side of his mouth at the woman to his left: "Dewey Wainwright reported a disturbance. Shootin' disturbance. Me and the boys was waitin' out the storm in the jailhouse. Didn't hear a thing."

The sheriff was a tall, blond man with a brick-red, clean-shaven face and broad nose. He set the butt of his Winchester on one hip, his gloved fist on the other, spreading the flaps of his duster wide, and looked around the room, whistling. "I'll be damned." He canted his head at Hawk. "That the perpetrator of this hoedown?"

The brunette, inspecting a bullet hole in a brocade-upholstered chair, narrowed an eye at Sheriff Wiley. "Well, I didn't do it."

Wiley gave a caustic chuff as he started walking toward Hawk, keeping his rifle on his hip, the barrel aimed at the ceiling.

"For what it's worth," the brunette said to his back, "they started it."

Wiley slowed his step for a second before continuing toward Hawk's table. He glanced at the barman, who was dragging one of the dead men outside by his stockinged feet — he'd removed the man's boots and set them with the rest of his loot on a bloodied fainting couch — and glanced at his deputies, "Louis, Joe — give Ingram a hand."

He stared at Hawk, who held the stare, as he crossed the room. Stopping a few feet from Hawk's table, he glanced at Hawk's Henry and narrowed one eye.

"Why don't you slide that rifle a little

37

farther across the table?" he growled. "And to the left. Your left."

Hawk leaned forward and, with his left hand, slowly slid the rifle in the direction the sheriff had ordered. "How's that?"

"That'll do just fine . . . long as you keep both hands where I can see 'em."

"All right." Hawk lifted his shot glass and looked at the dead man slumped in front of the bar to his left. "That there is Laramie Blaxton. Lead rider of the Stony Hills Bunch out of Wyoming. Robbed two banks in the Texas Panhandle last week, another in New Mexico, just north of Taos, last Saturday. Four townsfolk killed. And, like the lady said" — Hawk glanced at the brunette, who was holding the door open while the two deputies carried another dead man outside — "they busted the first cap here today."

The sheriff narrowed his eye again at Hawk. "Who are you?"

Hawk ignored the question. "If you look through your files, you'll likely find paper on 'em. A sizeable reward for each. I'd like for the lady to have it."

The woman looked at Hawk as she closed the door on the gritty, gnawing wind.

"Right neighborly," the sheriff said. "You a lawman?"

Hawk's eyes flickered. He glanced at the woman, who now walked past him to the bar. He threw back the last of the whiskey in his glass and set the glass on the table. "Some would say so. Some might have a bone to pick."

"What the hell kind of an answer is that?"

"The only one I got."

"How 'bout a name? You got one of those, don't you?"

"Yep." Hawk was slowly turning his glass around between thick, brown fingers on the table, and his lips were forming a cryptic half smile.

Wiley's red face turned redder, and his broad, pitted nostrils flared with exasperation. "You want me to guess? Or maybe I'll just throw you in the lockup till I can find out who you are my own self."

Hawk lifted his eyes from his glass. "Gideon Hawk."

The sheriff held his gaze before glancing at Hawk's rifle on the table, as though it had suddenly transformed into a coiled rattlesnake. His eyes returning to Hawk's, he grunted, "No shit?"

"No shit."

Wiley's eyes flicked across Hawk's rifle once more.

Hawk stared up at him, that ambiguous

half grin quirking a corner of his mouth. "I know what you're thinking, Sheriff — take down the crazy Rogue Lawman and maybe get promoted to mayor or even U.S. marshal. But the only name you'll make for yourself will be chiseled on a tombstone."

Wiley continued holding Hawk's gaze, his own eyes widening ever so slightly, anxiously, while a vein in his temple expanded and contracted.

"Don't do it, Day," warned the woman behind the bar. "You didn't see him shoot, but look around."

Wiley glanced at her, the skin above the bridge of his nose wrinkling. He flexed his fingers around the stock of the rifle still snugged against his hip, then gave a startled jerk as the saloon door opened behind him. He tossed a quick glance over his shoulder to see his two deputies and the bartender file back into the saloon, all three wearing owly looks, blood staining their clothes.

As they looked around grimly, trying to decide which stiff to haul out next, Wiley returned his frustrated gaze to Hawk and kept his voice low and taut. "Come sunup tomorrow, you make yourself scarce. You hear me, mister?"

Hawk saw no reason to argue. The man was just trying to do his job, keep a little self-respect. "Whatever you say, Sheriff."

Wiley flexed his fingers on his rifle again, seemingly regaining some confidence, and shifted his weight from one foot to the other. "And we got a law here against the dischargin' of firearms inside the town limits."

Hawk splashed more liquor into his glass. "Now you tell me."

Wiley's nostrils flared. He glanced once more at the woman behind the bar, then wheeled and strode back to the front of the room. He opened the door, and the wind nearly blew his hat off as he ducked into it, and instead of holding it open for his deputies who were half carrying, half dragging another dead man toward it, he pulled the door closed behind him.

Hawk threw back his whiskey shot, grabbed the bottle in one hand, his rifle in the other, and heaved himself to his feet with a low, weary groan. He turned toward the stairs, glancing at the woman, who'd started sweeping the floor behind the bar.

She returned the glance. "You always make so many friends?"

Hawk hiked a shoulder and started up the stairs. "Does it matter which room I take?"

"Take any one of theirs you want," she said, tossing a glance across the disheveled room. "The girls' rooms aren't numbered."

"Obliged."

He was halfway up the stairs when he stopped again. "You got a kitchen?"

The woman stopped sweeping again and nodded.

"Send me up a plate. I'll pay for the service."

"Anything else?"

"A girl."

The woman nodded. "Got a preference? Blonde or — ?"

Hawk looked at her quickly, angrily. "Not a blonde!" His voice echoed around the room. The woman gave a slight start, and the bartender, going through the pockets of another cadaver, looked up at Hawk in surprise.

"Not a blonde," Hawk repeated, more quietly, looking at the stairs again as he resumed climbing. "Anything else."

Hawk stepped over the dead man in the upstairs hall and pushed open the door of the room just beyond him. There was a saddle on the floor and an open war bag on the dresser. The bed was rumpled, obviously having been slept in, but Hawk didn't care. With the barrel of his Henry, he nudged the war bag onto the floor beside the rifle, then set his own rifle against the dresser, and sagged down on the edge of the bed.

He gave a long, weary sigh, doffing his hat, letting it fall to the floor and running his hands through his thick, dark brown hair that curled over his ears and his shirt collar and that was faintly streaked with gray. He leaned forward, set his elbows on his hips, and continued to scrub brusquely at his scalp as if to ease the hard tension knots in his skull and in the back of his bull neck.

As if to obliterate the echoes of the dead men's screams in his ears and to erase the images of bloody murder that danced around behind his eyes like snippets from a thousand waking nightmares. . . .

Always it was like this after a "job," as he called his unsanctioned hunts. A day or two, maybe even a week or two of self-recrimination, isolation, depression. A free fall into an abyss darker than the remotest regions of outer space. Into a world without sound, without color, without taste save the coppery taste of blood, without smell except the sweet, cloying odor of burned powder and death.

No sounds but his own remembered screams as he'd ridden up a hill in the driving rain trying to reach his son's hanging body while there was still a flicker of life left in it.

Worst of all was the knowing that no matter how many men he tracked and killed, his wife and son would still be dead. And that he would not, could not, stop tracking and killing — even though he'd tracked and killed those responsible for the murder of his family — because it was the only thing that tempered the images in his mind's eye of his young son's corpse hanging from that cottonwood atop that Nebraska hill in that hammering rainstorm, and the overexposed photograph image of his pretty blond wife hanging from another cottonwood in Hawk's own backyard.

Linda's blue, sorrow-racked eyes wide and staring.

Images of death replaced by more death. . . .

Of course, it didn't make sense. But in a world where little made sense, hunting outlaws that other lawmen had given up on or were afraid of made as much sense as anything else.

He was glad when a knock on his door plucked him for the moment from his morbid dwellings. The two boys he'd sent to unsaddle his horse stood in the dim hall. They'd brought his saddlebags and his supper — a steaming plate of beef stew and a schooner of frothy beer.

Hawk tipped the boys, tossed his saddlebags onto the bed, and ate hungrily, washing the stew down with the beer. He'd finished and was taking a sponge bath at the washstand when another knock brought him, bare-chested, wearing only his balbriggan bottoms and socks, a cocked revolver in his hand, to the door.

He opened it.

The brunette stood in the hall before the door.

Her hair was down, splayed across her naked shoulders. For a time she didn't say anything but just stood in the open doorway, staring at Hawk's broad chest and flat belly, both of which, bearing the grisly white knots of a dozen bullet and knife scars, were like a contour map of these past few savage years.

Finally, she lifted her eyes to his and arched a brow. Her eyes said nothing, but a faint, pink blush rose in her cheeks. "You said you didn't want a blonde."

Hawk studied her with barely concealed bemusement. Finally, he nodded. "You got a name?"

"Folks around here call me Mrs. Parker."

Hawk stared at her.

45

"My husband's on boot hill," she said.

The half smile faded from Hawk's rugged features. He drew the door wider and stepped back. "Come in, Mrs. Parker."

4.
ROSE WATER AND TALCUM

Hawk closed the door, set his revolver on the dresser, and moved toward the woman standing before him.

Her hair was slightly damp from a recent bath, and she smelled faintly of rose water and talcum. She wasn't wearing the frilly, corseted affair she'd been wearing earlier, but a sheer, sky-blue wrapper over a nightgown of lighter blue. The gown was sleeveless and low cut, and it revealed nearly all of her cleavage while clinging alluringly to the full swell of her heavy breasts.

She frowned as Hawk moved toward her. Her eyes dropped to his belly then slightly lower — and apprehension flashed in her red-brown eyes as she stepped backward.

"Wait."

Hawk grabbed her arms and drew her toward him. "No. There's no waiting." A muscle beneath his right eye twitched, and his green eyes blazed like agates set in tarnished copper. "If you wanted a gentleman this evening, you came to the wrong room. What I need, I need now."

She looked up at him. Her lips parted slightly. Her breasts swelled and she nodded.

Hawk leaned forward and kissed her. At first she was stiff in his arms, but gradually her body relaxed, and she wrapped her arms around his neck and rose up on her toes to return his kiss.

Kissing her, he lifted her hair in his hands, then set his hands atop her naked shoulders and slid the straps of her nightgown down her arms. It and the wrapper fell with a sibilant whisper, and then she was naked and supple in his firm embrace, running her hands across his shoulders and pressing her breasts against his chest.

Finally, he pulled back away from her. Reluctantly, she let him go and stood, her chest rising and falling sharply, staring at him from between the mussed tresses of her hair framing her face as she crossed her arms beneath her breasts. Chicken flesh rose on her arms.

Hawk tossed his head toward the bed. He slid his fingers behind the waistband of his balbriggans, and slipped the wash-worn garment down his legs.

The woman turned to the bed, brusquely threw the covers back, and crawled in. Her heavy breasts, with their large, dark rosettes, sloped toward the mattress, the nipples pebbled. She flattened her left hand on her rising and falling belly, and when he came to her, his manhood jutting, she took it in her hand. She rolled onto her back, spread her legs, lifted her knees, and guided him without further ado inside her.

Hawk grabbed the spools of the bed's headboard and, propped on his elbows, thrust his pelvis against hers. She groaned, threw her head back on the pillow, and ground her fingers into his buttocks as her bent knees flapped like wings, and the bed shuddered and creaked like a sloop on choppy seas.

"Oh," she said breathily. "Oh . . . Christ. . . ."

The first time, Hawk took his pleasure quickly, almost violently, and without apology. The second time was slower, less desperate, and while he held her hips in his hands and ground against her from behind, she tossed her hair back from her shoulders so that it slid in rich, brown cascades across her curving, creamy back. It dropped all the way to her full, sweat-glossy rump when she lifted her head and arched her back and moaned loudly, half laughing, half sobbing, at the height of her passion.

Himself spent, Hawk pulled away from her and leaned back against the headboard, stretching his long, lean, muscled legs down the length of the rumpled bed, and crossed his ankles. Sweat shone on him. His flat belly, taut as braided rawhide, rose and fell as he breathed. He fingered his shaggy hair back from his face and reached for his tobacco makings on the small table beside the bed.

As he built a smoke, Mrs. Parker rolled toward him, throwing an arm across his waist and staring up at him wonderingly, her cheeks still flushed from their coupling. "You're a man of many talents, Mr. Hawk. I don't normally entertain, but you're making me think I should start to on a regular basis."

Hawk glanced over the cigarette paper at her.

She laughed at his stoicism and shook her head, ran the first two fingers of her right hand down the center of his chest. "Why are you giving me all that money?"

"I don't need it."

"Who doesn't need money?"

Hawk held the open cigarette paper with its line of tobacco in one hand. He took the tie strings of his makings sack in the other hand, gave them a jerk to close the bag, then swung the sack back onto the nightstand. "Me, I reckon. I only need enough to get me from here to there."

"Between killings?"

"That's right."

She narrowed an eye at him. "Why?"

He twisted the cylinder closed and stuck it in his mouth to seal it. "It's what I do."

"Just born nasty, huh?"

"I reckon."

She lowered her eyes to her fingers, absently playing with a curl of the dark brown hair on his belly. Hawk fired the quirley with a match from the night table and exhaled smoke from his nostrils, setting the spent match on the table. "What's Mr. Parker doin' on boot hill?"

"Fell into the wrong crowd after we came out here from Tennessee." She kept her eyes on Hawk's belly, an oblique smile quirking her lips. "We'd settled on a ranch, was out there about a year before he got restless. Chet came from rough stock around Chattanooga. Robbed a mercantile and got shot by a posse up from Alamosa. Deserved it, as he killed a shopkeeper and wounded a deputy town marshal." She sighed. "He'd found a little gold on our claim, and I used it to put a down payment on this place. At least he gave me that much."

"You come up with the name?"

"A Thousand Delights?" She laughed. "That's what Chet used to call me."

Hawk took a deep drag off the quirley. The wind had died after the sun had gone down, and it was so quiet in the room that he could hear his cigarette burning.

She looked up at him. "You really that Rogue Lawman Laramie was talking about?"

Hawk snorted. "I'd just as soon that didn't get spread around."

"Oh, don't worry. I think with men like Day Wiley running around with badges cut out of peach tins on their vests, we need more of you, though . . . uh . . . not in my place." Mrs. Parker chuckled, then narrowed an eye at him. "What happened to make you so good at killing?"

Hawk looked at the smoking coal of his quirley, and his jaws tightened slightly. "Watching a guilty man walk away from a murder charge because a county prosecutor got him off on a loose stitch in the law."

"Who'd he murder?"

"My son."

Mrs. Parker scowled. "I'm sorry." She looked away. "How'd your wife take it?"

"Not too well," Hawk said. "She hanged herself."

Mrs. Parker stared at the wall on the far side of the bed. "I see." After a time, she dropped her legs to the floor and began to push herself to her feet. "It's been nice knowing you, Mr. Hawk. Safe travels to —"

Hawk touched her arm. "You in a hurry?"

She looked at him across her shoulder, shook her head. She leaned down and kissed his belly, then farther down. "For you, Mr. Hawk, I got all night."

Before he'd even realized why, Hawk's Russian was in his hand and cocked. He was sitting up. Mrs. Parker groaned beside him but continued sleeping.

Just outside the door of Hawk's room, which was revealed by bright morning light pushing through the two sashed windows, a floorboard creaked. A shadow moved under the door. Quickly but soundlessly, Hawk threw the blankets back and bounded out of bed. Two long strides, and he was at the door.

He set his hand on the knob, turned it, and threw the door wide.

"Whoa!" the man standing on the other side of the threshold said, but not before Hawk had grabbed the collar of the man's duster and swiveled his hips. Kicking out his right leg, he jerked the man toward him, and the man gave another cry as he stumbled forward, hit the floor of the room on both knees, twisted around, and piled up against the washstand.

On the bed, Mrs. Parker awakened with a clipped scream and drew the blankets up to cover her breasts, her sleep-mussed hair in her eyes.

Hawk set his bare right foot on the man's holstered six-shooter and aimed his Russian at Sheriff Day Wiley's scowling, tomato-red face as the man squeezed his eyes closed and raised a defensive hand, "Don't shoot, fer chrissakes! Don't shoot me, goddamnit!"

"What the hell're you doing, lurkin' around outside my room, Sheriff?"

"I wasn't lurkin'! If you'd given me time, I was about to knock!"

"The hell you were."

"I was." Wiley looked up at Hawk's imposing, naked figure through one slitted eye, keeping his right hand raised in front of his face. "Christ, if I'd been trying to bushwhack you, don't you think I'd have my gun out?"

Hawk looked at the holstered gun beneath his bare foot. He removed his foot from the

54

gun but kept his cocked Russian aimed at the sheriff's head. "Well, if it's Sunday and you're wakin' me for church, you're wasting your time, Sheriff."

The fear in Wiley's eyes was quickly tempered by fury. He glanced to his right, saw Mrs. Parker scowling at him through the hair hanging down over her eyes, and a deeper flush rose in his cheeks.

He glanced at the big, silver-plated pistol aimed at his nose and shuttled his angry gaze up past the gun and Hawk's muscular arm to the Rogue Lawman's sparking green eyes. "Very funny, you sonofabitch. Get that gun out of my face. Man downstairs wants to see you."

"Who?"

"Muckety-muck from Denver. Flashed a badge at me, told me to fetch you pronto. Three of 'em, matter-of-fact."

"Three? All with badges?"

"Yeah, but they ain't here to arrest you. Leastways, they said they weren't. One said he's an old friend of yours. Said his name was Spurlock, from Denver."

"Spurlock."

"That's what he said. Now will you kindly get that iron out of my face? Don't much appreciate bein' some three-piece suit's errand boy, then havin' your big horse pistol stuck up my nose."

As Hawk lowered the Russian, Wiley began climbing to his feet, his voice pitched high with exasperation. "Goddamnit, I'm the sheriff of this county!"

"You sure the man said Spurlock?"

"What — you think I made up Spurlock off the top of my head?"

Hawk went to one of the room's two windows and looked down into a fifty-yard gap between the brothel and the next building. Nothing there except morning shade, brush, and trash. No badge-toting gunmen.

Hawk glanced back at Wiley, who was still standing in the middle of the room looking indignant.

"All right, you did your job, Sheriff." Hawk waved the Russian toward the open door. "Tell Spurlock I'll be down shortly."

"He said I was to wait for you."

Hawk just stared at him.

"Christ." Wiley moved to the door, glanced from Mrs. Parker to Hawk, who was still standing naked, his silver-plated pistol in his hand. The sheriff gave a caustic, exasperated chuff, shaking his head, and stomped out.

"Who's Spurlock?" Mrs. Parker asked. In spite of last night's intimacies, Hawk had seen no reason they should get on a first-name basis.

Hawk closed the door, set the Russian on the dresser, and plucked his balbriggans off the floor. "Old friend of mine," he said, brows mantled in deep thought. "What the hell he's doin' out here — I can't imagine."

She lowered the quilts from her chest and cupped her heavy breasts in her hands, canting her head and squinting an eye at Hawk. "You're not gonna shoot up my place again, are you?"

"I told you," Hawk said, sitting on the edge of the bed to pull his socks on. "Spurlock's an old friend of mine."

"Then what were you looking out the window for?"

Hawk looked at her as he stood and grabbed his black denim trousers from off a chair back. She was still absently cupping her breasts, rolling her thumbs across the nipples jutting from the large rosettes. Now she arched a brow at him.

He chuffed ironically as he pulled the jeans up around his hips and buttoned the fly. "I'll probably head out soon. For what it's worth, it's been a long time since I spent the whole night with a woman."

"For what it's worth," she said, "it's been a while for me, too."

When Hawk had finished dressing and

hitching the buckle of his double-rigged cartridge belt, he donned his hat and grabbed his rifle and saddlebags.

If he were walking into a trap, he likely wouldn't have time to retrieve his possibles later. Racking a cartridge into the Henry's breech, he moved to the door, glanced once more at Mrs. Parker, who leaned back against the bed's headboard with an ambiguous expression on her pretty face, her hair tossed straight back over her head.

Hawk opened the door, looked both ways along the hall, and went out.

5.
DEADLY PREY

Hawk stopped at the top of the brothel's rear stairs and removed his spurs. He dropped the spurs into a saddlebag pouch, then started down the steps, moving quickly but quietly in spite of an occasional squawk of a loose riser and a belch from the rickety railing along which he ran his left hand.

The stairwell was still dark, but the window in the door at the bottom shone with intensifying morning light. He stopped before it and peered out. Seeing nothing more than freshly scalloped sand and a thick pile of tumbleweeds blown in on yesterday's wind, he opened the door and went out.

Holding his rifle straight out from his hip, he gave the area around the brothel a careful scouting.

Satisfied for the time being that he wasn't about to be dry-gulched by federal marshals armed for bear and packing a death warrant like the one four territorial governors had recently armed a U.S. marshal named Flagg with — a man whom Hawk had dispatched along with six others in southern Arizona — he made his way to the front of A Thousand Delights. He peered in a window to the right of the door, then opened the door quickly but quietly and stepped just as quietly inside and drew the door softly closed behind him.

The sun blazed in the front windows, leaving the area directly in front of the windows in inky purple shadow.

Keeping to those shadows and stepping around the furniture that had all been properly arranged though bearing the bloodstains and bullet holes of yesterday's dustup, Hawk made his way toward the rear of the room, toward the bar and the stairs, where three men sat playing cards and sipping coffee from large stone mugs and liquor from large snifters.

Two had their backs to him. The one who sort of faced him from the other side of the table — a well-set-up gent with a clean-shaven though deeply lined, blue-eyed face under a cap of wiry, silver hair — he recognized.

Gavin Spurlock had given Hawk his first job as a deputy U.S. marshal out of Yankton, Dakota Territory, nearly fifteen years ago, when Hawk had returned west from the battlefields of the Civil War. Hawk's own father, an old war chief who had fallen in love with Hawk's mother, a pretty blond Scandinavian girl named Ingrid Rasmussen, had died when Hawk was still a child. The chief had many wives, and Hawk had been one of many children, so the chief hadn't paid much attention to his half-breed offspring.

For all practical purposes, Hawk had been fatherless . . . until Gavin Spurlock had taken him under his wing, given him a job, and made him an expert at it. He'd also given the young veteran cavalryman a place to call home, a place to, as Spurlock had once said, "sink a taproot," which Hawk had done when he'd married Linda and fathered Jubal.

Gavin Spurlock.

The name burned on a wand of fiery guilt across Hawk's brain. When he'd turned rogue, he'd become in essence a traitor to the one man he'd respected most in the world — a venerable chief marshal who held no laws more sacred than those laid out by the Constitution of the United States of America. A man in whose house on the outskirts of Yankton hung portraits of both Washington and Jefferson, and whose supper prayer consisted of four simple words, "God bless this land."

His guilt for the past three vigilante years now swept through Hawk to his belly, where it boiled like water, as he stole quietly up to the table where Spurlock perused the cards in his hand while puffing a long stogy angling down from one side of his short, resolute mouth, beneath the straight, broad line of his judicial, lightly veined nose. As Hawk stole up behind a brick ceiling joist ten feet from the table, one of the men sitting with his back to Hawk slammed his cards down on the table and looked up at the second-floor balcony.

"Where is he, damnit? Who in the hell does he think he is, keepin' us — ?"

"Oh, I think he knows exactly who he is," Gavin Spurlock said, not raising his eyes from his cards, which he was shifting around in his hands. "And as far as where he is, I believe he's right behind you, Deputy Stuart."

Both men who had their backs to Hawk jerked their heads around. Finding that the Rogue Lawman had, indeed, flanked them, their eyes snapped wide, then hooded with incredulity. Both had automatically slapped their hands to their holsters but froze when they saw Hawk's rifle extending straight out from his right hip.

"At ease, gentlemen," Spurlock said, casually shuttling his cool gaze from his cards to Gideon Hawk standing in the shadows beside the brick pillar. "You didn't think such a savvy hunter . . . and such deadly prey . . . would actually enter the room with the turgid predictability of taking the main stairs, did you?"

Both men were well dressed, one in his middle thirties, the other early forties. Cold weather coats hung over the backs of their chairs. They continued glowering up at Hawk. The one on the left, the older one, removed his hand from his six-shooter first. The other glanced at his older partner, skepticism flashing faintly in his brown eyes, then followed suit.

Both men held their hands up where Hawk could see them. Moon-and-star badges of deputy U.S. marshals shone on their wool vests.

Hawk glanced behind him at the door, then at the windows, again making sure he wasn't walking into a trap.

He vaguely, absently realized that some small component inside him had, surprisingly, been untouched by the wildness that had otherwise reshaped his character in recent years. This throwback trait to a more civilized time made him want to trust the older man before him now. But the dominant feralness, cultivated by his overwhelming urge to track and kill killers while dodging bona fide lawmen so that he could continue to track and kill, would not allow it.

At least, not yet.

He let his saddlebags and coat slide down his arm. As they hit the floor he stepped forward and crouched slightly, keeping his rifle aimed at the men at the table while his eyes scanned the second-floor balcony for ambushers.

"Gideon," Spurlock said sadly. "You know me better than that."

Hawk looked at the man. Spurlock's face was a little more lined, his gray hair perhaps a little grayer and thinner, his shoulders a little sharper and more pronounced beneath his black, broadcloth coat. But he was still the man Hawk remembered, right down to the genuine warmth and affability spoking his clear, intelligent eyes.

Guilt bubbled in Hawk again, but he didn't let it show on his face. He took another step forward, keeping his rifle aimed between the two younger lawmen while looking at their older, more seasoned and time-tempered superior. "What're you doin' here, Gavin?"

Spurlock set his cards down on the table carefully, as though he intended to pick them up again and resume play a little later. He crossed one arm on his broad chest and, with his other hand, plucked the stogy from between his lips and held it close to his face, narrowing his eyes slightly as he stared through the smoke at his one-time apprentice.

"I didn't come to kill you, Gid. And I didn't come to bring you in."

"That's good. Because I wouldn't let you do either." Hawk glanced at the older deputy, who had a thick dragoon-style mustache, and then at the younger one, who had a week's growth of sandy beard on his pale cheeks. "But since you got two gun-hung coyotes tagging along, I figure you're not here for tea and pound cake."

"They're merely my escorts," Spurlock said. "You wouldn't expect a man of nearly sixty-five years . . . one who's put away as many red-tailed, shaggy-faced lobos as I have . . . to make the trip from Denver alone, would you? No one to back my play . . . ?"

He indicated the chair to his right. "Sit down."

"I'll stand."

Spurlock smiled bemusedly as he studied Hawk for a moment before glancing at the two lawmen across from him. "Gentlemen, why don't you go out and get some air?"

The older deputy glowered up at the Rogue Lawman, then turned to his boss. "You sure about that?"

Spurlock nodded as he returned his eyes to Hawk. "Go on. I'll be out shortly."

The deputies shoved their coins and bank notes into their pockets. The older man plucked a loosely rolled quirley from an ashtray, and then he and his young partner slid their chairs back and gained their feet. The older man stepped in front of Hawk and furrowed his bushy black brows. His soup-strainer mustache was a straight line across his mouth.

His voice was a low growl. "You're damn lucky I was never assigned to your trail, Hawk. If I had been, you wouldn't have been runnin' off the leash half as long as you have."

Hawk smiled grimly. "I don't doubt it a bit."

The older lawmen held Hawk's gaze for a moment, then hitched his gun belt up his hips, straightened his ribbon tie, took a drag from the quirley in his right hand, and turned away.

He and the younger deputy, who was a little flushed with apprehension but taking all his cues from the older man, strode off toward the front of the room. Glancing over their shoulders, they headed outside. Seeing the two of them together — a mentor and an apprentice — sparked a memory of the young deputy he himself had trained and gotten to know like he and Spurlock had known each other once, and Hawk silently ground his teeth against the pain of it.

He'd killed the deputy, Luke Morgan, in western Colorado two winters ago, when Morgan had been sent to track him because Morgan, who'd been trained by Hawk, had known the Rogue Lawman best and would supposedly know best how to take him down.

Hawk turned to Gavin Spurlock sitting back in his chair with that somber, knowing smile on his mouth. "Don't believe I know those two," Hawk said.

"The younker is Jimmy Pfiefer. The older gent is Knut Nicholson. He was a stock detective in Montana before he joined the marshals. Right effective lawman."

"I bet he is."

"We're alone now. No gunmen skulking around the balconies or anywhere else. I told the apron to keep the room clear, though I must say that the two girls I saw when I first walked in were right impressive. You chose your lodgings well. Or . . ." Spurlock glanced around at the bullet-pocket, bloodstained furniture and looked over his shoulder at the back bar mirror. ". . . Did the lodgings choose you?"

"The Stony Hills Bunch," Hawk said, dropping into the chair the younger deputy had vacated.

"I know who they were. Following them is how I found you. I'd gotten word you were in this area, and, knowing you — or having gotten to know the man you now are from newspaper accounts and even a few penny dreadfuls based on your exploits — I figured you'd sniff out their trail sooner or later."

Spurlock leaned forward to bring his coffee to his lips. "Maybe you're not as wily as you thought, Gideon."

Hawk beetled his brows slightly with self-reproof. "Gettin' careless."

"I'm sure you'll remedy the problem." There was a silver coffee service on the table, as well as a stout brandy decanter, a stone mug, and an upside-down snifter. Spurlock glanced at the service. "Coffee and brandy? Or maybe you're still not imbibing this early in the day."

Hawk leaned his rifle against the table,

sort of half resting it against his knee, within fast reach. "I changed that, too. Coffee and brandy sound good."

Spurlock set his cigar down to pour coffee into the mug and brandy into the snifter. As he did, Hawk studied the man's aging face, trying to uncover some hint about what the man was doing here. He hadn't had any contact with his old boss for years; well before Hawk had gone rogue in the wake of his son's murder and his wife's suicide, Gavin Spurlock had accepted a presidential appointment to the chief marshal's office in Santa Fe. He and Hawk had corresponded a few times, but their paths hadn't crossed . . . until now.

And now was no accident.

Spurlock slid the mug and the snifter through the strewn playing cards, then took a long puff from his cigar and leaned back again in his chair. "So, how you been, Gid?"

"Busy," Hawk said. "And as long as there's bronco cutthroats tearin' down their corrals, I aim to stay that way. So let's cut to the main camp, Gavin. What do you want from me?"

Spurlock picked up his brandy glass, swished the brandy around, and lifted it to his lips. "I'd like you to do what you do best, Gideon."

69

Hawk stared at him through the thin tendrils of steam lifting off his coffee mug.

Spurlock sipped the brandy and lowered the snifter halfway to the table. He lifted his cheeks with a bizarre smile. "I want you to kill a man."

6.
A KILLER CALLED KNIFE-HAND

Hawk laughed for the first time in years. "No shit?"

Spurlock said, "I'm gonna reach inside my jacket, Gideon."

Hawk nodded his approval.

Spurlock hauled out a quarter-inch-thick sheaf of folded papers and tossed them onto the table in front of Hawk, scattering pasteboards. Hawk let his smile dwindle as he regarded his old boss skeptically. Reaching forward, he slid the packet toward his chest and opened it. It was an assignment file like those he used to be furnished with when he'd been working as a bona fide lawman for Spurlock and Spurlock's successor in the Yankton office.

There were about thirty carbon copies of neatly typewritten pages and a few hastily scribbled maps of what appeared to be desert country, though Hawk didn't give any of the pages much of a look. He riffled through the file quickly and looked up again at Spurlock, who continued to regard him with that off-putting, semi-bemused smile between occasional puffs of his stogy and sips of either coffee or brandy.

Hawk said, "All this for one owlhoot?"

"That's not the half of it, but remembering how you used to work, I figured it's all you'd take the time to read." Spurlock's smile brightened slightly, like a low fire fed a twig. "And the information collected isn't about just any owlhoot, nor is it about even one man but about the movements of an entire gang. A gang of bloodthirsty wolves led by one Wilbur 'Knife-Hand' Monjosa."

"That's a hell of a name," Hawk said. "Why 'Knife-Hand'?"

"Lost his left hand to a Mojave Indian's war ax. The Mojave was tracking him across the devil's dance floor in southern Arizona Territory . . . after Knife-Hand had broken out of Yuma Pen. He killed the Mojave tracker, so the story goes, with the sharp end of his hacked-up wrist bone and got away. Down in Mexico, he had the hand replaced with a knife blade. Not a hook, but a knife blade. One he's said to keep razor-edged."

"Right handy," Hawk said. "No pun intended. White man or Indian?"

"Half Americano, a quarter Apache, a quarter Mex."

Hawk glanced at the file, riffled a corner with his thumb, and shook his head. "Damn . . . I thought I'd heard of 'em all."

"It's not so odd you haven't heard of Knife-Hand, given that he disappeared in Mexico about five years ago and just recently resurfaced in western Arizona. He was once a tracker for the army, helped 'em corral quite a few Apaches onto reservations. He and the army had it out over something or other, and he became a turncoat, organized a group of bronco Lipan Apaches to take down an army payroll shipment. They massacred all thirteen soldiers. Old Wilbur Monjosa — as he was more simply known at the time — got himself wounded, and the cavalry ran him down around Benson. That's when they shipped him off to Yuma, where he spent a year before he and a handful of other wildcats sprang themselves."

Hawk had sipped his coffee down, and now he poured his brandy into it and drank. Swallowing the bracing brew, he ran the back of his hand across his mouth, leaned back in his chair, and hiked a boot onto a knee. "I can't imagine what all this has to do with me, Gavin. I sorta pick my own targets these days — remember?"

Spurlock took a last drag from his stogy and scraped the smoldering coal into his ashtray. He picked up his brandy glass, slid his chair back, and stiffly gained his feet, his old bones popping faintly. His brows hooded thoughtfully as he strolled casually toward the bar. Hawk could see the man's darkly troubled face in the back bar mirror.

Spurlock drew a deep breath. "He's become a *contrabandista,* Gid. A very deadly man. The deadliest in the Southwest right now. He runs rifles across the border to a stubborn band of bronco Apaches holed up somewhere in the desert south of Yuma. He steals the rifles from army pack trains that feed the frontier forts down there.

"Sometimes he even attacks the forts themselves — overruns them with his own band of Mexican as well as gringo cutthroats, including several ex-Confederates with axes to grind against the current American government. With the stolen rifles and even a couple of very troublesome Gatling guns, the Apaches continue to raid along the border and well into both Mexico and Arizona. They raid towns, villages, roadhouses, even mission churches. You name it, they raid it. They raise hob with ranching, stagecoach lines, the U.S. mail, and even railroad lines.

"Everything's in chaos down there now. Many, many soldiers have been killed — butchered — in the past three months alone. Countless others — entire patrols — have simply disappeared. Their numbers are nothing compared to the droves of innocent civilians who've been brutally cut down by those loco Apaches — ranchers, townsmen, stage and railroad travelers. . . ."

Spurlock rested an elbow on the bar, crossed one boot over the other, and regarded Hawk, who sat listening patiently at the table, severely.

"It's been decided that the dust isn't going to settle down there until old Knife-Hand is put out of commission. Only after the Indians' supply line has been breached can the soldiers begin to work on the renegades themselves."

Hawk hiked a shoulder. "So, put him out of commission. There must still be enough soldiers down there to do the job, if they're working with the right trackers."

"They've tried that. They sent men by tens and twenties, then smaller bands of sharp-shooters led by the best Mojave and Apaches trackers in all of Arizona and California. Half of them disappeared. Those were the lucky ones, judging by the ones that were found tortured and killed."

Spurlock sipped his brandy, smacked his lips, and hooked a thumb behind the waistband of his tailored gray trousers. He wasn't wearing a gun or a cartridge belt — just a simple black belt for keeping his pants on his narrow hips.

He said darkly, "Wilbur 'Knife-Hand' Monjosa is one slippery man. He has a series of hideouts somewhere out in those wild volcanic mountains of western Arizona, eastern California. North of Yuma, along the Colorado River. The army intelligence boys figure he ventures as far into Mexico as the Sea of Cortez, as far north as Las Vegas, Nevada. It's believed he has a half dozen mountain hideouts, but in the three years he's been running like a wild, bloodthirsty lobo across that devil's playground, not one of his hideouts has ever been discovered. At least, not by anyone who's lived to tell about it."

Hawk was more than a little puzzled. "So, how is it you're trying to involve me — a man who's wanted by the law his own self. And what does this have to do with you, Gavin? Your office is in New Mexico Territory — not Arizona."

"One question at a time, Gid. Your name came up during a meeting of the four territorial governors of New Mexico, Arizona, Utah, and Colorado. You see, the trouble in Arizona and California has long tendrils, reaching far up into the surrounding territories."

Hawk was smiling without humor. "Those are the four governors who issued a death warrant on me two years back. The death warrant that got my good friend, Deputy Luke Morgan, killed."

Spurlock nodded soberly. "The irony isn't lost on me, Gideon. Of course, they're the same men. I reckon they figure if they can't beat you, they might as well employ you . . . when there's no one else qualified for the job."

"Qualified?"

"By that I believe they mean a professional, well-seasoned tracker and killer. Someone so reckless, so careless of his own fate, that he'd have a better chance of accomplishing his objective than would a man who gave a good goddamn about his own hide. A man who cared about nothing so much as he cared about the hunt and the kill. Not even the law."

Hawk drew a deep, woeful breath.

"You see, they want Knife-Hand killed. Not captured. Not taken into custody. Dispatched. Sanctioned. Turned toe down and inside out." Spurlock's lips spread. "That would be another of your areas of expertise, would it not? Vigilante justice?"

"I prefer to call it *effective* law enforcement."

"Call it what you will. The governors figure that by killing Knife-Hand you'll be for all intents and purposes cutting off the snake's head. The gang that surrounds him won't know what to do without him, and they'll disperse into smaller, poorly organized groups that the army will be able to run to ground themselves later on."

Hawk took another sip of his coffee and brandy, slid his chair back, grabbed his rifle, and stood. "Tell the governors to go to hell, Gavin."

Hawk stooped to retrieve his saddlebags from the floor.

"That was my response to your first question," Spurlock said. "You haven't heard why they sent me to talk to you."

Hawk froze, glanced over his shoulder.

Spurlock lowered his eyes to his glass and swirled the brandy around in front of his belly. His voice was low and suddenly very thick. "Knife-Hand killed Andrew."

Hawk felt a quickening pulse beat in his temples. He wanted to say something, but no words would come.

Spurlock's jaws tightened. He glowered into his brandy snifter. "He wanted to be a soldier, get some dust under his nails before reading for the law. Wouldn't go to military school; wanted to go in as an enlisted man — a grit-chewing, shit-shoveling private. I couldn't talk him out of it. He was stationed at Fort Colorado, north of Yuma, and was on one of the patrols searching for Knife-Hand's group. They were ambushed, everyone killed but one lone soldier who managed to survive by playing possum. Andrew had survived the initial attack, and when he was crawling off for sanctuary in a ravine, Knife-Hand himself rode his horse in front of him. That killer stepped down from his horse. . . ."

Spurlock's voice grew thicker, and his Adam's apple swelled. He ground his teeth, trying to compose himself, and then continued in a voice raspy as a file blade. "He grabbed Andrew's head by his hair, pulled him up, and sank that knife in Andrew's belly. Gutted him like . . . like a damn . . ."

Spurlock's jaw hinges dimpled, and he tossed back the last of his brandy with a desperate air.

Hawk stared at him.

Andrew. Spurlock's only offspring. The boy's mother had died of an infection the week after the boy was born and, as far as Hawk knew, Spurlock had never remarried.

Hawk remembered a rawboned, sandy-haired younker around twelve when Hawk knew him, who spent most of his time either tending his father's three prized Thoroughbreds or reading a book from his extensive, eclectic library. A good-natured kid, bookish and smart as a whip without being cocky or exclusive. A loner without being reclusive. Shy but affable. Andrew had been good with a whittling knife, too, and had even taught Hawk's boy, Jubal, how to carve figures out of cottonwood and pine.

A well-grounded kid on the path of building a good life for himself.

Hawk turned full around to face Spurlock and rested his rifle on his shoulder. He still didn't know what to say to the man. His heart was heavy for any man who lost his son. He knew the toll it took on the emotions, the soul. The yoke-heavy weight that forever resided in the shoulders. Nothing could ever again be right after such a loss.

Spurlock mistook Hawk's silence for something else. "So I lost my boy, too, and I came here to ask you to kill the man who killed him. Go ahead and gloat. It doesn't justify what you did, and I can't say as I'm proud to make the request. But goddamnit,

I want Andrew's killer dead!"

Spurlock set his glass down on the bar and strode toward Hawk. He stopped two feet in front of him. His mouth was a knife slash across his lower face, and his eyes were as hard polished as two stones at the bottom of a fast-running stream. "The governors sent me because they figured you'd trust me. And because, after what Knife-Hand did to Andrew, they knew I'd agree to make the offer. And that you'd likely agree to do it. Now, will you accept the assignment?"

An inexplicable sadness had filled Hawk like a poison quickly replacing the blood in his veins. It was sadness for Spurlock's loss, but it was caused by something else, too. If he could have put his finger on it, he would have said that it was the loss of what he'd admired most about the man — his integrity.

But he couldn't probe himself that deep. Not after learning what he'd learned about Spurlock's boy. Hawk loved Spurlock like a father, and, in light of the reason, there was nothing that would keep him from doing what the man wanted him to do.

Despite the cost to them both and to Spurlock most of all.

Hawk picked his saddlebags off the floor, set them on his shoulder. "I'll do it."

He glanced at Spurlock standing red-faced before him, tears dribbling down the man's cheeks. Unable to bear the man's keen sorrow, Hawk turned away quickly and began striding for the door.

"Don't you want to know about payment, Gideon?" his former boss asked quietly behind him.

"No."

Hawk went out.

7.
UNDIVIDED ATTENTION

"I sure wish somebody'd bury those sons o' bitches before they smell up the whole town!"

Sitting the saddle of his grulla, Gideon Hawk turned to see a wheelchair-bound old man in the dusty, rutted street behind him. The oldster had only one leg, and he couldn't have weighed much more than a sack of flour. He wore threadbare Confederate-gray trousers, a wolf coat, and a soiled, funnel-brimmed Stetson, which sat back off his bulging, age-spotted forehead. A sawed-off shotgun jutted from a leather sheath dangling from an arm of his chair, and he wore a big knife on his waist. The knife looked inordinately large on his wasted frame.

Hawk shuttled his gaze from the oldster to the three corpses he'd been studying in bitter bemusement.

He'd just ridden into the little town of

Saguaro, in southern Arizona, having hopped the train from Durango over a week ago. A scrap of information he'd picked up in Las Cruces had brought him here. The corpses were no clue to the whereabouts of Wilbur "Knife-Hand" Monjosa, but Hawk looked them over just the same.

They were three Mexican men and a woman reclining against pine planks that had been propped against the wall of the town's adobe-brick bank. The woman's long, black, gray-streaked hair blew in the breeze. She was dressed like the men around her in dusty, bedraggled trail clothes bloody from the bullet wounds that had torn her body and theirs.

The corpses wore cartridge belts and holsters, but their guns and ammunition were gone. The dead woman stared up at Hawk through half-shut eyes, and an oblique death smile twisted her lips, showing a glimpse of the front teeth behind them.

"They try to rob the bank?" Hawk asked the wheelchair-bound gent.

"That's right. But the good citizens of Saguaro didn't like the idea of their hard-earned money goin' out so easy." The oldster wheezed a laugh and sniffed.

Hawk turned to the man. "This dump have a sheriff?"

"Sure."

Hawk hardened an eye impatiently. "Would you mind tellin' me where I'd find him?"

"Wouldn't mind a bit." The oldster turned his wheelchair, rocked back, and jutted his chin toward the hill rising behind the high false fronts on the other side of the street — a low, brown, rock-and-cactus-spotted hill sprouting stone markers and crosses among large rocks, cat's claw shrubs, and barrel cactus. "We planted ole Roy Marquardt on boot hill a little over two years ago last Christmas eve. Never could find another man with the cojones to replace him."

"You don't say."

"Just said so."

"Where's the best place in town for harvesting a little information?"

"What kind of information might that be?"

"The kind not readily available elsewhere."

"Oh, that kind." The oldster tugged on his beard. With another quick maneuver, he aimed his wheelchair up the broad main street, toward the center of the ancient border town. "You'll find the Dandy Dog Inn on the left side of the street. Across from the main square and the church. I'd think twice about payin' a visit, though . . . especially if you're in the market for infor-

85

mation."

"Oh?" Hawk had removed his hat to mop the sweatband with the tail of his neckerchief. "Why's that?"

" 'Cause men that go in there lookin' for anything but hooch and cooch often don't come out again. Leastways, not walkin'."

Hawk set his hat back on his head and plucked a gold piece from his trouser pocket. "Mister, you've been a wealth of information. Have a beer on me."

The old man caught the coin one-handed as Hawk turned the grulla up the street.

"Maybe you better tell me your name, friend," the old man called behind him.

Hawk said nothing as the grulla clomped along the dusty street, between adobe-brick shacks and the gaudy false facades of business establishments. There were a handful of horseback riders on the street — mostly well-armed Mexicans, a few *norteamericanos.*

Scantily clad girls lounged on porches or balconies, plying their wares. There were dogs, chickens, goats, and even a few pigs scrounging the trash-strewn areas between buildings. Somewhere, a baby was crying.

"You don't wanna be planted without a name, do you?"

Hawk only vaguely heard that last yell

from the wheel-chair-bound oldster. He'd turned his attention to the weathered gray shingle jutting into the street from a left-side boardwalk, its black, blocky letters announcing simply DANDY DOG.

Six or seven sun-seared hombres lounged about the saloon's broad gallery speckled with sunlight streaming through the gaps between the branches forming its roof. They were all so darkly tanned and dust-caked that it was hard to tell if they were American, Mex, Indio, or an amalgam, but which side of the law they rode was made plain by the amount of guns and cartridges weighing them down and the sharply penetrating, perpetually sneering casts to their drunken gazes.

Glasses and bottles in various stages of fill sat along the brush arbor's cottonwood rail or were held in brown fists, a few seated on leather-clad thighs near jutting pistols.

The sweet, green smell of marijuana laced the slightly rancid odor of liquor and tobacco.

As Hawk rode up to the saloon — a long, low building constructed of sandstone blocks but patched here and there with mud adobe brick — he heard a din to the right. He swung his head to see a brown-skinned, round-hipped Indian whore bent forward over a rain barrel, her heavy, bare breasts jouncing, a soiled gray skirt bunched around her waist. A burly, bearded Mexican, pants fallen around his high, black boots, hammered her from behind while holding a bottle in his left fist, her black hair in the other.

He wore a grand, black, silver-trimmed sombrero, and two thick bandoliers were crossed on his broad chest and bulging belly. He and the whore were both laughing in drunken glory. If they'd noticed Hawk, neither let on.

As they toiled, water in the barrel sloshed up across the whore's bouncing bosoms. Behind the two fornicators, another man sat slumped against the next building, legs stretched out before him, chin tipped to his chest. Deep in drunken slumber.

Hawk swung down from his saddle, shucked his Henry repeater, looped the reins over a hitch rack at which half a dozen mounts stood swishing their tails, and mounted the gallery. His eyes swept the group lounging around him quickly, and then he was pushing through the batwings and striding through the dingy main saloon hall in which someone strummed a guitar just loudly enough to be heard above the rumble of conversation and occasional bursts of roaring laughter.

The rough-hewn bar stretched along the room's right wall. Over it ran a balcony upon which whores of every age, shape, size, and color hovered like exotic birds, some calling down to the men in the main saloon hall and giving alluring glimpses of a bare thigh or a breast.

A stairway climbed the rear wall, half hidden in shadows, and more men and women — some in love's embrace — lounged across the stone steps. Two girls there were playing keep-away from a snickering, inebriated young firebrand with his high-crowned leather hat.

"Give me a beer," Hawk ordered the frizzy-haired, blue-eyed bartender.

Hawk was dry from the long ride. The odor of marijuana and Mexican tobacco peppered his nose beneath the fetor of ancient, spilled liquor and human filth.

He threw back the tepid beer in one, long draught. The din in the room had quieted slightly when he'd entered, and several pairs of eyes watched him incredulously — this tall, dark rider with a finely chiseled, green-eyed face, wearing a fleece-lined bull-hide vest, two big pistols on his hips, a Henry rifle propped on his right shoulder.

When Hawk finished the beer, he pivoted,

flung his empty schooner into the air over the room, and raised his Henry.

Boooommmm!

The blast echoed off the adobe walls like a ricocheting cannonball.

The glass shattered as it started its drop from the ceiling into a million glittering shards, raining down on several tables but on one most of all. The broken handle plunked off the brim of a broad-brimmed gray hat with a snakeskin band, and the hat's wearer jerked his head down with a start, then shot a fiery glance across the room to Hawk.

He was on his feet in a wink, his right hand shoving back the flap of his spruce-green duster and closing over an ivory-handled Colt.

"Just wanted to get everybody's attention," Hawk said one notch louder than his normal volume, when he saw that he had it.

The gray-hatted gent stood tight-jawed and glaring, his right hand squeezing his pistol's grips so hard that his knuckles turned white.

Loudly, Hawk ejected the spent brass from the Henry's chamber. It clattered onto the bar top behind him as he levered a fresh round in the breech and regarded the indignant gent mildly.

"Amigo, if you got something to say, say it, or remove your hand from that hogleg and sit your ass down."

Hawk aimed the smoking Henry from his chest. The gray-hatted gent flicked his eyes toward the gun. One hard eye twitched, as did a muscle in his right cheek. His nostrils flared.

The room had suddenly become so quiet that Hawk could hear the gray-hatted gent's bitter, raspy breaths as well as a moaning breeze shepherding a dust devil along the street out the Dandy Dog's front windows.

Several pairs of eyes shifted back and forth between Hawk and the gray-hatted gent. Finally, keeping his threatening eyes on Hawk, he slowly lowered his tall bulk into his chair, doffing his hat and shaking the bits of shattered glass from the brim and crown.

"Obliged."

Hawk nodded to the man, then swept his gaze across the still, quiet room and the others, including the sporting girls, glaring at him through the wafting tobacco and gun smoke.

"Now, I realize you folks are all pretty flush at the moment, but just in case anyone wants to make a little extra spending money — say, five hundred dollars' worth — here's how. I'm lookin' for an hombre who rides under the handle of Kid Reno. You don't need to know why I'm lookin' for him, so don't bother askin'. You can speculate all you want. But I'm offering this five hundred dollars here for information — good information — about his whereabouts."

Hawk had plucked a roll of one-hundred-dollar bills — reward money from a recent batch of wanted deadmen he'd hauled to a sheriff and had collected on to keep himself fed, clothed, and dusting the owlhoot trail. He ran his thumb across the end of the bills as he held the wad up for inspection.

He noticed that several pairs of the eyes fixed on him had turned incredulous. A couple of men sneered and glanced at each other. A blond sporting girl snapped a surprised glance to one of her colleagues in a see-through cream shift adorned with several hoops of fake pearls.

"Five hundred dollars," Hawk said, again running his thumb across the bills then stuffing the wad back into his shirt pocket. "Think about it. I'll be around till tomorrow. Got a feelin' you'll know where to find me."

He set the butt of his Henry on his hip and strode across the crowded room toward the batwings, the heads around him swiveling as though they and he were connected by hidden strings.

The men who'd been spread out across the porch had gathered around the batwings when Hawk had shattered the beer schooner. Now as he approached the doors, the small crowd, including the big Mexican and the Indian whore who'd been fornicating over the rain barrel, bulged out away from the doors and split in two.

Hawk tipped his hat to the whore, who regarded him contentiously as she held her skimpy, unbuttoned dress closed across her breasts, and moved across the porch and slowly down the steps. He'd just started to turn toward his grulla when his well-trained ears heard the faint *snick* of a pistol being slid from a leather holster.

He wheeled as a big hombre in a cracked leather jacket, high-crowned hat, and billowy red neckerchief palmed a Frontier model Colt. Before the man could get the gun leveled, Hawk fired his Henry from his hip.

The man said, "Hu-uh!" and fired his Colt into the porch floor as Hawk's .44-caliber round hammered his breastbone and punched him straight back against the Dandy's Dog's front wall with a loud thud and cracking of bones a quarter second after the whip-crack of Hawk's rifle.

To that man's right, another hard case jerked a long-barreled .45 up from a holster thonged low on a deerskin-clad thigh, and Hawk sent him hurdling, screaming over the porch rail and into the gap between buildings.

Hawk ejected the spent brass, seated fresh, and looked at the other men on the porch. They all stood hang-jawed and white-faced, by ones and twos slowly lifting their hands above their holsters. One of the sporting girls — clad in nothing more than a man's wash-worn longhandles and a silk duster, with pink ribbons in her thick blond hair — also raised her hands and jerked back with a start.

The second man Hawk had shot groaned in the gap off the end of the porch. He rose up on his hands and knees, coughed blood into the rocks and sand beneath him, then dropped with a final sigh.

Hawk regarded the group facing him distastefully. "Anyone want to try it from the front?"

They all looked as sheepish as scolded schoolkids.

"Had a feelin'."

Hawk grabbed his reins off the hitch rack and stepped into his saddle.

Keeping his rifle aimed one-handed at the porch, and casting cautious glances toward the batwings, he backed the grulla away from the hitch rack and the other horses. He turned the horse toward the other side of the street, then, casting one more glance toward the porch where the hard cases and sporting girls only watched him with dubious expressions, hands still raised above shell belts, he booted the horse down the cross street.

When he'd put a harness shop between him and the Dandy Dog, he depressed the Henry's hammer, turned his head forward, and looked around. There wasn't much out here at the north edge of town — a livery barn and a near-empty corral, some sun-blasted shacks nearly buried in tumbleweeds, and a high, narrow, white-frame building with a red front porch and red window trim.

The shabby shingle hanging over the porch announced simply ROOMS.

Hawk turned in.

8.
JUBAL'S STALLION

Two pale eyes shone in the hotel's dingy shadows, beneath a narrow, low-slung stairs. There was a potted palm at one end of the plank-board counter; it was only three feet high and there was more brown on its leaves than green.

Coming in from the harsh light, Hawk couldn't see who belonged to those eyes until he got right up to the counter. Then he saw the whipcord-lean gent with a witch's nose and chin and a bulging fore-head, gaunt cheeks tufted with patches of gray bristle. He wore a red-and-white-checked shirt buttoned to his prominent Adam's apple.

Perched on a high stool behind the counter, fronting a row of small, numbered cubby holes, he rasped, "A dollar fifty fer a double. Two dollars fer a single."

Hawk glanced at the stairs slanting over his head. The place was as quiet as a mortu-

96

ary. "Any other boarders?"

"Not yet." The birdlike old gent leaned forward to take a bite from a crusty ham sandwich. "But later, around midnight, they come trampin' in from the saloons in droves."

"I'll take a single," Hawk said.

Fishing coins from his denims' pocket, he glanced through a dusty window at the livery barn across the street. There were only two horses in the corral, and a mule he hadn't seen earlier.

"The barn open for business?"

The birdlike man nodded as he chewed with his mouth open, his tongue flapping like a wing inside. "That's mine, too, and it is open." His thin, colorless brows hooded his eyes. "Say, what was the shootin' about? I keep attuned to the killin's. My brother's the undertaker."

Hawk scratched a fake name in blue-green ink in the ragged register book. "Two men dead over to the Dandy Dog."

The birdlike gent's cheeks dimpled with either joy or dismay — it was impossible to tell. "Who shot 'em?"

"I did."

"You don't say?"

"They'd been needin' it fer a long time," Hawk said, tossing the pen against the spine of the register book. "Since they were out of rubber pants, most like."

The old man croaked a chuckle.

"You got a man over there?" Hawk said, canting his head at the barn.

"I do."

"Will you have him take my horse? Give him a good rubdown and feed, plenty of water. And I'd like a bath in my room, if you're set up for it."

"I am set up for it," the birdlike gent said, sliding stiffly off his stool. "The barn and the bath will cost you one dollar extra . . . if you're only staying the night. . . ."

Hawk went back outside to retrieve his saddlebags from his horse. He picked up the key that the birdlike old man had left on the lobby counter, then tramped up the rickety stairs to room number three and tossed his saddlebags on the bed.

The room wasn't much bigger than a broom closet — boasting only a sagging bed with a tarnished brass frame, a dresser with a cracked mirror, and a wooden washstand with one broken leg leveled with a box of playing cards. There were a few wall pegs behind the door for hanging clothes.

When the old man hauled a copper tub up the steps and filled it with water, Hawk undressed and crawled in. He was running a cake of lye down an arm when the old man returned with another bucket of steaming water.

"What was the shootin' about?" The stoop-shouldered old gent poured the hot water into the tub, sending steam into the stale, dingy air. He'd rolled a quirley, and it sagged from the right side of his thin-lipped mouth. "If you don't mind my askin', I mean. . . ."

"Well, first," Hawk said, resting his elbows on his upraised knees and cupping water over his head and face, "I needed to get their attention. I had a question, you see, and figured it was the best place in town to ask it."

The old man held the empty but still-steaming bucket straight down by his side. He plucked the quirley from his mouth, letting smoke trickle out his broad nostrils. "What question was that?"

"About a killer named Kid Reno. I heard he used to run with another killer called Wilbur 'Knife-Hand' Monjosa down Arizona way."

The old bird was laughing so softly and hoarsely he was almost silent. His slumped shoulders shook. Finally, he sucked a sharp breath and shook his head.

Scrubbing his hair with the soap, Hawk

glanced up at the man. "You've either heard of Kid Reno or Knife-Hand, or both. . . ."

"Hell, mister," the old bird croaked, "once you get down south of the Colorado-Utah line, most folks you run into have heard of Kid Reno. He's been runnin' afoul of the law in these parts for the better part of ten years. Can't say as I ever heard of this . . . this, uh . . . Knife-Hand fella, though."

"Figured," Hawk said. "Knife-Hand's been in Mexico. Just surfaced in the southwest corner of Arizona Territory about a year ago. You'll hear about him soon, most likely."

"Kid Reno," the old bird said, giving his bony head another shake. "Land sakes, the Dandy Dog sure ain't the place to go whisperin' his name, much less sayin' it up loud and clear."

"Know where he is?"

"Hell, no, not me!" The old man jerked with a start and wheezed another laugh. "But a few of them curly wolves over to the Dandy Dog just might!"

"That's kinda what I was hopin'."

"And you really think they're gonna *tell* ya?"

"That's kinda what I was hopin'," Hawk repeated.

The old man was exasperated as he

headed for Hawk's open door. "The only thing you're gonna get out of askin' questions around the Dandy Dog is a bullet."

"They done tried that. Those were the last two shots you heard." Thoroughly lathered, Hawk rested his elbows on his knees. "I'm ready for a rinse. And if you got any cigars downstairs, I'll take two."

The birdlike gent went downstairs and came back with another bucket of hot water and two cigars. He dumped the bucket over Hawk's head and bent down to light one of the cigars for him.

"You want me to send up some vittles?" he asked, straightening and waving out the match. "Might not be too safe for you on the street."

"No, thanks," Hawk said. "I'll be dining out this evening."

The old gent wagged his head, hefted his bucket, went out, and closed the door behind him. Hawk lounged back in the tub and puffed the cigar, feeling the trail fatigue begin to leech from his bones. Idly, his eyes swept the room as he listened to the distant sounds from the lawless town; they weren't many or loud now, but they'd likely grow in number and volume once the sun went down.

Maybe soon one or a couple of the cutthroats would get drunk enough, and/or the five hundred dollars would look attractive enough, that Hawk would learn something about Kid Reno. Once he found Reno, he'd probably find —

Hawk's eyes had drifted to his saddlebags on the sagging bed. One of the pouches had opened, and a small wooden horse had tumbled out. It leaned upright against the bag, the small, black carving flailing its carefully, precisely scaled hooves toward the darkening ceiling, its indigo mane ruffling in an invisible wind.

The horse was so lifelike that for a moment Hawk thought he could hear the wild bugle shepherded on a sage-scented gust from the open prairie.

Hawk's eyes glazed slightly. A tear formed in the inside corner of the right one, down near his broad, wind-and-sun-blistered nose. In the last light angling through the room's lone window, it glistened like liquid gold.

Jubal hadn't been good in school. In spite of Hawk's and Linda's efforts at tutoring the youngster nights at their kitchen table, his reading and math scores had remained low. The other kids had teased him, called him "Cork Head" and "the Marshal's Moron." Hawk didn't know who felt worse —

Jubal or Linda, who, tortured by their son's travails, often cried herself to sleep at night in Hawk's arms.

But either in spite of his slow academic abilities or because of them, Jubal could look at a cabin or a tree or a hill when he and his father were out fishing, which they did together a lot, and go home and draw the setting effortlessly and perfectly, so that a photograph couldn't have done the subject more justice than Jubal's hand.

He'd been just as good with wood.

The rearing black stallion had been one of his last efforts before "Three Fingers" Ned Meade had lured the boy off the school playground and hanged him from the cottonwood atop that stormy hill . . . while Hawk had galloped up the hill howling and screaming only to arrive after Jubal's neck had snapped, and his limbs in their little wool jacket and knickers hung slack toward the ground.

Then Linda had hanged herself after the funeral, and Hawk's life was over.

He'd been half dead when Jubal was murdered.

Linda's suicide had finished him.

Only, unlike his wife and son, he hadn't been returned to the earth. Another man had arisen from Hawk's ashes. A man who looked like Hawk, who talked and walked and rode like him. But one who hardly ever smiled, who was uncannily good with his guns, and whose green eyes burned like twin fires of jade.

A hunter of hunters. A killer of killers.

A lone, fearless, stalking wolf of the deserts, mountains, and plains . . .

Hawk stared at the rearing horse. The lone tear dribbled down his cheek.

Jubal.

Hawk groaned, squeezed his eyes closed, and rested his head back against the tub.

When would the memories ever stop haunting him? Would he ever find peace again like other men knew it, or must he die to attain such sanctuary?

If so, he'd take one more man with him before he went. The one who'd killed Andrew Spurlock and turned the boy's father, Gavin, into a vigilante like Hawk.

Wilbur "Knife-Hand" Monjosa.

Hawk slumped in the bath until the water turned cold.

Then he hauled himself out, dried with a scrap of towel, and dressed in fresh balbriggans and socks from his saddlebags, and the black denims, blue shirt, and green silk neckerchief he'd had laundered by a Chinese couple in Alamosa.

He used a brush on his black hat and his cracked bull-hide vest, then donned both, shouldered his Winchester, and left the hotel and the old birdlike gent snoring in a Windsor chair under the stairs.

He found a tonsorial parlor and had to wait twenty minutes for a shave. The wait was fine. He read a paper while casting frequent, hopeful glances out the window, where the street turned dark and gradually more boisterous. He wanted that information. Surely someone who knew Kid Reno would give it up for five hundred greenbacks. When it came to money and women, there was little honor among killers.

But, while several hard-looking passersby glanced through the window at him — by now, word of his exploits in the Dandy Dog had likely made it halfway around the county — no one came in or looked even somewhat eager to deliver the informational goods.

An hour after he'd walked into the parlor, Hawk tramped out, rubbing a hand over his freshly shaven cheeks, his nose burning with the liquory, over-fragrant stench of the tonic the barber had doused him with before holding out his hand for payment. The barber glanced through the door glass at him skeptically, then, glancing quickly up and down the street, drew the "Closed" shade down over the door and extinguished his lamp.

Hawk walked around, weaving through the milling crowd whose din was growing louder and more rowdy by the quarter hour. Piano or mandolin music sounded from most of the saloons now, and there was the frequent roar of laughter — women's as well as men's.

A good distance from Hawk came the sound of a six-shooter fired twice in anger, and then a woman screamed in castigation. There were more arguments, more sporadic gunshots, and the smacks of fists against flesh.

Hawk smiled as he strolled, sliding his eyes around. On his third walk around town, he turned into a café in the middle of the ever-growing maelstrom and ordered steak and tequila.

When he finished, he strolled through the crowd again — several midsized groups of inebriated revelers of both sexes and several nationalities more or less clumped around Saguaro's three saloons, a dingy little shack flanked with plank, tin-roofed cribs that passed for a brothel, and a couple of cantinas from which emanated the din of Spanish conversations and raucous mariachi bands.

Hawk knew he was pushing his luck. At any time, he might feel the sharp gouge of a knife in the back, or the piercing burn of a bullet. There was no law to deter such an assault, and his death would likely be seen as a justification for even more revelry.

But while he kept his senses pricked, and watched the eyes sliding furtively toward him and then away, he knew no fear. Deep down inside himself, he dared anyone to try an assault. In fact, he welcomed one.

Any death he caused here could be nothing but good.

Around ten o'clock, deciding that if anyone wanted to talk to him, they'd know where to find him, he headed back toward the birdlike gent's hotel, choosing a route through hog pens and chicken coops that would put him at the place's back door. Since most folks likely knew where he'd landed a room, there was no point in taking unnecessary chances. An ambush would be easy to set up out here on the dark northern edge of Saguaro.

He was just passing a low shack and a dilapidated corral when he stopped suddenly. He'd heard something — the faint snap of a small branch or the crunch of a stone under a furtive boot.

Turning, he swept his eyes from left to right. The sky was tented with crisply glistening stars, but there was not yet a moon. Edges and flat surfaces were trimmed in silver, but there were more shadows than there was light.

A gun flashed, followed a quarter second later by a pistol bark. The slug plowed across Hawk's left shoulder and hammered the ground behind him.

Jerking his Henry off his shoulder, he thumbed the hammer back and bolted toward the corral corner just ahead and right, and started firing.

9.

Doris

He'd fired three times at the spot where the bushwhacker's gun had flashed. Another gun flashed and barked to the right of the first, and Hawk fired three quick slugs at the second shooter. He could hear the hollow barks of the two slugs chewing into wood and a groan.

He held fire. As he stared into the shadows behind him, there sounded the clatter of a gun hitting the ground. It was followed by a louder, more solid thud.

Hawk ejected the last spent cartridge, sent it smoking into the darkness behind him, and levered a fresh one. He waited, staring into the milky wash of moonlight and shadows. There were several small huts back there, as well as brush-sheathed boulders and a couple of stock pens.

Hearing nothing more, Hawk stepped out from behind the dilapidated corral and tramped slowly back the way he'd come.

He hadn't walked far before he was standing over the first shooter, who was slumped against a stock tank, chin dipped to his chest. Blood shone darkly on his shirt, between the flaps of an open denim jacket, just beneath the tail of a knotted red bandanna. The dead man's hat lay beside him, and his hair shone sandy and matted down in the moonlight, curling down over his collar.

Hawk used his rifle barrel to lift the man's chin. He didn't recognize the raw, unshaven features. Letting the man's chin dip back toward his chest, Hawk walked over to where the other man lay belly down against an empty chicken coop. Hawk's rifle bullet had taken half the man's head off and spewed it over the low, gray fence and into the dung-and-corncob-littered pen.

Most of his face was intact, however. Hawk didn't know this man, either, but he remembered the face from one of the saloons he'd visited earlier. The man had been playing poker, and by his sour, worried expression, he'd been in over his head, his coins slipping away like the sand in Father Time's hourglass. Likely, he'd seen Hawk and remembered the five hundred dollars the Rogue Lawman had flashed around the Dandy Dog, and had summoned a friend to assist him in shadowing Hawk's trail.

Hawk gave a caustic grunt as he turned away from the dead men and continued toward the hotel, thumbing fresh cartridges into the Henry's loading rod. He approached the rear of the building without further trouble, and tramped along the south side to the front veranda.

All the windows of the hotel were lit, and the hum of conversations punctuated with laughter sounded from inside. Hawk kept his rifle on his shoulder as he pushed through the front door.

A bracket lamp guttered on the wall to his left, another on the wall behind the desk. Also behind the desk was not the birdlike gent but, apparently, the birdlike gent's replacement — a lanky younger man with long, straight blond hair and a sandy mustache and sideburns. He was kicked back in the Windsor chair, resting his head against the key boxes behind him, shabby boots crossed on the counter.

There were a dozen key boxes, and there wasn't a box left with a key in it. The place had filled up.

Hearing men talking and laughing in the second story, and the thumps of boots in the creaky ceiling, Hawk turned to the stairs and stopped suddenly. One more step and he would have kicked the girl sitting on the second step up from the bottom.

"Well, if it isn't the five-hundred-dollar man," the girl said in a slightly jeering tone.

She was a small girl, and young, with dark brown hair cascading to her shoulders. It was a cool night, but her shabby dress was skimpy, and she had only a ratty cream sweater wrapped around her shoulders. Under the sweater was a light pink corset that tried to make her breasts look large. On her legs were black net stockings, and on her feet were pink, high-heeled shoes adorned with fake blue flowers.

Hawk started to go around her, but she grabbed his pants leg and gazed up at him, faint beseeching in her eyes. "Need a woman?"

"No."

Hawk lifted his left boot onto the step beside the girl, but she tightened her grip on his pants leg. "You wanna know about Kid Reno?"

Hawk looked at her, frowning.

"Well?" she said. He noticed that she had a faint bruise on the nub of her right cheek, and a small scar on her bottom lip.

Hawk continued staring down at her, measuring her, trying to decipher the thoughts in her eyes. A sporting girl was as likely as anyone to know where the outlaw was hanging out. Maybe Reno liked them young and flat-chested. Hell, maybe this little waif with more hair on her head than tallow on her entire frame was his favorite.

"You better not be hornswogglin' me, girl."

"Take me to your room," she said softly, flattening her hand out on Hawk's thigh and slowly sliding it up toward his crotch. "And I'll tell you what I know about Kid Reno."

Hawk pulled away and continued up the dark, narrow stairs. He could hear the clumsy clomping of the girl behind him and glanced back to see her climbing the steps, head lowered to watch her feet as she held her dress up with one hand and clutched her sweater with the other.

Voices grew louder above him. As Hawk gained the second story, he turned to start down the narrow hall and stopped.

Just outside the door of his room — the *open* door of his room — a man in long-handles, boots, and a shabby Stetson looked up at him. He'd been talking with his head turned toward Hawk's open door, but had swung his head toward Hawk when he heard Hawk's tread at the top of the stairs.

The man held an uncorked bottle in his hand, and he hung both pale arms over his knees. His lower jaw dropped slightly, and a chagrined look washed over his eyes. His cheeks flushed behind their three-day growth of dark brown beard. Slowly, keeping his eyes on Hawk, he reached behind him with one hand and lightly rapped his knuckles against Hawk's door.

"Ahh . . . Pope . . . you best come on outta there."

"What?" came a man's voice from inside Hawk's room.

"Come on out."

Hawk could see the man through the cracked door. The man said, "Why . . . ?" and let his voice trail off when he swiveled his head to look into the hall. He froze, and his eyes snapped wide. He'd been going through one of Hawk's saddlebag pouches on Hawk's bed, and cooking gear from both pouches and other possibles were bunched on the frayed top quilt.

The man in the room scowled as Hawk stepped forward. He moved past the man sitting on the floor, who didn't appear to be armed, and shoved the door wide with his Henry's barrel. The man in the room was fully dressed in rough trail clothes, with a holstered Colt hanging from a low-slung shell belt. As Hawk approached him, hard-eyed, Henry extended from his hip, the man stepped back and raised his hands shoulder high.

"Hold on now. . . ."

"Find what you're lookin' for?"

The man stammered, licked his chapped lips, his eyes darting around like hunted gophers.

The man stammered some more. Then his eyes slid to the unarmed, half-dressed gent whom Hawk had half turned toward, keeping the gent in the field of his vision. "You were supposed to watch the goddamn door, Sanchez, you —"

Hawk cut him off. "I asked you a question."

"Look," Pope said wearily, shrugging. "We wasn't lookin' to rob ya. We was just curious, that's all. Ain't too many hombres go flashin' five hundred dollars around the Dandy Dog, much less askin' questions about fellas like . . ." Mentioning the name seemed difficult, troublesome. "Like . . . you know. . . ."

"Kid Reno."

"Right," Pope said, nodding.

He looked at Sanchez, who stood in the doorway, chin dipped shamefully toward his chest. The girl stood behind Sanchez, back pressed to the hall's opposite wall.

"So, we was just curious, that's all."

"Did you find what you were looking for?"

Pope stared at Hawk, his fingers curled toward his palms. The skin between his eyes wrinkled. "No."

"Mighta been easier just to go ahead and ask me straight out than slinkin' around like a couple of skunks in a spring-house."

Pope swallowed and tipped his head back, frowning as though something pained him terribly. "You . . . you a lawman, mister?"

"Some might say so. Some wouldn't." Hawk waved his rifle toward the bed. "Now, if you wanna save yourself from getting drilled through the heart, which I have every right to do, you comin' in here and messin' up my things and all, you'll put everything back nice and neat, the way you found it. Then you and Sanchez'll go on back to your room and go nighty-nighty, and I won't hear another peep out of you . . . or see your ugly faces ever again."

Pope went to the bed and, casting wary glances at Hawk who stood watching him statue still, the rifle aimed at Pope's chest, started shoving Hawk's possibles back into the saddle pouches. When he was done, Hawk ushered him and Sanchez out the door and watched until both men had hurried into a room down the hall.

They closed and locked the door behind

them, quietly arguing like an old married couple in the presence of strangers.

Hawk lowered the Henry and turned his attention to the girl. She still stood on the other side of the hall, back to the wall, hands behind her, chin dipped shyly toward her corset. She had skin like ivory, with a few light freckles in her cleavage and across her shoulders, and her eyes were as brown as fresh-roasted coffee.

"What's your name?" Hawk asked her.

"Doris Hoffman."

Hawk pulled back into the room. "Come on in, Doris Hoffman."

When the girl had clomped into the room, in shoes that Hawk judged were a size too large, Hawk lighted a lamp, closed the door, dropped his rifle on the bed, and moved to the washstand.

"Glass of water?" he said, holding up a water glass.

"No, thank you."

"Whiskey?"

She shook her head.

"Have a seat."

Hawk didn't indicate where she should sit. There was a rickety, straight-back chair and the bed. She chose the bed, slowly lowering her rump to the edge, hands in her lap. She kept her brown eyes on Hawk and a wistful smile on her full, wide lips.

Hawk poured a glass of water and sagged into the chair. It creaked uneasily beneath his weight. He stared at her, waiting.

She returned the stare, trying for all she was worth to be coquettish, sensual, but she was like a little girl playing make-believe in a tree house. She slid off the edge of the bed, dropped to her knees, and crawled toward him, placing a hand on his left knee.

"Wanna do it first?"

"Nope. I want you to tell me about Kid Reno, and then I want you to go."

"Come on," she said. "I'm young. Not even fourteen yet. My skin's really smooth." With one hand, she nudged her sweater off her shoulders, laying them bare. She leaned a little farther forward, giving him a better look down her shallow cleavage, and shook her hair away from her face. "You can do whatever you want. Might cost you a little more, 'cause I'm so young. . . ." She paused. "I won't even stay and pester ya afterward."

Hawk felt the nip of anger in his head and hardened his jaws. "You don't know a damn thing about Kid Reno, do you?"

She frowned. "Sure. But wouldn't you like — ?"

"No, I wouldn't like. What I would like is for you to haul your little ass out of here."

She winced as though slapped, then pushed up off her knees and sat on the edge of the bed. Anger flashed in her eyes. "What . . . you don't like girls?"

"Not as young as you." Hawk suddenly realized something that he'd only half noticed when he'd first seen the girl. He looked down at her belly. It was slightly swollen in contrast to the rest of her.

His anger ebbed and he drew a sharp breath. "Where's your family, Doris?"

She frowned. "Why?"

"Where?"

Her eyes went to the door, and the corners of her mouth pulled down. "Dead."

"All of 'em?"

She nodded slightly and stared at the door. She licked the scar on her lower lip and began to push herself up. Hawk stuck his leg out, resting his boot on the bed, blocking her way to the door.

"You're alone. . . ."

"All right," she said, her voice hard, shuttling her angry gaze to him. "I don't know where Kid Reno is. But I seen him once . . . three months ago. He came through town with five other men, and I don't know why you're lookin' for him, but you sure as hell better hope you don't find him. He'll kill you deader'n hell, mister!"

She tried to stand but came up against Hawk's leg and fell back down on the bed, her glare growing sharper. "Let me go, you son of a bitch!"

"You got one in the chute, Doris?"

She looked startled. She dropped her eyes suddenly to her belly and pressed her hand against it, as though caressing the baby inside her.

"What're you gonna do — have the kid here?" Hawk jerked his head toward the window, indicating the stinking town.

The girl just stared at him, incredulous. She needed money. She probably thought that using her body was a good way to get it. After she got it — by rummaging through Hawk's clothes after he'd fallen asleep, maybe — she'd slip off into the night, five hundred dollars richer.

Hawk cursed. He reached inside his vest and fished the wad of greenbacks from the breast pocket of his shirt. He peeled off several bills, dropped his leg from the bed, and held the money toward the girl.

"Take it."

Doris glanced skeptically at the money, like a coyote being lured into a trap with scraps of fresh meat.

"Take it," he said, waving the bills at her.

Slowly, she lifted her hand, accepted the

120

money, and inspected it quickly.

"It's a hundred dollars," Hawk said. "Take it and get out of here, Doris. Take it and go have your baby a goddamn long ways from Saguaro. Do yourself and the kid a favor, and don't come back."

Doris was still skeptical, wary. She glanced from the money to Hawk. "You . . . don't want anything for it?"

"I want you to hop the next stage out of here."

Doris continued to frown at him. From the rooms around them filtered the din of bawdy male conversation. There were several cracks of a distant pistol, and a dog was barking on the town's far edge.

Finally, Doris lowered the money to her lap and, keeping her eyes on Hawk, rose and clomped over to the door. She set her hand on the knob and turned it slowly, watching him as though expecting him to stop her and tell her it was all a joke: "I'll be needing the money back."

When the bolt clicked, she jerked the door open, clomped out, closed the door quickly behind her, and clomped off down the hall and down the stairs.

Hawk threw the last of his water back and set the glass on the dresser. With a ragged sigh, he rose from the creaky chair, went

over to the window, and stared out at the
raucous night.

10.
RIDE TO SWEETWATER

Hawk's gun was in his hand before his head had risen from his pillow. The ratcheting click as he cocked the hammer echoed around the shabby room that was lit with bloodred light washing through the single, drawn window shade.

He looked at the door.

He'd heard something in his sleep. Probably someone in the hall, possibly another bushwhacker hoping to catch him snoring. He'd been expecting it all night, slumbering the way in which he'd become accustomed — light as a long-lived bobcat.

The hall floor creaked. A spur trilled faintly. Beneath the door, a shadow flickered. There was a soft scraping sound, and then a small slip of paper slid into view through the crack beneath the door.

A sliver of morning light burnished a corner of the paper. It was a small, manila-colored envelope with writing on it. The writing was in shadow, and Hawk couldn't make it out from the bed.

He waited, keeping his big, silver-chased Russian aimed at the door. When the shadow beneath the door vanished and soft footsteps began to retreat, Hawk pushed out of bed, crossed the room barefoot, and pressed his left shoulder against the wall beside the door. He turned the key in the lock, drew the door open quickly, and thrust the Russian through the opening.

The hall was empty. Men snored behind closed doors on both sides. Soft footsteps faded down the stairs, with the occasional soft chimes of a spur.

Hawk looked down. His last name was penciled on the envelope — large, blocky letters. He picked it up and strode down the hall to the top of the stairs, arriving just in time to see a long-haired girl turn at the bottom toward the hotel's outside door.

She stopped with her hand on the latch, and turned an Indian-dark face toward Hawk, glancing at him sidelong, expressionless — a round-faced girl in a cream-and-brown calico blouse under a wool vest and beaded necklace. She wore a bullet-crowned brown hat, and a gun and shell belt on her hips. Before Hawk could say anything, she moved on out the door and latched it behind her.

His eyes heavily mantled by his dark brows, Hawk depressed the Russian's hammer, tore open the envelope, and removed a scrap of plain, lined notepaper. He shook it open, and held the dark-penciled words up to the light.

RIDE TO SWEETWATER

He recited the words aloud and lowered the paper.

"What's in Sweetwater?" A moment later, staring blankly into space, he said, "And who in hell are you, girl?"

He hurried down the stairs and looked through the window right of the door. The late-dawn light showed the back of the long-haired girl riding away on a brown-and-white pinto pony, heading back toward the main part of town. As Hawk watched, she booted the pinto into a trot, and a moment later she disappeared behind some falling-down mud huts and dilapidated stables.

Gone.

Hawk turned toward the hotel's front desk. The long-haired gent who'd been lounging behind the desk last night, asleep, was lounging there now in much the same position as he had last night, asleep, his arms crossed on his chest. He snored softly, chin lifting as he inhaled, lowering as he exhaled. He probably wouldn't know who Hawk's messenger girl was, anyway. Something told Hawk she was a stranger around here.

He looked at the front of the small envelope in his hand, on which had been scrawled: HAWK.

But she, or someone she knew, knew him. . . .

He went upstairs and dressed.

At the livery barn across from the hotel, Hawk had to saddle his own horse, as there wasn't a hostler to be found. He led the grulla out through the barn's double doors, and stepped into the saddle, reining the horse south — the direction his caller had ridden.

It was after seven, but the town owned a funereal silence in the wake of last night's frenetic revelry. Hawk was glad he'd awakened the desk clerk for directions to Sweetwater, an abandoned stage relay station in the hills about six miles south of town.

He'd have gotten no such help in the streets of Saguaro. He didn't see a single soul out and about even as he headed back through the business district, and on the southern outskirts he saw only a couple of mangy coyotes and one skittish rabbit.

The only man he saw on the street was dead — a scrawny half-breed sitting against the porch of a run-down cantina, his hands cupped around the knife in his guts, chin dipped to a shoulder.

Someone had run off with his boots, half removing one filthy sock in the process.

The ragged shacks at the town's edge fell back behind Hawk as he followed an old freight trail and stage road over the rocky southern hills. He assumed that the freshest horse tracks in the trace's finely churned powder were those of the girl who'd delivered the note.

They were easy to pick out, as there were none even two days fresher, and there weren't that many to begin with. The trail obviously wasn't used much — probably only by saddle tramps and, a couple of times a month, by freighters delivering supplies to the small army outpost that straddled the Arizona/California border.

Hawk wasn't far from town before he slipped the Henry from its sheath and rammed a live round into the chamber. He knew he could very well be riding into an ambush. A man with as many enemies as Hawk should have burned the note and forgotten about it. A normal, cautious man. Hawk was neither.

Besides, someone might be genuinely looking to collect on the five hundred dollars he'd offered and didn't want to be seen with Hawk in town.

He'd followed a sign for the Sweetwater Station down a left tine in a trail fork and was about to leave that secondary trail and circle the station to approach from the opposite direction when he spied a man standing in the high rocks off the trail's right side. A lone gunman with a rifle and a hat with its brim curled sharply on both sides.

Hawk tightened his grip on the Henry, jerking the grulla to a halt. Before he could raise the rifle, the lookout turned to face in the direction of the station. He waved his arms above his head broadly — a signal wave. Hawk considered the man for a moment, then, resettling the Henry across his saddlebows, booted the grulla forward.

Ten minutes later he came upon another lookout standing in cactus-studded rocks not far from the trail, on its left side. This was a burly gent with a red bib beard and dressed in black bull hide, bandoliers crossed on his stout chest.

The man held a Sharps rifle across both shoulders. He grinned toothily as Hawk approached, then lowered the rifle and gave a mock, graceful bow, throwing a pale, freckled arm out to indicate the trail ahead.

Again, Hawk booted the grulla forward, and presently the Sweetwater Station appeared among large red boulders strewn like the toys of a giant, temperamental child on both sides of the trail, in a depression lime green with creosote, cat's claw, and time-worn saguaros. A windmill and a brush arbor fronted an adobe stable and a couple of corrals formed from woven ironwood and ocotillo branches. The station itself — a long, L-shaped, adobe-brick structure with a brush roof and a wide front veranda — nestled in the chaparral on the left.

A large sign above the veranda, so faded that most of the letters had disappeared, announced SWEETWATER STATION.

A half dozen men milled under the arbor of cottonwood poles, around a smoky coffee fire. A dozen or so saddled horses were tied to cottonwood-rail hitch racks fronting a stock trough over which the wooden blades of the windmill turned, squawking like a dying chicken.

Some of the mounts ate from feedbags draped over their ears. Others lazed in the sun, their hides dusty and sweat lathered, saddle cinches hanging free beneath their bellies. The men beneath the brush arbor watched Hawk with mute interest.

They were all well armed with pistols and knives, some carrying rifles, but no offensive moves were made. It was almost, Hawk mused, as though they'd been warned not to make any, or to even seem to make any.

Another man, closer to Hawk and acting as a third lookout, leaned his butt against a boulder fronting an armless saguaro. He was a little, craggy-featured man with longish, light-red hair spilling down from a shabby derby hat, and holding a Winchester across his thighs, aimed away from Hawk. As Hawk approached, the man tipped his head to one side and gave the newcomer a slit-eyed, dimple-cheeked smile against the sun.

It occurred to Hawk, as he rode past, who the hard case was: Seymore T. Lindley. A slippery desperado from far west Texas, and wanted in nearly every frontier territory from Dakota to Texas.

Hawk allowed himself a bemused grin as he angled toward the station house, in front of which three saddled horses stood, tied to one of the two hitch racks, idly swishing their tails. One of the mounts, a sleek buckskin, turned its head toward Hawk, flicked its ears, and whinnied.

The grulla responded in kind.

130

Hawk's eyes were on the cabin, in the open front door of which a tall, rangy young woman appeared. She stood with both hands on the door casing, her long, straight blond hair sliding around in the wind, a thin cigar clamped between her white teeth as she appraised the newcomer with a cool, faintly haughty expression.

Hawk's grave eyes belied the recognition behind them.

He said her name to himself silently, and his loins heated instantly, aching. His gut tightened in revulsion against the sudden, physical response, denying it.

Saradee Jones.

Christ.

"Well, look what the old bobcat dragged in."

The girl sauntered out the door, spurs ringing, in men's dusty trail garb including a low-cut, pin-striped shirt showing the lacy edge of a camisole beneath, and a small silver cross dangling from a rawhide string to nestle in her deep, tan cleavage. She wore tan chaps over blue denims, a cartridge belt from which a hand-tooled black holster hung, thonged low on her right thigh, a pearl-gripped Colt jutting above its keeper thong.

She kicked out her worn brown boots with

undershot heels, tucked her thumbs behind her cartridge belt, and favored Hawk with a knowing, smoldering smile around the cheroot in her teeth. "Been a while, lover."

"Not long enough."

"Don't be that way." Sunlight angled under the brim of her tan Stetson and flared across her lilac-blue eyes. "We got history, you an' me."

"I take it you were on the prowl in Saguaro last night." Funny he hadn't seen her, though. Tall, buxom blondes dressed like male gunnies stuck out in crowds like red silk in a funeral procession.

"Nah, not me. Some of the boys." She lifted her chin slightly, to indicate the men behind Hawk.

Hawk glanced over his shoulder toward the hard case guarding the trail at the edge of the yard. "Like Lindley."

"Can't keep Seymore from a party. I've done tried. Towns — even one as wide open as Saguaro — ain't no place for wanted killers. But some men just won't listen to reason."

Just then a figure moved behind Saradee Jones, and Hawk saw the girl who'd delivered the note to his hotel room slip through the station house door, sort of slither around the casing as though she were making brief love to it. Her big, brown, Indian eyes were on Hawk, and they bespoke as little emotion as her broad, dark red lips.

As she flanked Saradee, another figured moved out of the cabin — a man dressed in an expensively cut black suit with a crisp white shirt and a ribbon tie blowing around his neck. He was a dark-haired, dark-mustached gent — not a Mexican, maybe a Scot — with oily black eyes and a grim smile. His pale skin was sun-blistered beneath the shade line of his hat. Three pistols, including a belly gun, bristled around his hips and breeze-whipped flaps of his black frock coat.

Hawk's busy mind flipped through the sheaf of names in his brain, and clicked like a roulette wheel making a sudden stop on a winning number. Melvin Hansen.

Not a Scot. A dark Swede from Wisconsin.

Hawk's eyes must have betrayed his recognition. Saradee chuckled, spreading her lips, removing the cheroot from her teeth, and spitting a fleck of cigar skin from her lips. "Melvin, meet Gideon Hawk."

Hansen dipped his chin slightly.

Saradee jerked her left thumb over her shoulder at the Indian girl. "This is April. I sent her with the note after my boys got back and told me a tall stranger with two big pistols, a Henry rifle, and five hundred greenbacks was makin' fast friends with the local undertaker. I figured you were less likely to shoot a girl skulking around your room than a man . . . and you wouldn't know April's deadlier'n a coiled rattlesnake."

Saradee smiled flirtatiously. "I would have come myself but there's folks there who might recognize me — folks whose fur I rubbed in the wrong direction, time or two."

"Imagine that."

"The way I remember it . . . you sorta liked the way I rubbed your fur . . . when I'd come skulkin' about your room." Saradee took a long drag from the cheroot and let the wind tear it away from her red lips. "Remember?"

Hawk's throat grew heavy. His undeniable lust for this woman made his anger flare. He should have killed her when he'd first met her down in Mexico, where he'd chased her and another, now-deceased gang after she'd murdered and robbed an army payroll and kidnapped a Mexican whore Hawk had rescued from an overzealous posse. He should have put a bullet between those big, saucy breasts she was shoving toward him now and kicked her out cold with a shovel.

He'd known that, letting her live, she'd

come back to haunt him. And she had haunted him, several times. Trouble was, she'd also saved his life a time or two. . . .

Hawk rested a forearm on his saddle horn. "You shadowin' me?"

"Nah." Saradee took another puff from her cigar. "I think our paths are just naturally meant to cross. Must be something in the stars, Hawk. What do you say you light and sit a spell, join me for a drink?"

Behind her, Melvin Hansen said tightly, molasses-dark eyes pinned to Hawk, "I don't see why. . . ."

"Shut up, Melvin," Saradee said with a smile.

Melvin's pink-splotched tan cheeks turned pinker, and his chin dimpled as he slid his eyes to Saradee and then returned them to Hawk. They were as flat as those of a Mojave rattler.

"Melvin's new to the gang," Saradee explained to Hawk. "He still can't get used to a woman runnin' things."

Hawk wanted to ride on. Or part of him did.

Another, smaller but insistent part — a breathless voice in the back of his brain — urged him to answer her siren call.

He glowered across the grulla's twitching ears at the pretty, lightly tanned blonde regarding him with infuriating frankness and female understanding and decided — or part of him did, anyway — that giving his horse a rest couldn't hurt. Since she was one of the curly wolves he spent his lonely days hunting, it couldn't hurt to hear what she had to say, either.

She might even put him on Kid Reno's scent.

Hawk lifted his Henry from his saddlebows and, keeping his eyes on Melvin Hansen, who returned the favor, swung his right boot over his saddle horn and dropped to the ground. He tossed his reins over the hitch rack, mounted the veranda's cracked, rotting steps, tipped his hat to the silent, expressionless April, and turned to the black-clad gunfighter.

"Would you mind watering my grulla, Melvin? It's a hot day, and he hasn't drank since Saguaro."

Hansen gritted his teeth, but before he could speak, Saradee said with her petulant grin, "Do it, Melvin. Hawk here's a friend of mine, and any friend of mine is a friend of yours."

She turned and walked into the cabin.

11.
THE GIRL HE
SHOULD HAVE KILLED

Hawk gave the gunman from Wisconsin a phony grin, then followed Saradee into the station house's dingy shadows, the air stale and rank with the smell of dry rot and mice shit. There was a small bar consisting of planks laid over barrels, and a door to the left that probably led to a kitchen. A door on the right, partly covered by a ratty, dusty blanket, probably led to overnight sleeping quarters for stage passengers.

There were three or four small tables, some tipped over, and a half dozen chairs, some without backs and also tipped over. Dust lay a half an inch deep on everything, and enough cobwebs for a witch's lair hung from ceiling beams and support posts.

Saradee made her way to one of the few upright tables, around which several chairs were gathered, and on which was a clear bottle and three tin coffee cups. "Come on over and have some tequila. Picked it up in

Nogales. The dead worm on the bottom died with a smile on its face."

She kicked out a chair and plopped down, slapping her well-turned thighs. "That snake water's so damn strong it's like to put hair on my tits, but it's right refreshing. Make you see the world through a whole new pair of eyes."

Hawk kicked out a chair across from Saradee and slacked into it. "I doubt all the rotgut tequila in Sonora could make me see it any clearer. What the hell're you doin' here, anyway? And why'd you send that note? You're wasting my time, Saradee."

"How can you be so sure I'm wasting your time?" Saradee picked up one of the tin cups. "You all right with drinkin' after Melvin?"

"I reckon I'm no more particular than you are."

Saradee's lips quirked with satisfaction at that. Hawk's ear tips warmed. Was that jealousy he heard in his voice? He ground his jaws against it and accepted the cup from Saradee. He glanced inside at the clear liquor half filling the cup.

"Don't worry," Saradee said. "I ain't gonna get you drunk and take advantage." She nudged a chair to her right and crossed her boots on it. "Though it's right tempting . . . you bein' you, and me bein' me an' all. We got some history, Hawk. Don't tell me you don't think about it. I can tell you straight out that I do."

Hawk sipped his drink and started wishing he'd listened to the soft voice of common sense and ridden on.

"Answer my question."

"Which one?"

"How 'bout the first one? We'll mosey over to the second one after I've had enough sips of this coffin varnish to thin out your bullshit."

Saradee sipped her tequila and, smacking her lips, looked over the brim of her dented cup at him. "That's no way to talk to an old flame."

"Moment of weakness. Thank Christ it didn't last."

"Moments of weakness," Saradee said. "And they could stretch into a fair piece of time . . . if you'd take the hump out of your neck. Ain't no man more qualified to ride with my bunch."

Hawk chuffed an ironic laugh. "Shit, I kill men like your bunch. And women like you."

"Then how come none of us is dead yet?"

"I'm feelin' merciful today."

She tossed her head back, and thrust her shoulders against the slat-back chair.

Whether she was aware of it or not, her breasts pushed so hard against her blouse that the button over her cleavage popped open, revealing more of the crucifix over a smooth stretch of snow-white camisole. She was a fair-skinned girl, but the sun had turned her olive. The camisole stood out against it . . . alluring.

Against his will, Hawk's brain tossed up a picture of her naked and straddling him, those large, cherry-tipped breasts jostling an inch in front of his face. He drew a ragged breath, and winced against the memory, turning away from it as he lifted his gaze to Saradee's glowing blue eyes.

"You ain't changed a bit." She pouted. "Just as stubborn as ever. Oh, well, you and Melvin would just fight over me, anyway. I'd have to have Lindley shoot you both to put you out of your misery like moon-crazed wildcats."

Hawk lifted his cup to his lips for another sip of the heady, astringent brew. "Back to the subject."

"Ah, shit, I'm not followin' you, Hawk, though it wouldn't be difficult except for hopscotchin' my horse over all the dead men you leave in the trail. I had business over in California and this is the best *back* trail from California; the U.S. marshals and

140

Pinkertons preferring not to get beefed out here where no can find and bury 'em."

"What kind of business?"

"That's one question too many."

"All right." Hawk shrugged. "Let's get back to one already asked but not yet answered."

"Kid Reno?" Saradee smiled like a little girl offering to sell a rose for a penny and a tousle of her cornflower curls. "Shit, he's in Ehrenberg. Never met the man, but I saw him there. Figured to ask him to join up with me — you know, safety in numbers — but, now, there's a problem I don't need."

She squinted an eye and held up her shot glass, poking her index finger around it at Hawk. "He must have half the marshals, Texas Rangers, Arizona Rangers, county sheriffs, and Pinkerton agents in all the frontier dusting his back trail. And then, when you have to make a fast dip into Mexico . . . well, the man wouldn't be fit company in Mexico. Not if you don't want every *rurale* and *federale* and any other kind of 'rale' in Sonora and Chihuahua clinging to you like the lice clinging to the Kid's rancid hair!"

She threw back the last of her shot and slopped more tequila into her cup.

"Me and the boys lit out under cover of

141

darkness, left the Kid howling and bellowing like a poleaxed bull in one of the whorehouses in the company of his men. Christ — what a gang of miscreants and mangy coyotes."

"What was he howling about?" Hawk asked.

"Just drunk and stompin' with his tail up. Melvin and I heard he has the pony drip something awful, but it don't keep him from trying to spread his seed around, hot as it is. I don't reckon he can get it up or keep it up or at least bring the practice to completion. Too painful, I 'spect. I wouldn't know — I've never had the drip. You?"

"Knock on wood." Hawk threw the last of his own shot back and rattled the empty cup back down on the table. "Ehrenberg?"

"As of two weeks ago, anyway."

"If he's got the drip, he might still be there. I hear it's hell to ride with."

Hawk fished inside his sheepskin vest and dipped his fingers into his shirt pocket.

"I don't need your money," Saradee said with indignation.

She dropped her boots down off the chair and leaned over the table toward Hawk, resting her elbows on her knees. Her eyes were shiny, her cheeks flushed from the tequila. "What I would like is a long afternoon under some cool cottonwoods. I know a creek near here. We could slip away, just the two of us. Take a little dip. . . ."

Hawk glowered at her. His heart shuddered. Hot blood jetted through his loins.

No woman aside from his wife had ever had such a grip on him. But she was nothing like Linda. She was some wild creature of the southwestern deserts and mountains. A she-cat with the perpetual springtime craze crawling up a dry, sun-blasted arroyo looking for a mate as hot-blooded and feral as she.

Try as he might, he could not keep his mind from remembering the radiant mounds and knolls and plains of her porcelain-smooth body. Nor the fierceness with which she'd writhed beneath him, her arms and legs entangled with his, her heels grinding into his rump, her fingernails deliciously raking his back.

Her catlike howls and groans that set his male lust and passion exploding like a million pounds of black powder. . . .

She stared across the table at him, her eyes aglow with radiant knowing. "Come on, Hawk. You remember how it was. It could be like that every night. Hell, every morning."

Hawk wanted to run a hand down his face

as though to wipe her image from his retinas, but he maintained an impassive expression as he lounged back in his chair. "You talk like we got somethin' in common. Like I said, I kill folks like you."

"That's what we have in common, Hawk."

"Thieves, rapists, murderers. You'd kill your own mother for a plug nickel and a shot of rotgut tequila."

"We're flip sides of the same coin, lover."

The word bit him like a razor-edged blade twisting deep in his guts. He swallowed, and his brows bunched like stormy mountains. He was repelled by the brittleness, the faint desperation he heard in his own voice. "One of these days, Saradee, I'm gonna come gunnin' for you and your boys. I'm gonna run you down."

"If you'd really wanted to beef me, you'd have done it two years ago in Mexico."

"The time wasn't right then. We had to throw in together to stay alive. But we ain't in Mexico anymore, and your days are numbered."

She stared into his eyes — a diamondback mesmerizing a cat. Her tongue darted deliciously across her lips as she spoke. "Our hearts are the same, Hawk. You think you ride for some noble cause, but it's even *less* noble than mine, because I don't pretend I'm some kinda saint with a six-gun. And you'll never be able to kill me because you remember what it was like to *fuck* me!"

Hawk kicked his chair back and heaved himself to his feet.

Saradee laughed. "A man like you is dangerous, Hawk. You oughta be locked up . . . or go ahead and admit what you are — a cold-blooded killer. Come on, lover. Throw in with Saradee, and let's have some *fun!*"

Hawk gritted his teeth against the throbbing in his temples. He wheeled and started for the door, clenching his fists above his guns.

Saradee rose from her chair and called behind him, "Well, you think on it and let me know. I got a feelin' our paths are gonna cross again real soon."

Hawk stopped at the door. His jaws were tight, and his nostrils flared as he breathed. He couldn't help taking one more look behind.

Saradee stood staring after him, fists on her hips, breasts jutting against her blouse. Her gaze met Hawk's. She grinned.

"Tell Melvin to get in here," she called as she sank back down in her chair, suddenly pouting again. "I ain't done drinkin' yet, and I'm not the kinda girl who drinks alone."

Hawk turned his head forward and walked through the door. He stopped on the other side. Melvin Hansen sat against the veranda's front railing. He stared gravely at Hawk.

"Boss's callin'," Hawk said.

He started toward the veranda's steps. In the corner of his left eye, Hansen stiffened. Hawk stopped again and looked at the gunman. Hansen's right hand had slid toward the walnut grips of his Colt Army positioned for the cross draw on his left hip.

Hawk met the gunman's flat, hard, wide-eyed gaze.

All sound and all thoughts dwindled to vapor in Hawk's head. He became conscious of only his right hand and Melvin Hansen, whose own right hand had flattened out across his brown wool vest and watch chain, halfway to his Colt.

Hawk waited. Half consciously he felt his cheeks lift with an eager, encouraging grin. Hansen's eyes gained a wary cast. The skin above the bridge of his nose wrinkled slightly, and slowly, he let his right hand fall away from his belly and drop back down to his side.

Hawk canted his head toward the station house's open door. "Boss's waitin'."

Chagrin blossomed in Hansen's burned cheeks, and the man's fury returned. Keeping his eyes on Hawk, he rose from the veranda's rail and, hooking his thumbs behind his cartridge belt, stomped off into the station house.

"Where the hell you been?" Hawk heard Saradee say. "I don't like to be kept waitin', Melvin."

Hawk allowed himself a faint smile as he continued down the steps and into the yard, where April stood with his grulla. A bucket of water sat on the ground in front of the horse. The saddle's latigo strap dangled toward the ground, and its bridle bit had been slipped from its mouth, as well.

"Obliged," he told the girl, who stood holding the grulla's bridle with one hand and regarding Hawk with customary dullness.

He buckled the belly strap, shoved the bit into the horse's mouth, and stepped into the saddle with a squawk of sun-cured leather. Saradee's men continued to regard him with faint curiosity from the shade beneath the brush arbor.

Hawk pinched his hat brim to April. "Obliged."

April released the grulla's bridle and stepped back. Hawk reined the grulla away from the station house and booted it into a gallop past Saradee's men and the windmill and stock tank, and southwest along the seldom-used stage road toward Ehrenberg.

12.
KID RENO RIDES

Kid Reno was Hawk's only clue as to the specific whereabouts of Knife-Hand Monjosa.

According to an old sheriff he'd met — a wizened old desert rat, long retired, who kept his ear to the outlaw-trampled trail out of habit — Kid Reno had been Knife-Hand's first lieutenant down in Mexico but had recently fallen out of the murderous half-breed's favor. They'd somehow not killed each other but parted ways.

The sheriff figured the Kid would be holed up somewhere in Arizona, as he was said to have a Lipan Apache wife he felt some loyalty to and vice versa. As Kid Reno was nowhere near the recluse Knife-Hand was, and had many friends and acquaintances in Arizona, the sheriff didn't think he'd be as difficult as Knife-Hand to run down.

And the Kid would know the whereabouts

of Knife-Hand's several mysterious hideouts along the Colorado River, might even know which he was currently calling home. Getting the desperado himself, a notorious thief and killer, to divulge such secrets would be a trick in and of itself, but the sheriff was confident that Hawk's best chance of locating Knife-Hand would be to run down the man who knew him best.

Hawk wasn't thinking such thoughts on his second day out from the Sweetwater stage station, however. He'd thought them all through, shuffled them, and set them aside days before. No, Kid Reno wasn't on Hawk's mind this day, though of course he should have been, as the Kid had many ears listening for him, and there was a good chance the Kid knew by now that he had a shadow.

At the very least, Hawk should have been paying careful attention to the rolling, sun-blasted terrain around him, as this was as much Apache country as the hideout territory of law-dodging cutthroats from America as well as Mexico.

What he was thinking about as he traversed a broad, sandy arroyo between two rocky, creosote-and-mesquite-stippled cutbanks, was Saradee Jones.

For the third or fourth time that day, he

found his mind harking back to her sprawling naked in his soogan blankets down in Mexico — that wanton succubus, that golden-haired, high-breasted Circe who knew better than any ten-dollar whore how to drive a man to the end of his wits with aching need and howling desire.

And this careless inattention to his immediate surrounds was why, just as his nostrils detected the faint smell of wood smoke on the warm, early-afternoon breeze, he heard a sudden, faint whistling too late to prevent a careening rope loop from falling down over his head and shoulders. The broad, revolving noose drew taut so suddenly and with such force that, before he could so much as lift his hands, he found himself hanging in midair three feet behind the grulla's ass and lazily swishing tail.

His wind gushed out of him in a sudden whoosh and then the ground rushed up from below to hammer him brutally about the back and shoulders. Before he could do much more than lift his head and blink his eyes in an attempt to clear them, the rope drew taut again, pinning his arms to his sides.

Someone gave a victorious howl.

Hawk grunted loudly as the rope jerked him straight back along the arroyo in the direction from which he'd ridden. The rocky, sandy ground slid away beneath him, scraping his butt, and he reached up to grab the rope and turn belly down to keep from being taken for a Dutch ride over rocks on his back.

Ahead, at the end of the rope slanting down from the left hip of a lineback dun, a man in a dusty cream slouch hat adorned with silver conchos whooped and hollered as he ground his black, spurred boots into the mount's lunging flanks. Hawk groaned as the ground shot out from beneath him, and horse and rider galloped off down the arroyo, Hawk fishtailing along behind, blinking against the sand and rocks being kicked up by the lineback's hammering hooves.

"Got me a big ole fish on the line!" the rider whooped, showing tobacco-stained teeth inside his scraggly beard.

Hawk gritted his teeth as the horseman dragged him along the arroyo. He could feel his sleeves and jeans tearing, feel the burning of the rocks and sand rawhiding his knees and elbows.

In spite of the pain and the violent hammering, he lifted his forearms and grabbed the taut rope with his hands, pulling, trying futilely to unseat the rider. Hawk couldn't see much through the sifting dust and flying gravel, but the rider had apparently dallied his lariat around his saddle horn.

After he'd galloped a hundred yards, whooping and yapping like a crazed coyote, the rider swerved his horse up the arroyo's low right bank. Hawk followed about fifteen yards behind the horse, his hat off, his hair in his eyes, his knees and elbows on fire, the rope cutting into his arms. Fishtailing up the bank, Hawk lowered his head as the horseman dragged him through mesquite snags and over greasewood shrubs and hard-edged chunks of black volcanic rock.

Branches snapped. Rocks rattled. The dun's hooves thudded loudly.

The mesquite and greasewood branches clawed at Hawk's face and scalp. He felt the icy burns oozing blood.

When he was clear of the shrubs, he looked up and peeled his eyes half open. The rider swerved just left of a saguaro, almost hitting the tall, one-armed cactus. The near collision startled the gent, and he jerked sideways in his saddle, nearly toppling his horse.

On impulse, Hawk leaned as far right as he could without rolling over. The movement was enough to angle him over to the saguaro's right side. He could hear the horse whinny angrily, its hooves raking the ground.

Working quickly, Hawk set a shoulder snug against the base of the saguaro and peered around the front of it. His tormenter had regained his balance and was savagely raking the dun with his spurs.

Behind him, the rope sagged slightly.

The horse lunged off its rear hooves.

Hawk felt the violent jerk as the rope pulled taut once more, but he ground his left shoulder into the saguaro, ignoring the thorns gouging through his shirtsleeve. Desperately, he ground his boot toes into the sand.

The horse screamed again, and as Hawk peered across the front of the saguaro at it, the horse jerked hard right. The saddle slipped down its right side a quarter second before the horse hit the ground on its right hip as it twisted its neck and head up, trying in vain to keep its balance.

The rider gave an indignant cry as he rolled down the side of the horse, still clinging to the saddle. He gave another cry as the floundering horse's right shoulder fell atop the man's right leg, pinning it between the stirrup and the ground.

He bellowed, gritting his teeth and throwing his head back on his shoulders.

The horse whinnied and struggled to right itself, the saddle falling farther and farther down its side, the rope raking across the left side of the rider's neck. Hawk scrambled back on his hands and knees. When he had enough slack in the rope, which the horse continued to jerk as it tried to rise, jostling the half-attached saddle, he whipped it up and over his head and tossed it away.

His knees burned like liquid fire, and the ground pitched and swayed beneath his boots. But Hawk sleeved blood from his left brow and staggered around the saguaro just as the horse gained all four hooves with a final lunge and galloped away.

The dragger screamed as the weight lifted from his right leg, and rolled onto his butt, propping himself up on his elbows. His hat was gone, and sandy-blond hair hung in his eyes. He stretched his thick, bearded lips back from his teeth painfully and panted.

His right leg was bloody where the bone had pushed through his deerskin breeches, just above his knee.

"*Ayyy!*" the man cried, throwing his head back on his shoulders, sobbing. "Oh! Oh! Oh, mercy, Jesus!"

Both of Hawk's six-shooters remained in their holsters. The Rogue Lawman unsnapped the keeper thong and slid the Russian from its cross-draw holster, raising the silver-chased iron and ratcheting back the hammer.

Hawk snarled, "He ain't here, friend. It's just me and you."

"Not quite!"

Hawk wheeled. His ears were ringing. That must be why he hadn't heard the clomps of the horses that were now moving up out of the arroyo from which Hawk himself had been dragged.

They were seven men on well-set-up mounts, some Mexicans, some Americans. They rode abreast, all clomping through the mesquites and creosote shrubs at the same time, spaced from eight to fifteen yards apart.

All holding either rifles or pistols aimed with casual menace at Hawk.

All except the man who rode slightly ahead of the others and whom Hawk took to be the leader. He held a Winchester straight up, its butt snugged against his buckskin-clad thigh. He was a tall, rangy man with anvil-wide shoulders and long silver-gray hair gathered into several thin, rawhide-wrapped braids. His gray hair was in stark contrast to his clean-lined, brick-red face that boasted a brushy gray mustache, its ends upswept and waxed to fine points.

His eyes were blue as the desert sky on a windswept winter day, and they surveyed Hawk and the fallen dragger from deep sockets mantled by grizzled brows.

Hawk held his cocked Russian half out from his side as the gray-haired man and the others closed on him in a sauntering, shambling pace. Their horses blew. Tack creaked. Shod hooves clipped stones. Dust rose, gilded by sunlight.

"Fuck," groused one of the riders approaching from the leader's left flank. "What'd he do to you, Merle?"

On the ground behind Hawk, Merle groaned and panted. "Ah, Jesus, my horse fell. Oh, God, I've never known pain this bad!"

"You were supposed to lasso the son of a bitch and drag him to *us*, Merle," the leader said. "Why in the hell did you cut up this way?"

"Didn't mean to," Merle sobbed. "My horse spooked at a rattler, so I figured I'd circle around. Then this goddamn saguaro got in the way, and that son of a bitch wrapped the rope around it, and sure as hell, my dun went down on top of me!"

Merle kicked his good leg and threw his

head back on his shoulders, gritting his teeth. "Oh, please, boys! For chrissakes, don't just sit there. Help me!"

Hawk waved the Russian around uncertainly as the men slowly circled him, the leader heading around Hawk toward the sobbing man on the ground behind him.

Hawk's belly was tight. He was worn out and beaten up from the dragging, and he blinked blood from his left eye. He'd need that eye when the shooting started, or he'd go down fast without taking so much as one of these cutthroats with him.

"How bad you hurt, Merle?" the leader said, and Hawk turned to see the man sitting on his steeldust gelding over the dragger, leaning forward against his saddle horn and regarding Merle with bemusement. "You gonna make it?"

Merle's voice was losing its vigor. "My leg's broke, Kid. Can't you see the blood? I'm gonna need a doctor. Shoot that son of a bitch and take me to a doctor!"

Inwardly, Hawk had flinched at the name by which the dragger had addressed the gang's leader. No. Couldn't be. He couldn't have let himself get run down by the very man he'd been tracking.

He wasn't that goddamn careless. . . .

"Ah, hell, Merle — look at you," the

leader said. "You're a goner."

He raised his Winchester to his shoulder and fired. His horse barely flinched. The bullet plunked through Merle's right temple and exited the opposite rear corner of Merle's skull to smack the ground with a little dust puff.

Merle's head jerked as though he'd been slapped, and then he collapsed, dead before his right shoulder hit the ground. The men sitting on their horses in a semicircle around Hawk stared at their dead *companero* with expressions on their craggy, hard-planed faces ranging from mild concern to sneering amusement.

The leader ejected the spent cartridge, seated fresh, and pulled his steeldust's head around, spurring the mount back toward Hawk. With a clattering of hooves and a rattle of bridle chains, he turned the horse so that he sat among the others, slightly ahead of them and between a rail-thin Mexican with long, black sideburns and a white-haired American with a yellow Vandyke beard and a string of Indian-dark human ears around his neck.

The leader leaned forward on his saddle horn again, resting his Winchester barrel across his left forearm, and regarded Hawk severely. "Now, friend, I'm going to ask you real nice to throw that hogleg off in the brush over there — as far as that cholla there — see? And then I'm gonna ask you to follow it up with the one still at peace in its holster."

Hawk caressed the hammer of his cocked Russian with his thumb as he glanced around the hard-eyed group before him. Aching and sore and more than a little addled from the dragging, he was still trying to figure out if he'd made the dunderheaded mistake of becoming his quarry's prey. At the same time, vaguely, he considered his options against this bunch of obvious killers.

There weren't many. Instead of dying in a hail of lead without even a chance of running Knife-Hand to ground, he depressed the Russian's hammer and tossed it into the brush. He followed it up with the Colt. Then he stood there, looking grim and not a little chagrined, hands raised to his shoulders.

13.
A Friend of
Galvin Woods

"Now," the gang's leader said in his resonate, authoritative voice as he continued leaning forward and narrowing one eye at Hawk, "please tell me who in the winds of blazing fury you are, and why you're trackin' me."

"Kid Reno, then," Hawk said. Odd to see a man of Reno's years — at least as old as Hawk — called "Kid."

"Kid Reno." The man winked and smiled proudly. He had a wasted face, and Hawk remembered Saradee telling about the Kid's health problem. "But you haven't done me the courtesy of telling me who you are."

"Hall," Hawk said. "Gideon Hall."

If Reno had heard of Hawk, like so many others had by now, the outlaw would likely know why Hawk was tracking Knife-Hand. Hawk wanted to keep that card facedown as long as he could.

"And your business?"

Hawk hiked a shoulder slightly. "I heard you were a man who knew your business. Sorta thought you might be someone I'd want to throw in with."

"Oh, you wanna throw in with me, huh?"

"That's right."

"Throw in with me for what?"

"For . . . whatever it is you got goin'," Hawk said.

Reno frowned with mock sincerity. "And who is it who told you about me?"

"Fella by the name of Galvin Woods out of Tucumcari." Hawk's mind was working fast. "Told me he'd ridden with you once . . . under a different name."

Reno stared at Hawk, not buying it. "Galvin Woods."

"That's right. Can't remember what handle he said he went by back then."

"Galvin Woods," Reno said. "Hmm." He paused. "And he gave me a good recommendation, did he?"

"Fair enough."

Silence.

Reno and his men stared at Hawk.

None of them was buying Hawk's story. Oh, well, Hawk thought. It wasn't a bad story, or a bad alias, on short notice. Galvin Woods was an old Welshman who'd farmed near Hawk's old ranch in Dakota Territory.

Hawk could tell Reno why he was really looking for him, but then they'd all know who Hawk really was. Likely their knowing he was no friend to outlaws wouldn't put him in any more favorable light than that which he was already in — no matter how Reno felt about his former partner, Knife-Hand.

If Reno wanted Knife-Hand dead, he likely could have killed him himself. He didn't need Hawk to do it for him. Besides, Hawk had sort of figured he'd kill Reno when he'd gotten the information he needed. . . .

Kid Reno glanced at the men to his right. He returned his gaze to Hawk and fashioned a menacing half smile on his sharp, pasty face. "Mister, I believe you're a bounty hunter. Pinkerton, maybe. No man who'd want to ride with me would be announcing my name around the territory. Especially no man who'd ever ridden with a man who'd ridden with me." He blinked. "If you catch my drift. . . ."

He glanced to his left, then tossed his head toward Hawk. "Fellas, you've handled bounty trackers before. Been a while, though. Time to get back in trim."

Hawk chuckled dryly to himself as the men began to dismount, looking eager.

Maybe he should have just gone ahead and told the truth. Instead, he'd bluffed himself into drawing on an inside straight.

Seven men against one. And he was still addled from the dragging, not to mention stove up and sore. . . .

They moved in on him quickly, circling, a couple glowering hatefully, a couple of others grinning devilishly. Hawk backed up and shuffled around slowly, trying to get his feet firmly beneath him, raising his hands.

He glanced at the pistols on their hips. They'd left their rifles in their saddle scabbards. Maybe Hawk could get his hands on one of the pistols and take a few of these rawhiders to hell with him. . . .

Kid Reno remained on his horse, leaning forward and grinning down with expectant satisfaction, like a Roman general at a gladiatorial match.

Reno's men moved closer, closer, starting to feint and raise their fists, shuffling their feet. In the corner of his left eye, Hawk saw a man lunge toward him. Hawk leaned back, and the fist only grazed his jaw. Wheeling, he raised his own right fist and felt the man's nose give with a chewy crack of breaking gristle, blood flying across the man's face in all directions.

The man grunted and stepped back, eyes

crossing slightly as he continued moving his balled fists out in front of him. His nose began swelling, turning a dull purple.

A couple of his compatriots chuckled, but he only glared at Hawk and hardened his jaws, nostrils flaring.

"That's it, Santos," Kid Reno encourage from his saddle. "Stay with it. Stay with it, now."

Another man lunged in suddenly and hammered a right cross against Hawk's cheek. Hawk ducked an attempted left follow-up, then rammed his right fist into the man's gut. The man groaned and staggered backward, sucking wind.

Another man stepped toward Hawk and landed a sound right cross on Hawk's chin. Hawk's jaws clattered together, and for a moment the men jostling around him, trying to gain position, blurred and doubled. Fury burned through Hawk, and he ground his heels into the sand and gravel, and bolted forward, straight into a Mexican in a straw sombrero.

The sudden offensive took the man by surprise, and he gave a little cry of alarm as Hawk head-butted him, driving the man to his knees, then smashing his right fist into the man's cheek, opening a four-inch cut spurting blood. Pivoting right, Hawk drove his left fist into a fat belly clad in a faded blue shirt and, as he heard the deep-throated groan, pivoted to his left, and broke another nose, feeling the warm blood bathe his knuckles and wrist.

"Son of a bitch!" he heard behind him as he ducked a fist adorned with three silver rings and a miniature pinky pendant.

The fist whistled over Hawk's head, and when he came up, he slammed both his own tightly clenched fists into the underside of the beringed gent's chin, hearing the teeth clatter and crack and seeing the blood from the man's tongue dribbling over the man's lower lip.

As the man spit out several bits of broken teeth, cursing, Hawk grabbed the bone-handled Colt in the man's cross-draw holster. He'd gotten it out and half raised it before a gun butt slammed against the back of his head. He stared at the ground, and the rocks and tufts of wiry brown grass shifted and pitched wildly.

A rooster crowed in his ears, and his knees turned soft as axle dope.

"Ouch!" someone whooped. "Damn, Ed, you smacked him good."

A delighted laugh.

Hawk dropped to his hands and knees, gritting his teeth and blinking his eyes, trying to clear them. He gave a savage grunt as he tried heaving himself back up, but he hadn't risen two inches before someone drove the toe of a boot deep into his ribs. Suddenly he was on his back, goatheads and sharp pebbles cutting through his shirt, and far up in the brassy sky, a dot-sized hawk soared.

Hawk's side was on fire. He could do little but stare up at the sky, waves of pain washing through him on a tide of raw fury. And then he felt brusque hands pulling him up, and a fist smashed deep into his solar plexus, forcing the breath from his lungs with a loud, *"Haaah!"* of exploding air.

He bent forward. A pin-striped knee smashed his forehead. He flew up and back. Arms caught him under his own arms, and he was hauled back to his feet.

He had only just started to set his boots and regain his balance when someone clobbered his right ear. Someone else clobbered his left, and Hawk spun, hearing himself groaning and sighing, his boots crackling gravel and creosote branches.

His attackers grunted and swung, grunted and swung, laughing, hooting, howling like lobos. Their fists connected with Hawk's cheeks, chin, and temples with solid, crunching smacks. Hawk staggered this way and that, stumbling, the blows steering him in circles like a weather vane in a fickle gale, and when he'd fall his assailants picked him back up again and started the entire savage dance over.

In the midst of it all, his senses dulled. All but his hearing and the ringing in his ears, that was. Below that, he could hear the cacophony of the jubilant savages, the thumps of boots — his own and those of the men around him — and the raucous chings of ground-raked spurs.

His eyes swelled and knots sprouted on his head. The cool wetness of blood trickled from his torn lips and brows. His ribs felt as though they'd been pierced by a half dozen Apache arrows, and he found himself no longer even trying to raise his hands to deflect the blows, but only wishing to fall and remain fallen and to sleep.

Finally, when either his eyes swelled shut or he'd simply lost consciousness, welcome darkness came like hot, black, gravelly tar.

The darkness was shot through with near-relentless agony. Between bouts of nearly unbearable, overwhelming pain in every bone, muscle, and sinew of his body, he slept so deeply that in some squalid corner of his subconscious, he figured he was dead.

But a pain spasm shooting up like a

splintered lance head from his groin or belly or ribs or from deep in his skull always returned to remind him that he somehow still lived. He yearned for death, for only then would the pain finally abate for good, and he could curl up in a tight ball and sleep out the infinite ages.

At times, his own cries woke him.

Or the clatter of his own teeth as he shivered against an impenetrable chill.

An eon of misery broken by only intermittent snatches of restive sleep passed. There was the cold of outer space and then the heat of hell's blazing ovens. It was hard to tell how long each interval lasted. At the time it seemed just short of forever. Each period dwindled almost imperceptibly, dovetailing gradually into the next building agony.

Hawk tried to reposition himself, to find some comfort in his own limbs, but he could get nothing except a few fingers and toes to move. Even his head was fixed as though it were encased in solid stone.

Somewhere between the apex of agonies, a pain sharper and somehow more immediate than the others woke him. His swollen eyes slitted enough to see, as he stared down his naked chest to his bare feet, a hawk perched on his right thigh, digging its talons into his flesh. The hawk lowered its head to peck at the soft skin above his hip, and when he felt the sharp, savage nip of the bird's beak, he screamed and tried to move his hands and feet.

He could do little more than ever-so-slightly bend his knees.

"Get off me, you goddamn carrion eater!" he heard himself rasp.

The bird fixed its pellet-like eyes on him. It jerked its head this way and that, befuddled. Then it gave a near-deafening screech, spread its wings, and gave Hawk's thigh another miserable pinch as it stretched its hair-tufted legs, rose, and fluttered up and away, the sinewy sounds of its wings dwindling quickly behind it.

Hawk's vision quickly began dimming again, but in the waning seconds before unconsciousness swept over him, he looked down the length of his naked body to see that he lay spread-eagle on the desert sand, his ankles bound with straps of rawhide to buried stakes.

He couldn't move his head enough to see to either side, but he was aware suddenly that his arms were stretched out to either side, slightly above his shoulders. They, too, were likely bound to stakes, as he couldn't move either hand a bit.

A momentary shudder of bald horror swept through him, and then, mercifully, the tar washed over him once more.

He slept.

And he dreamt. Mostly fleeting images from his past. Some made some sort of dim sense to his slumbering mind; others were nonsensical and either uplifting as sunny days from his childhood, or as terrifying as snarling wolves' heads lunging toward him, attacking.

At one point, he was suddenly convinced that Linda and Jubal were not dead. Jubal had not been killed on that storm-brushed hill, and Linda had not hanged herself from the cottonwood in Hawk's backyard. They'd been alive all this time while he'd been living as though they were dead, and he just hadn't realized it.

Some horrible trick had been played!

While Hawk had been off hunting bad men to somehow get even for their deaths, they'd been living back on the farm that Hawk and Linda had rented in Dakota Territory, just after they were married and before Hawk had gone to work for the U.S. marshals service.

That's where Jubal was born one cold winter night after Hawk had ridden four miles to bring the German midwife out from the settlement called Napoleon, and where he and Linda had spent the previous nine months as excited as schoolchildren upon hearing the circus was coming to town.

They were about to start a family. And when Hawk made enough money from his corn and wheat and the steers he'd trailed from Kansas, he'd invest in seed bulls and heifers, and he'd build one of the largest ranches in the county.

Linda and Jubal were back there, on the little ranch they'd rented from old Sam Jahner, on the banks of Juneberry Creek. They were waiting for him there. . . .

He couldn't ride fast enough. The long gallop took forever, up and down the chalky buttes and across the shallow rivers and streams.

He was about to be reunited with his family!

Finally, he rode through the gap between hills stippled with bur oak and chokecherry and into the yard.

The buildings — the small dugout cabin, brush-roofed barn, windmill, and corrals — were tumbledown and overgrown with thistle and lamb's ears. Hawk could see through the cracks between the cabin's broad, rough-sawed plank walls. Linda's

172

pumpkin and potato patch was all wiry brown weeds and gopher holes.

No one had lived here in years.

Hawk leapt off his horse, ran up the porch steps, and threw open the rickety door, the hinges screeching like magpies. He yelled for his family as he bolted across the doorjamb.

He stopped suddenly. His heart leapt. Horror gripped his gut in an iron fist, eyes snapping wide, lower jaw falling.

Hawk dropped to his knees, wailing and stretching his arms up toward his wife and boy hanging slack and doll-eyed from the ropes dallied around the rafters above his head.

14.
LAST CHANCE RANGE

"Jubal." Hawk lifted a hand to smooth a wing of auburn hair back from the boy's right eye.

"Name ain't Jubal, mister."

Hawk froze, his hand only half raised. His mind was wrapped in gauze, and there was a thick, opaque lens over his eyes. "Jubal?"

The boy, whose sunburned, lightly freckled face hovered over him, shook his head, frowning. "I ain't Jubal. Name's Harry." The boy leaned back slightly, warily, and called over his shoulder, "He's awake, Ma!"

The boy's voice kicked up an anvil-like ringing in Hawk's ears. He heard quick footsteps, and a curtain was pulled back from the low, narrow doorway behind the boy.

A woman peered into the room, a white towel in her hand that held the curtain back, a small tin teapot in the other. Her eyes met Hawk's, and she stepped slowly through the

174

doorway, setting the pot and the towel on a small dresser wedged into the pantry-sized room.

"Hello."

She stood beside the boy, who'd gotten up from the stool he'd been sitting on while sponging Hawk's face. He held a small bowl and a sponge.

Hawk tried several times to speak, but his lips were dry and crusted with blisters, his throat constricted. Inexplicably, he detected the smell of butter and mint. Finally, he managed, "Where am I?"

An eager cast brushed across the woman's dark blue eyes, and she gently shoved the boy aside and sat down on the stool. She took the sponge from the boy, dipped it into the basin, and leaning toward Hawk, ran the cool, refreshing sponge gingerly along his right cheek.

"Last Chance Range." The woman smiled. "At least, that's what my man called it."

She had coal-black hair gathered in a tight bun behind her head, and skin nearly as dark as an Indian's. She was fine-featured, almost beautiful, with small lines around her eyes and mouth that betrayed her age to be in her late twenties or early thirties. Her dress was simple, conservative, with a white collar and sleeves, and a cameo pin secured

175

at her throat.

"I'm Gloria Hughes," she said. "This is Harry."

The boy said, "We found you staked out in the desert. Was it Injuns?"

Hawk's mind was slow to process the boy's words. Even when he did, he wasn't sure at first what he was talking about. Staked — out — in — the — desert? Slowly, the memory came to him. He'd made the unforgivable error of letting himself get caught by the very man he'd been trying to catch.

His face warmed with chagrin. "No. It wasn't Injuns."

He tried to move his arms and legs, and he winced at the multiple pain spasms shooting through him, and the raking sunburn that scraped like coarse sandpaper from his hair to his toes.

"Best not to move around too much," the woman said, squeezing water from the sponge, then laying it gently against Hawk's neck. "You have several broken ribs, and I've never seen man or beast so bruised. Bruises take longer to heal than breaks, so you'll be right where you are for a good while longer."

Hawk sniffed the not-unpleasant aroma.

"That's the crushed mint from my kitchen

garden," the woman said. "I've rubbed that with butter over your burns. Best sunburn cure I know."

"How long . . . ?"

"Almost three weeks." She dabbed at Hawk's forehead with the sponge. "Thought we'd lost you several times. I even had Harry dig a grave last week, when you seemed about to go. Your breathing was so shallow, and I couldn't hear your heart beating. You needed a doctor, but there isn't one in fifty miles, and the trails aren't safe. I couldn't send Harry, and I didn't dare leave you."

She shook her head and smiled. "You're waking now means you must be out of the woods. But I have a feeling the real pain is about to begin."

"Got me a feelin', too," Hawk managed, gradually becoming aware of an all-encompassing misery. He licked his lips, feeling the hard roughness of scabs and dried blood.

"Not to be nosy, but it might be easier to address you if I knew your name."

"Hawk," he said, his brain too dull for lies. Likely, she wouldn't have heard of him, anyway. "Gideon Hawk."

"Are you hungry, Mr. Hawk? I've been forcing broth down you, but some solid food would do you good."

Hawk shook his head. "I'll take a shot of hooch, if you got it."

"I have that." She looked at the boy. "Harry . . ."

When the boy had left, Gloria Hughes set the sponge in the washbasin and rose from the stool. "You've gotta be tough, I'll give you that. You were out in the desert at least three days when we found you. We were out looking for mavericks that might have strayed from our mountain range."

She set the basin on the dresser, then, as the boy pushed through the curtain with a bottle and a small water glass, she took the bottle and splashed whiskey into the glass. "Bobcat tracks around. You might have been about to become that wildcat's supper. A female, by the size of the prints. Probably with several little mouths to feed."

"Ma thinks she was layin' around, waitin' for you to die," the boy said, proud of his knowledge.

Hawk gave a snort. "I sort of remember a cold nose sniffing me out. I wonder why she didn't go ahead and dig in."

He winked at the boy. Then the woman sent Harry out to gather firewood for the supper fire.

When the boy had gone, she helped Hawk

take a sip of the whiskey. He got half a shot down, and smacked his lips. "Not bad."

"There's not much more," the woman said. "My husband's old stash. I don't imbibe. I've been pouring it down you with the broth. You've been in a lot of pain, crying out."

"Hope I haven't kept anyone awake."

She raised the cup. "More?"

Hawk nodded. The pain was welling up inside him like a physical thing. He hated to think how badly he was bruised and how many ribs were broken.

Likely he wouldn't be back on the trail for weeks. When he was, he'd have to give his think box an overhaul. It was Saradee Jones who'd distracted him. He should have killed her back in Sweetwater, even if it would have meant shooting it out with Melvin Hansen and the rest of her gang. . . .

The second whiskey shot helped ease the physical fires inside him, as well as the deep searing burn of the sun over every inch of him, and he found himself drifting off, eyes closing as Mrs. Hughes set the bottle on the dresser, glancing over her shoulder at him, frowning with curiosity.

When he woke again, it was morning, and when Mrs. Hughes had helped him use the thunder mug beneath the cot, turning him just enough that he could urinate on his own albeit with extreme self-consciousness, she brought him a cup of coffee and a bowl of oatmeal. He ate a few bites of the breakfast before his insides recoiled.

He took a couple sips of the coffee that went down more easily with the shot of whiskey he tasted, then set the cup on his belly. He couldn't sit up, but only hike his shoulders a little. During his set-to with Kid Reno's bunch, he must have wrenched his neck and back.

"Forgive me for prying again, but who's Jubal?"

Hawk winced inwardly. The dream of the old ranchstead ached as badly as any of his wounds or broken bones. "My boy."

Mrs. Hughes was standing with her back to the dresser, wearing a purple dress today, as fresh and crisp as the one she'd worn yesterday. It highlighted the indigo black of her hair, which appeared not quite as tightly wound behind her head as yesterday, a few wisps hanging loose about her face.

Hawk wasn't sure where he was; she'd mentioned mountains. He also remembered that she'd used the past tense when mentioning her husband. The ranch had the feel of an isolated backwater, probably not many men around.

"And Linda?" she asked, flexing her fingers uncomfortably along the edges of the dresser behind her.

Hawk lifted his cup to his lips, his hand shaking slightly. "Wife." He sipped, swallowed with effort, and set the cup back down on his belly. "She's dead, too."

Mrs. Hughes nodded sadly. "My husband, Romer, died last spring. He was prospecting, and a rock fell on him. It crushed his skull."

He just looked at her. He wasn't up to hollow words of apology.

She looked down at her hands. "He wasn't really a very good husband — more dreams than common sense, just like my father warned me back in St. Joseph — but I loved him."

Hawk glanced at the room's sole window covered with a sackcloth curtain letting in lemony light around its edges. "What mountains are we in?"

"The Vultures. We're near Eagle Eye Peak. We have a little cattle ranch, Harry and me. Some chickens and a milk cow. I do some sewing in the winters."

"When I can," Hawk said, though at the moment he couldn't imagine being able to leave the bed, nor of ever facing the sun again, "I'll do some work around the place.

I'm very grateful for your help."

"Don't be silly," Mrs. Hughes said. "I'd have done the same for a dog I found in a trap."

Hawk noted the guarded, slightly admonishing tone.

She fidgeted with the cameo pin at her throat. "Whoever it was that worked you over, they must have really had it in for you — staking a man naked in the desert so he couldn't even move his head from the sun. They weren't Apaches or you'd have been even worse off than you were."

"They weren't Apaches. The gang of Americanos and a few Mexicans I was tracking. Their leader's a man named Kid Reno."

Her voice acquired a hopeful tone. "You're a lawman?"

Deep down even he himself knew that he was merely a vigilante, as much on the run from the law as the men he hunted.

He settled for a simple, honest reply. "No." And he left it at that.

She stared at him grimly, her chest falling slightly as she exhaled. "I see." She turned to the door. "I'll bring your lunch in a couple of hours."

Hawk slowly, gradually healed. As he did,

his days on the Hugheses' Last Chance Range turned to weeks. Days as well as nights slowed down, and boredom set in.

The aches in his body ebbed and dulled, but because he had too much time to think, his mind grew tender and raw.

When he could start walking again, he did so eagerly. At first he had to use a cane — a knotted oak branch that the boy, Harry, had found for him — but he couldn't walk far. Every day he pushed himself a little farther until finally he was making it out to the hay barn roughly sixty yards from the tight little log cabin, in the small yard ringed by rocky peaks and piñon pines.

From the barn he made it to the creek running along the base of a slope, through cottonwoods. Here he sat every day around three in the afternoon, perched on a large rock, leaning forward on the cane, resting and thinking. . . .

Of course, recuperating here with a pretty widow roughly his own age, and a boy roughly the age Jubal would have been if his son were alive, he couldn't help wondering what might have been. He found himself attracted to Gloria Hughes, as any man would have been, and he grew close as a stepfather to the boy, Harry. They often fished together along the stream, and the boy was always close when Hawk tried to push his walks a little longer, in case Hawk should fall, which was always a risk with his slow-healing ribs, knees, and hips.

He sensed that his feelings for Gloria went both ways, and he couldn't help taunting himself with the possibility of his staying here, of becoming Gloria's husband and Harry's father. Of giving up the stalking trail for a settled life here on Last Chance Range.

The possibility of such a change toyed with him as he toyed with it, and he found himself vaguely considering it more and more as he abandoned the walking stick and started working about the place — slowly at first, bringing in wood, forking a little hay, and currying his own grulla as well as the Hugheses' four ranch ponies.

But the stronger the possibility grew inside him, and the more he favored Gloria with speculative glances, the more she seemed to withdraw from him. She spoke to him less. And her eyes retreated from his gaze.

Most nights after supper, the three of them sat around the cabin's stone hearth, reading the newspapers that a friendly old hand from a neighboring ranch dropped off once a week on his return from visiting the saloons in Prescott. More and more often, when it was time for bed, Gloria retreated silently to her own room, bidding good night to only Harry and quietly latching her bedroom door behind her.

One night, however, she sat up later than her usual nine o'clock. After the boy had eaten his customary before-bed gooseberries and cream and retreated to his room in the loft, Mrs. Hughes set aside the afghan she'd been crocheting and turned to Hawk, who sat with a newspaper folded in his lap — he'd read every word of the outdated paper twice — and staring wanly into the fire.

It being winter, there was a chill in the air that not even the large fire of stout mesquite and piñon logs could ward off completely.

"Gideon?"

Hawk turned his head to her.

"Tomorrow, I'd like you to leave."

Hawk studied her closely. His face must have betrayed his shock.

Understanding flickered in his haunted eyes when he realized that the man she was looking at was not the Gideon Hawk of years ago, before Linda and Jubal had passed. Not the family man, Hawk. The man she saw sitting here in her candlelit parlor was Gideon Hawk, the outlaw lawman.

Hawk found that he had tightened his

belly. Now he released it along with a held breath. His soul felt like lead — an anvil-like depression hammering his shoulders straight down without mercy. He nodded.

She rose slowly and moved toward him, staring down at him grimly, the flames sliding shadows across her face, showing in her eyes. The fire cracked and fluttered. She pressed her hands together, mashing her fingertips together nervously, pensively.

"This last night, Mr. Hawk, you're welcome to share my bed."

Hawk arched a shocked brow. For several seconds, words defeated him. "You don't have to do that."

"Men," she scoffed. "What makes you think I'm doing it for you?"

She turned and, holding his gaze with hers, walked across the cabin to her room. She disappeared inside, leaving the door open behind her.

Hawk sat there for a time, elbows on his knees. Finally, he ran his hands back through his hair, heaved up from his chair, and followed her. Inside the small but neatly appointed bedroom, she'd lit the red lamp on the table beside the bed. She stood beside it naked, reaching up to let her hair down.

Her body was heavy-breasted and willowy,

and in the lamp's red glow her skin shone like polished brass.

Letting her hair, as black as crow's feathers, tumble down across her shoulders, she walked toward him. He placed his hands on her slender shoulders. She closed her eyes and set her cheek against his chest, and then he felt her hands slowly, expertly unbuttoning his pants.

They made love hungrily, tenderly, wordlessly. When they finished, she rolled away from him. Hawk got up, gathered his clothes, and returned to his own room.

In the morning, before dawn, he left.

15.
BUZZARD BAIT

Two weeks later, camped by an unnamed creek in the lonely wilds of central Arizona, Hawk drew deep on a half-smoked quirley and let the smoke out slowly through his nose that bulged where it had been broken and had not healed properly. The nose complemented the pocked and pitted scars of his cheeks and lips, and the short, hoof-shaped knot of gristly white tissue hanging like a half-moon above his left brow.

His back to his fire for its warmth this crisp mountain night, he stared into the night-shrouded pines and rocks that tumbled off toward the murmuring stream.

He felt hollow and used up, but he'd gotten used to it before. He'd get used to it again. Though now there seemed a hard finality about it.

After leaving the ranch of Gloria Hughes — or, rather, seeing that last sad, faintly accusing look in the woman's eyes — he'd realized there was only one clear path for him from now on. Really, he'd been on that path for a long, long time while only a small part of him had believed he was still partly the man he'd been before Linda and Jubal had died.

Now there was no doubt. There'd never again be any hope of his ever returning to a less violent life.

And that was all right now that it was straight in his head. There was no more Gloria or Harry Hughes, but only another couple of men to kill — Kid Reno and Wilbur "Knife-Hand" Monjosa.

And so it was with an ear-ringing tolling of fate's bells that he took another drag from his quirley and opened the newspaper he'd picked up when he'd passed through Prescott earlier that day, and saw a headline near the bottom of the second page: "Quartermaster Depot at Fort Bowie Robbed."

A caption just below the headline announced: "Six Cases of Winchester Repeating Rifles Stolen by Eight Murderous Desperadoes!"

Hawk's heart thumped, nearly drowning the ringing in his ears. Quickly, eyes blazing and quirley smoldering between his lips, he scanned the article.

The robbery had occurred the day before

the paper had been printed, sixteen days ago. The rifles had been taken by eight men masquerading as cavalry soldiers. They'd killed half a dozen soldiers at Fort Bowie and busted out the stockade gates with the aid of a team of army mules and the Gatling gun they'd also stolen from the depot.

A contingent of soldiers had been dispatched to "run down the thieves and return the guns and ammunition safely to Fort Bowie before the feral Apaches can get their hands on them." As the robbery and butchery had occurred on a moonless night, none of the thieves had been identified. When the article had been published, the wagon had been seen by several ranch hands heading southwest via old Indian trails in the region of the Gila River.

Hawk lowered the paper slowly and closed it. He removed his quirley from between his scarred lips and stared off through the pines and the creek twinkling in the milky light of a powder horn moon.

The only reason rifles were stolen around here was so that they could be sold to bronco Apaches or Yaquis. Was it just a coincidence that Hawk had had only a couple of months ago run into Kid Reno out here in the high-desert hills and mountains, only about a hundred miles from Fort Bowie?

Reno was the most notorious *contrabandista* in the entire Southwest, and until recently he'd been in cahoots with another gunrunner just now building a name for himself along the border.

Either with or without his partner, it looked very much like Kid Reno was back in business.

Hawk's mind churned as he walked off to check his horse and evacuate his bladder. He was glad to feel the old pull of the trail again. Now, he just needed some fresh sign.

He went back to his bivouac, kicked dirt on his fire, and rolled up in his soogan. He thought for a while, and then he slept.

Three bodies, partly clad in soldier blue, twisted and swayed in the hot, dry breeze.

The ropes stretching their necks from the branch of the lone cottonwood creaked and squawked beneath the barks and mewls and bizarre, frenzied chortling of the half dozen buzzards that, spooked by Hawk's approach, flew up to perch in the tree's higher branches, staring hungrily down at the corpses.

Two young men with corporal's stripes on the bloody sleeves of their blue wool tunics and an older gent with a silver spade beard, brushy mustache, and sergeant's stripes. All three had been hanged and shot several times, right here by the road where they'd be seen by anyone who might be following.

A warning.

Hawk looked the bullet-riddled corpses over. They didn't appear too stiff yet, and the zopilotes had only just started working on them. This had probably happened less than three hours ago.

Hawk looked around for the other members of the patrol. Odd there weren't more bodies. Maybe the patrol had split up and only these three had been bushwhacked. That would mean the others were still after Kid Reno and the stolen rifles.

Hawk had picked up their trail a couple of days ago. It hadn't been all that hard to find; he'd been down here before, hunting outlaws, and he'd suspected Reno's bunch would be following one of the main wolf trails across Arizona and into Mexico. A couple of prospectors who'd seen both the wagon and the soldiers shadowing it had put Hawk on the right one.

Now he swung the grulla away from the cottonwood and gigged it into a lope down the trail, over the rocky, cedar-stippled shoulder of a steep volcanic mountain, heading southwest.

It wasn't long before he checked the mount down again, stopping dead in the trail and staring ahead, reaching down to slide his Henry repeater from the boot under his right thigh. Less than fifty yards away, a horse lay in the trail.

Hawk raked the brush and rocks on both sides of the trail with his gaze. The only sound was the eerie piping of warblers in the creosote shrubs. Nothing except the birds themselves moved.

Hawk walked the grulla ahead. The fallen horse grew large in the trail before him, until Hawk could see a boot poking out from beneath the white belly. The boot was attached to a leg, and on the other side of the horse, a young, red-haired soldier lay belly up on the trail, pinned beneath the horse.

Corporal stripes marked the young man's sleeves. He had a broad, freckled face, and his light blue eyes were wide and death-glazed.

A Colt Army with a seven-and-a-half-inch barrel lay in the dust just ahead of the corporal's outstretched right hand. He'd been shot through his right temple and no telling how many times in his blood-bibbed chest.

Looking around again, a worm of apprehension lifting its tail in his belly, Hawk saw two more buzzards waiting nearby — one perched on a boulder, another on the tall saguaro beside it. The carrion eaters mewled repellently, ruffling their feathers and shifting their weight from foot to foot, eagerly awaiting Hawk's departure.

Carefully, Hawk rode on. He found no more bodies until he pushed through gnarled mesquites lining the bank of an ancient riverbed paved in black volcanic rock washed down from a low, distant sierra. Halting the grulla at the edge of the wash, which was nearly a hundred yards across, he stopped again and stretched his gaze across the dozen or so men and horses strewn about the rocks in a shaggy line.

Hawk grimaced and shook his head.

The soldiers had been cut down from the opposite bank, most likely. Judging from how they lay, hardly having been given time to break formation, they'd been cut down quickly by the stolen Gatling gun.

Hawk toed the grulla out onto the riverbed, zigzagging around the fallen men and horses. Buzzards flapped and squawked around the carrion, several holding their ground defiantly until Hawk was right up on them, then leaping airborne in a hammering whoosh of large, dusty black wings, viscera trailing from their long, hooked beaks.

"Christ," Hawk said, seeing how young some of the dead men were, lying sprawled in every position imaginable, some pinned beneath their horses in thick, still-wet blood pools.

When he was nearly to the far bank, he stopped suddenly and whipped the grulla to the right. An ocotillo stood nearby with its drooping, slender branches. On the other side of the ocotillo, something moved. A buzzard squawked. A man cursed shrilly, and then a gun spoke twice, the slugs wailing off the rocky riverbed.

The bird screamed, and then Hawk saw the black bedraggled body bounce like a ball and lay quivering, one wing extended like a shroud.

Grinding his heels into the grulla's flanks, Hawk galloped toward the ocotillo, swinging around the plant, turning the horse, and extending his rifle out from his right hip. Several feet from the still-quivering bird, a burly man was on his hands and knees, an Army .44 in his right hand against the ground. He was trying to get a cavalry boot under him, to push himself to his feet.

He must have seen Hawk in the periphery of his vision. He turned his head quickly, his thin, light red hair flying about his broad, craggy face, and losing his balance, he plopped down on his butt, raising the Colt.

"Hold it," Hawked warned, aiming the Henry at him. "I'm friendly . . . long as you are."

The man blinked. His face was freckled, with a two-day growth of red beard stubble. He had a high, freckled forehead with a receding hairline, and a slight jowl. A not-so-slight paunch stretched his army-issue yellow suspenders forward. Sergeant's stripes shone on the wash-worn sleeve of his unbuttoned tunic. A bad bullet burn across his left temple had attracted flies that weren't as easily discouraged as the buzzard.

The sergeant's bleary, close-set, light blue eyes bored into Hawk. His Colt sagged, and he depressed the hammer. "Who're you?"

"Hawk." He was in no mood for made-up names. "How long ago they hit you?"

The sergeant looked around, blinking hard and shaking his head as if to clear it. "I don't know. I reckon I was out for a while. Maybe an hour."

"How bad you hurt?"

The sergeant winced as though the words themselves drilled at the wound across his bloody temple. He pressed the heel of his hand against it, then looked at his hand. "That damn Gatling gun." He looked toward the near bank. "They bushwhacked us from them mesquites." He looked at Hawk again. "It was Kid Reno. You a lawman?"

"I asked you how bad you were hurt, mister."

"Why?"

"Because if you can make it on your own, I'm gonna leave you here and try to catch up with Reno. Appears all your horses are dead."

The sergeant looked around, wincing and muttering.

Hawk said, "I'll be back after I run Reno down."

He'd started to spur the grulla ahead when he heard the ratcheting click of a gun hammer. Hawk stayed his spur, and turned to the sergeant.

Still on his butt, the man glared at Hawk. The Colt was in his hand, aimed at Hawk's chest, the hammer locked back.

"I do apologize," he said with no apology in his voice, "but I'll be confiscatin' that mount, mister."

Hawk pressed his lips together. "I don't think so, friend."

"Step down. Official army business." The

sergeant grunted as he heaved himself to his feet, wincing and blinking and keeping the Colt aimed unsteadily at Hawk.

"Don't be a fool, sergeant. You're in no condition . . ."

Hawk didn't have to finish the sentence. The sergeant had no more gained his feet before he gave a pained yelp and, lowering the Colt and clapping a hand to his battered forehead, stumbled sideways and hit the ground hard on his back. The gun clattered to the rocks beside him. He grimaced, and then, gradually, his face fell slack.

His broad chest rose and fell slowly, deeply.

Hawk chuffed as he glared down at the man coldly. "Goddamn fool."

He looked around, pondering the situation.

Finally, he stepped down from the grulla, grabbed the sergeant by both ankles, and dragged him over to the bank, depositing the comatose soldier in the shade beneath the mesquites. He wrestled him into a half-sitting position against the bole of one of the trees, then retrieved a nearly filled canteen from one of the dead horses and propped it beside the sergeant's bulging belly.

That should do the fool until Hawk got

back with a horse of one of Kid Reno's bunch. With any luck, the copper-plated tinhorn would die and save Hawk the trouble of figuring a way to get him to Fort Bowie.

Hawk mounted the grulla and loped off, following the alluringly fresh wagon tracks and the dozen or so sets of shod hoofprints showing plain in the sand and gravel, trailing off through the chaparral.

16.

RECKONING

It took Hawk less than an hour, urging the grulla hard, to push within view of the Kid Reno bunch. At the rear of the pack, the high-sided wagon, a dirty cream tarp tenting its box and driver's boot, lurched and bounced across the stark, stony desert between tabletop mesas angling trapezoids of purple shade onto the trail.

Hunkered low between cracked boulders on a hill shoulder, Hawk saw that most of the pack trotted their mounts ahead of the wagon. A single point rider — to Hawk's naked eye little more than a dark speck on the powdery trail — rode a hundred yards ahead of the main bunch. Another single rider rode drag, staying about a hundred yards behind the wagon and pulling up every few yards to peer cautiously along his back trail while holding a carbine barrel-up on his thigh.

The flanker was the tall Mexican in the

steeple-crowned sombrero whom Hawk had head-butted at the beginning of the set-to that, while having occurred a couple of months ago, was so fresh in his mind it could have happened only yesterday.

Hawk narrowed his eyes and tightened his jaws. A snarl pulled at his upper lip. They'd beaten him and left him for dead. They no doubt thought he *was* dead. By rights, he *should* be dead. Thanks to Gloria and Harry Hughes, he wasn't dead, and Kid Reno's bunch was in for one hell of a surprise. . . .

Hawk waited until the gang had dropped out of sight behind a distant rise, then jogged back to the grulla, mounted up, and started a minor rockslide as horse and rider dropped down the hill to the trail.

He continued shadowing the bunch, staying at least a half mile back at all times while keeping the flanking rider in near-constant sight. Near sundown, he watched the gang pull their horses and their wagon to a stop inside a broad, steep-walled canyon in which a small ruined church hunkered amid tumbled boulders, brittlebush, and cat's claw.

The church was little more than a brown adobe box with a bell tower minus the bell, and a few dilapidated stone-and-brush sheds flanking it. Another, slightly larger shed lay across the trail from the church, and into this the gang pulled the wagon. They drew two stout wooden doors closed behind the wagon and locked the doors with a rusty chain and padlock that Hawk scrutinized with his field glasses.

The flanking rider caught up to the others in the canyon between the church and the wagon shed, his dust brushed pink by the fading light seeping down the mostly shaded canyon walls.

Kid Reno gave orders, his jaws moving, hands gesturing, and then, while two men were left in the yard to keep watch and the others turned their horses into a rickety corral formed of ironwood poles, Reno and one of the other men fished bottles from their saddlebags and headed into the church, slapping dust from their pants with their hats.

Hunkered atop a stone thumb protruding from the canyon's north wall, the grulla grazing galleta grass below, Hawk watched until the other men had finished tending their mounts in the corral. One remained in the yard, resting his Winchester across both shoulders behind his neck and draping his arms over it, rolling his head around as though to work kinks from his neck. The others headed inside the church.

The yard went dark and quiet. In the corral, a couple of horses rolled. The lookout walked around, kicking stones with a desultory air, yawning, then finally leaning back against the corral and crossing his boots to leisurely roll a cigarette.

Hawk waited.

The canyon filled with darkness rushing down the steep, copper-colored walls like tar from heaven. Stars kindled. Coyotes screeched. In the heavily shadowed bell tower over the arched front door, a pinprick of light shone intermittently, moving slowing from side to side.

A picket up there, Hawk thought. The fool had lit a quirley.

The gang thought it was safe out here in one of likely a good number of their hideouts, with their only known pursuers lying dead in the ancient river bottom.

Hawk dropped his gaze to the man by the corral — an inky purple shadow in the thickening darkness. A light shone around the man's figure as he smoked. Soon his shadow slid away from the corral and sauntered toward the stable in which the gang had secured the wagon with the stolen rifles and Gatling gun.

Hawk climbed down the back of the stone thumb and dropped his field glasses in a saddlebag pouch. He removed his spurs, dropped them into the pouch, as well. Having already slipped the grulla's bit and unbuckled its saddle cinch, he shucked his Winchester from its boot, patted the horse on the rump, and stole under cover of darkness along the base of the canyon wall until he was about fifty yards from the back of the wagon shed.

He saw the lookout's cigarette glow to the shed's right. The man was milling there amid the boulders and what looked like an old wagon chassis. Impossible to tell what he was doing or which way he was facing.

Drawing a deep breath, feeling his blood running warm through his veins, Hawk pushed away from the canyon wall and, running nearly soundlessly at a crouch, gained the stable's left side. He stopped to hunker low and to look around and prick his ears, listening.

There was a nearly inaudible murmur of voices from inside the church. He could see a window in its right wall, marked by the glow of lantern light. Shifting his gaze to the bell tower, he couldn't see the guard. He wished Reno hadn't thought to put a man in the tower. While he couldn't see the lookout up there, that didn't mean the man couldn't see him, though the shadows up along the wagon shed were heavier than out away from it.

Gravel crackled behind Hawk. A spur trilled. He pressed his back flat against the wagon shed, near the rear corner. The crunching and trilling grew steadily louder. The other picket was moving toward Hawk from around the stable's rear.

Hawk held his breath, crouching and waiting, pressing his back hard against the wall, as though to become one with the ancient mortared stone. A tall figure came around the corner. The man smelled like sweat, wool, horses, and harsh Mexican tobacco. Holding his rifle over his right shoulder, partly blocking his own view of Hawk, he angled from the Rogue Lawman's left to his right.

Quickly deciding how he was going to make his play, Hawk leaned his rifle against the wagon shed. Just as the man started moving beyond him, Hawk lunged toward him and grabbed him from behind. Clapping his left hand around the man's mouth and pulling his right arm and rifle down with Hawk's own, Hawk hauled him straight back the way he'd come.

The man grunted and groaned, jabbing at the ground with his boots as he fought to regain his balance. His face was bristly and sweaty under Hawk's left hand, which he closed over the man's nose as well as his mouth. The man's rifle clattered to the ground, and the man's right boot heel and spur clipped it with a raucous, ringing rake.

Hawk gritted his own teeth, hoping the sound hadn't been heard in the bell tower. Then, just as he'd pulled the lookout back behind the stable shed, he jerked his head back sharply, hearing the grinding crack of the neck bones.

The man gave another, shriller yelp under Hawk's hand, and he stiffened, again desperately grinding his heels into the ground before the tension left his body.

Hawk hurled the man back away from him. The man hit the ground with a thud. Quickly, glancing toward the dark bell tower, Hawk retrieved his own rifle and smashed its brass-plated butt against the lookout's forehead. Probably unnecessary, as the man lay unmoving, but Hawk wasn't taking any chances.

Hawk stole up to the stable's rear corner and edged a look toward the church. The pinprick glow of a smoldering quirley shone. It didn't move. The man seemed to be staring toward the wagon shed.

Hawk's gut tightened. Had the bell tower guard heard the rifle hit the ground, or the dead lookout's groan?

Hawk looked at the dead man sprawled behind the wagon shed, one leg curled beneath the other. He wore a hat very much like Hawk's own — black and with a nearly flat brim. He was also close to Hawk's height — roughly six foot three.

The only difference was the dead man's gray serape.

Hawk quickly ripped the serape over the man's head and dropped it over his own shoulders. Nearly as quickly, he rolled a quirley from his makings sack, then, clamping the lit cigarette between his teeth, he set his rifle barrel on his right shoulder and walked out from behind the wagon shed. Moving slowly, taking short strides, he swung his hips with a desultory air, kicking an occasional stone.

His heart thudded anxiously.

Puffing the quirley between his teeth, he headed toward the church, keeping his hat brim low but rolling his eyes up toward the bell tower in which the cigarette still glowed. He couldn't tell for sure but the quirley seemed to dip lower as Hawk approached the church, as though the man were following him closely with his eyes.

Hawk's heart thumped in hard, measured beats.

In the bell tower, the quirley glowed, died, and glowed as the man puffed. Hawk saw the gray smoke billow in the darkness around the man's hatted head.

Only a few more feet, and Hawk would be too close to the church to be seen from the bell tower. . . .

"Hey, Rance — how 'bout sharin' some o' that Mex tobacco with your old pal, Rollo?"

The man's quirley sparked as he flicked it out of the bell tower. It showered sparks as it arced out from the church and then landed with a dull thump in the dirt five feet to Hawk's left. The wet, two-inch, brown-paper cigarette stub glowed briefly in the red gravel, and died.

Hawk caressed the Winchester's hammer with his thumb. Should he shoot the man out of the bell tower? Might be better to wait until Hawk had gotten inside. No sense tipping his hand before he needed to.

He kept his head down, wagged it slowly with feigned disgust, and continued toward the church's stout, weathered front door.

In the bell tower, Rollo chuckled.

As Hawk reached the door, he looked up. From this angle, he couldn't see Rollo and Rollo couldn't see him. Hawk took his Henry in his right hand, placed his left on the door's stout wooden handle, and pulled it slightly. It wasn't locked. The cords in Hawk's neck stood out, and his nostrils flared.

Here we go. . . .

He gave the door a hard tug, and as it opened, he stepped quickly inside and left the door standing open behind him.

The church lay before him — not large, only about twice the size of a modest-sized cabin, and longer than it was wide. Its walls were chipped and cracked, its ceiling high and also cracked, and where the worshippers once sat was a mess of gear and trash strewn by Reno's bunch and likely other passing wayfarers. Stone steps from the bell tower ran down along the wall to the right.

The nave fronting Hawk was lighted by several lanterns guttering here and there among the gang members scattered around tables and richly upholstered but badly worn armchairs and a few short, wooden pews. A couple of men slept in the pews. A couple more lounged on the floor, one resting against his saddle and trimming his toenails with a skinning knife.

At the back of the nave, near the low rail separating the nave from the chancel area and the altar, four men sat in richly upholstered, high-backed chairs around a low, rectangular table — probably an old packing crate — smoking cigars and arguing impassively as they tossed cards and coins around.

Another man lay atop the altar near the church's back wall, behind the pulpit and the lectern. His head with its several silver-gray braids rested back against his saddle, and Hawk recognized the hooked eagle's beak of Kid Reno poking out from under the down-canted hat brim. The Kid's boots were crossed, and his hands were folded as though in silent worship on his belly.

Hawk loudly racked a shell into his Henry's breech, holding the rifle up high across his chest and grinning darkly. The metallic rasp echoed cavernously off the high ceiling and the cracked walls.

All heads turned toward the front of the nave. One of the poker players looked at Hawk briefly, then looked down again at the cards in his hand, smoke puffing from the fat stogy wedged in a corner of his mouth.

He sniffed and growled around the cigar, "What the hell you doin' in here, Rance? You're s'posed to be . . ."

He looked up at Hawk again from beneath his bushy brows. His eyes widened slightly, and his cigar slipped from his lips to drop to the poker table with a wet plop and roll.

The others had looked away from Hawk, as well, and turned back.

The man who'd been trimming his nails against the stone staircase running down the nave's right wall inhaled loudly and dropped his skinning knife. It clattered against the stone floor. The stocky, black-mustached gent lifted his head, placing both hands on the floor beside him, and dropped his lower jaw to nearly his chest.

"Holy shit!"

17.
THE DEVIL IN CHURCH

One of the cardplayers, a scrawny little gringo with a mousy face and billowing green neckerchief, rasped, "My God — it's a devil!"

He'd been sitting with his back to the front door, peering at Hawk over his shoulder. Now, eyes wide, he bolted to his feet, kicking his chair back and twisting around. Before he could get his long-barreled Smith & Wesson raised, Hawk aimed the Henry quickly and shot the little turd through his chest. He gave another rasp, flew back against the baptismal font, and sagged to the stone floor, gurgling, blood staining his loosely woven tunic.

Grinning, Hawk ejected the smoking shell casing. The brass jacket hit the floor and rattled around as Hawk rammed a fresh one into the rifle's breech, the metallic scrape again echoing loudly.

All faces in the room were pinned to him,

expressions ranging from shock and horror to befuddlement and fury.

Still reclining atop the altar at the back of the church, Kid Reno slowly lifted his head from his saddle. He didn't look either fearful or angry. Mainly bemused, as though he'd just spied an old, long-lost friend.

Slowly, he sat up.

Hawk swept the other faces with his gaze and flexed his fingers on the Henry's stock with mute challenge.

Silence.

The men's eyes narrowed. Muscles in their cheeks or temples quivered. They swallowed or licked their lips or slid their gazes to each other in silent complicity.

One of the other cardplayers lurched to his feet. He already had a side-hammer Bisley out, and he ground his teeth as he raised it above the table.

Hawk's Henry roared.

The slug took the cardplayer through his leathery right cheek, just below his eye. He stumbled backward, triggering his Bisley through his fanned-out poker hand on the packing crate, causing greenbacks to fly and coins to rattle.

He grunted, turned, and dropped to his knees before falling flat on his face and lying there, shaking, spurs ringing as though attempting a little song.

The song hadn't died before one of the men in the pews made a sudden play, which Hawk's Henry rendered stillborn. Then a man on the other side of the room jerked into action, then a cardplayer, then another cardplayer, until the church was fairly filled with crashing echoes, billowing smoke, clipped screams, and bitter groans.

Rollo from the bell tower ran down the steps on the right side of the nave, raising a Spencer carbine in both hands, his boots and spurs ringing on the cracked stone. He got off a shot as Hawk turned toward him, the lookout's .44-caliber round sizzling across the side of the Rogue Lawman's neck.

Hawk fired twice from the hip, and as his spent brass jackets rattled around on the stone floor behind him, Rollo screamed and flew down the steps, dropping his rifle and piling up between the first riser and the front wall with a thud and a crunch of snapping back and neck bones. He sighed, sobbed once, miserably, and then his cheek smacked the floor.

Hawk cocked the Henry and swung the barrel toward Kid Reno, who had sat up to dangle his legs clad in checked wool trousers over the side of the altar. His expression was slightly more animated than it was before all his men were dead. But only slightly. He slid his eyes around the smoky room, almost as though he were hoping at least one man still had some life left in him. His gaunt, parchment-pale cheeks were flushed.

He glared at Hawk, his lips forming a knife slash across his lower face. Though he wasn't armed — at least, not that Hawk could see — he raised his hands chest high, slowly opening his long, thin fingers. Faint mocking shone in his eyes.

"Pinkerton's boys don't shoot unarmed men, now, do they?"

Hawk's Henry roared. The bullet sliced across the outside of Kid Reno's upper right arm before it ricocheted off the back wall with an angry screech. Reno yelped and, clapping a hand to his torn shirtsleeve, gritted his teeth so hard that Hawk thought he could hear the man's molars cracking.

"You son of a bitch!" Reno growled, an eye twitching miserably.

"I'm not one of Pinkerton's boys." Hawk waved his still-smoking Henry around the room. "This all of 'em?"

A low grunt sounded behind Hawk. He swung around, his cocked Henry extended from his hip. A big man with a Fu Manchu mustache and a shabby, feathered derby hat faced Hawk, the pistol in his right hand sagging as he staggered forward, his head falling back on his shoulders.

He turned right and, groaning, dropped to his knees. In the open doorway behind him, a broad, scowling face appeared under the leather brim of a dark blue forage hat, and the sergeant from the ambushed Cavalry patrol snarled, "No, it ain't, but this one is!"

The sergeant took one quick step to the big man on his knees, who was reaching around to grab the bayonet blade from his bloody back, and slammed the butt of a Spencer rifle against the back of the man's head. There was a cracking smack of splitting bone beneath the smashed derby hat. The big man jerked as though he'd been slapped across both cheeks.

Slowly, he sagged to the floor and expired with a loud fart.

Hawk scowled in surprise at the broad-shouldered, big-bellied, red-haired sergeant whose yellow neckerchief was wrapped tightly around his forehead, then swung his Henry back to Kid Reno who was still sitting on the edge of the altar clutching his upper arm, from which blood now oozed, and glared toward the front of the church.

"I take it you found a horse," Hawk said to the sergeant while keeping his eyes on the Kid, who looked even less like a kid now than he had before his gang was dead and he was nursing a wound inflicted by a man he'd left for dead.

The sergeant dismissed the question as, placing a boot on a shoulder of the derby-hatted gent and jerking his bayonet blade from the man's back, he looked in awe around the smoky, bloody room.

"Shit . . ."

"Yeah."

"Who the hell are you, mister? Lawman?"

Hawk only shrugged.

The sergeant gave him a skeptical glance. He used the derby-hatted gent's ratty suit coat to clean his bayonet blade before pointing the blade toward Reno. "That him? That Reno?"

Holding his arm, Reno dropped down off the altar, stepped over the low railing, and strode toward Hawk. "What now, amigo? If you're gonna kill me, get it over with."

Ten feet from Hawk, he swerved right and reached toward one of the short pews in which a dead man lay in a thickening blood pool.

"Uh-uh," Hawk warned, following the outlaw leader with his rifle barrel.

Reno stopped with his arm extended toward a pair of saddlebags and a pistol belt on the pew, near the dead man's legs. "I'm reaching for a bottle."

"Reach careful, and reach slow. You wrap your hand around anything but a bottle, I'll gut shoot you and leave you to die slow . . . like you left me."

Reno grinned. Shoving his hand into a saddlebag pouch, he raised a corked bottle labeled McCullough's Tincture of Zinc. The sergeant was moving around the room slowly, inspecting each of the dead men, angling his Spencer barrel low.

Glancing over his shoulder at Hawk, he said, "He bushwhack you, too?"

Anger liberally tinged with chagrin burned through Hawk. "Best head on back to Fort Bowie, Sergeant. Reno and the guns are stayin' with me."

Simultaneously, both the sergeant and Reno said, *"What?"*

Hawk looked at Reno, who was wincing again, having doused his arm with the zinc and taken a couple of pulls from the bottle. "You," Hawk growled, gesturing toward the door. "Get outside."

"Why outside? It's dark and it's gonna get cold." Reno curled his upper lip. "I ain't in the best o' health. Besides, I sorta feel like sendin' up a prayer for my boys."

Hawk glared at him. Reno glared back. Finally, the leader of the gunrunners ripped his neckerchief off his neck and began wrapping it around his bullet-burned arm, sauntering toward the door. Hawk followed, hearing the sergeant's footsteps behind him.

"What the hell's your game, mister?" the sergeant asked. "This here hombre bushwhacked my patrol. Now, I'll be takin' him and the wagonload of guns back to Bowie."

Hawk was only half listening to the sergeant's angry protests. He was watching Reno's back, noting the furtive movements of the man's left arm. Anticipating the gunrunner's play, Hawk stopped. Reno took two more steps into the dark yard fronting the church, ten feet in front of the door, then wheeled suddenly toward Hawk, crouching and snarling.

Starlight careened off the steel blade in his fist.

Reno froze, and his eyebrows lifted in surprise to see Hawk standing farther behind him than the gunrunner had expected.

"Reno, you got a bloated reputation."

Hawk slammed the Henry's barrel down hard across Reno's left wrist. The outlaw yelped. The knife hit the dirt with a thud.

Crouching, Reno grabbed his left wrist with his right hand, his braided hair dangling down over his eyes. Hawk stepped toward him. Switching his Henry to his left hand, he clenched his right fist, cocked it, and hammered it forward.

His bulging middle knuckle connected soundly with the gunrunner's right temple.

Reno's head jerked back. "Oh!"

When it came forward again, it was met again by Hawk's fist — two brutal, hammering blows that put the gunrunner's lights out almost immediately, and a third insuring he'd get a good, long night's sleep. He and Hawk had a long ride ahead of them tomorrow.

Reno piled up in the dirt like a fifty-pound bag of cracked corn tossed from a high-sided freight wagon.

"Jesus Christ!" the sergeant bellowed, incredulous, stepping around the comatose outlaw as though around a coiled rattler he'd just found in the trail.

Hawk strode back into the church. He came out a few seconds later with his Henry clamped under his arm, uncoiling the lariat in his hands. He stopped over Reno and thrust his rifle toward the sergeant.

"Hold that."

Frowning with befuddlement, the sergeant

took the gun.

Hawk crouched and quickly wrapped the lariat around both of Reno's wrists, slip-knotting it, then using it to drag the Kid over to one of the hitch racks fronting the church. He wound the lariat tightly around the rack until the Kid's wrists were snugged up against the worn rail, the Kid's torso stretched upward so that he was putting only about half his weight on his bent legs and knees. His chin dipped between his upraised arms and shoulders toward his chest. His breath came in rasps and half groans.

Hawk dropped the unused end of the coiled rope and took his rifle back from the sergeant, who stood staring down at the secured gunrunner with his lower jaw hanging, his eyes even more incredulous than before.

"I doubt he'll stir for a good long time, but keep an eye on that snake till I fetch my horse."

With that, Hawk tramped off toward the canyon's dark north ridge.

The sergeant ran a thick paw down his face and blinked at Hawk's back. "Just who in the hell *are* you, mister?"

18.

IRONSIDE

"Name's Hawk," he said as he approached the sergeant's campfire, having turned his horse into the corral with the sergeant's army bay and the gunrunners' mounts.

"You got a first name, Hawk?"

"Gideon."

Hawk dropped his saddle, saddlebags, and bedroll on the ground near the low fire that the sergeant had built beside the church, where several other fires had been built in the past, judging from the blackened stones comprising the fire ring. He knelt to untie the whang strings holding his bedroll closed.

The sergeant frowned at him. "Gideon Hawk . . . Where have I heard that name before?"

Hawk rolled out his blankets. "Got a name?"

"Ironside."

The soldier lay back against his saddle. His hat, Spencer, and holstered revolver lay beside him. So did a smoking tin coffee cup and a bottle of Old Bourbon. He was dabbing gingerly at the dried blood on his temple, wincing.

"Marion Jeffcoat Ironside, to come completely clean." He removed the wadded cloth from his temple and scowled across the fire at Hawk. "But anyone who calls me Marion gets a busted nose for their trouble, so just call me Sergeant or Ironside or Sergeant Ironside."

Hawk gave a snort as he dug a battered tin cup from his saddlebags and then used a leather swatch to pluck the sergeant's coffeepot from a rock near the crackling flames. He splashed the coal-black liquid, salted with ashes from the burning cat's claw branches, into the cup.

"What happened at the wash?" he asked, sitting back to let his coffee cool.

"A goddamn mess is what happened."

Sergeant Ironside pressed the bloody, wet cloth to his temple again and glanced toward Kid Reno's silhouette crouched as though in prayer beneath the hitch rack flanking the sergeant on his right.

"A green lieutenant to go along with about a dozen raw, blockheaded recruits still hungover from a stash of Apache *tizwin* one of the fool younkers had passed around

223

among 'em the night before. Sergeant Kaminsky and me was the only two who'd been stationed in Apacheria longer than three months."

"Kaminsky must have been the sergeant I saw dangling from the cottonwood."

"With the two whelps — that's right," the sergeant grunted. "He and the whelps left the main patrol to scout ahead. Kid Reno musta caught 'em flat-footed, though I suspect Kaminsky woulda been just fine alone. Him and me fought at Chickamauga together, and there weren't no savvier soldier."

Ironside poured whiskey onto the bloody cloth and once more pressed the cloth to his forehead, flushing and cursing briskly when the whiskey hit the bullet wound. "Anyways, the lieutenant refused to let me scout the wash before we pulled the patrol across. Said it was a waste of time, Reno's bunch wouldn't linger here after hanging Kaminsky and his two snot-nosed whelps.

"I should have shot the damn lieutenant off his horse and done what my good sense told me to do, but I didn't, and Kid Reno had set up the Gatling in the mesquites on the other side and cut us all down like ducks on a millpond."

Ironside loosed a long sigh, poured some

whiskey into his coffee, and offered the bottle to Hawk. Hawk took the bottle and added a jigger to his own tar-black belly wash, and sipped it.

"That's why I'm bringin' Reno and the guns back to Fort Bowie with me tomorrow." Stubborn challenge edged the sergeant's words. "Headin' out first thing in the mornin'."

Hawk shook his head and glanced into his coffee cup. "You make good coffee, but you don't listen for shit." He reached into his saddlebags for a small canvas sack and tossed it across the fire to the sergeant, who caught it against his chest. "Jerky?"

Ironside gave him a brooding, sidelong glance. He opened the bag, pulled out a couple chunks of the jerky, then tossed the bag back to Hawk, who fished a couple of pieces out for himself before returning the bag to his saddle pouch.

"You and me ain't fixin' to dance, are we, Hawk? I ain't seen no badge yet, and every time I ask if you're a lawman, you give a politician's answer. For all I know, you're a bounty hunter lookin' to collect a reward on the gang's head. This is army business." Ironside bit off a chunk of the jerky and chewed with his mouth open, narrowing a hard eye at Hawk. "I reckon you and that

Henry clean up right well, and I ain't no cold-steel artist. Just the same, you stay outta my way, hear?"

Hawk reached inside his vest, dipped his fingers into his shirt pocket, and tossed his old, tarnished deputy U.S. marshal's badge across the fire. He hadn't worn that badge in a month of Sundays, but now was as good a time as any to haul it out. Better to pass himself off as a bona fide lawman than to kill Ironside, likely a good soldier. There were too few good soldiers out here. Hell, there were too few good men, soldier or not, anywhere.

"Okay, so you're a federal," the sergeant said, tossing the badge back to Hawk after a quick look.

"On special assignment to kill Kid Reno's old pal, Wilbur 'Knife-Hand' Monjosa."

The skin above the bridge of the sergeant's broad, pink nose wrinkled.

Chewing jerky, Hawk said, "Mexican *contrabandista* who's moved his operations up close to the border and across the line around Yuma. Said to have several hideouts out there in that scorched country, and he's supplying the bronco Apaches with rifles. Reno rode with him for a time, after Knife-Hand started basing his operations in Arizona.

226

"Word has it they forked trails. Probably, the two old seed bulls couldn't get along on the same side of the fence. But Reno likely knows where Knife-Hand's main lair is, and I'm gonna have him lead me to it. With your guns."

Ironside's expression remained unchanged. Slowly, he nodded. "I heard of him. Stirrin' up the Lipan Apaches over there, raisin' a real bloody ruckus. Heard they ain't even sendin' trains out of Yuma no more." He turned his head sideways to give Hawk a skeptical look. "They sent you — one man — to kill him?"

"That's it."

"Who sent you?"

"Uncle Sam."

"Who signed your orders, and I'd like to see those orders."

"No papers," Hawk said. "And I'm not at liberty to tell you who sent me. But I know they wouldn't like it if I wasn't given your full cooperation. Likely the stage and railroad lines being harassed by the Apaches being fed guns and ammunition by old Knife-Hand wouldn't care for it, either."

Ironside stared skeptically over his cup as he took a long, slow, pensive sip of the smoking, whiskey-laced mud. Hawk was relieved to see that the man was buying it . . . or beginning to buy it. He'd hate to have to shoot him. He wasn't giving up those rifles and the Gatling gun, however. Nor Kid Reno. Altogether there was no better way — probably no other way at all — of running down Knife-Hand.

"You're an assassin," the sergeant said, pooching out his lips and chewing jerky as he continued digesting Hawk's story.

Hawk lifted his mouth corners. "I like to see my job as that of a problem solver."

"You see it however you want," Ironside grunted. "You're an assassin. But bein' as how Knife-Hand has been stirrin' up so many killin's down this way, I guess I can sorta see how Uncle Sam might have sent you. But I'll tell you one thing — top-secret mission or no, neither them guns or that prisoner is leavin' my sight. After you done killed Monjosa, I'm takin' both back to Fort Bowie. Ain't no way in hell I'm goin' back there empty-handed after that son of a kill-crazy bastard done wiped out my whole patrol."

Ironside threw back the rest of his coffee and tossed the grounds on the fire. He narrowed a stubborn eye at Hawk. "And there ain't no way around that bit of bonded fact, so don't even go thinkin' you're gettin' shed of me, Mr. Hawk."

He tossed his head toward the slumped and softly snoring Reno and then at the wagon shed. "Where he and that wagon go, I go."

"No arguments." Hawk swallowed a large sip of his own cooling coffee and bit off another hunk of jerky. "I'll likely need assistance with the wagon and the prisoner. I welcome your help, Sergeant."

"Welcome my help, huh?" Ironside grumbled, resigned but contrary, and used his empty cup to dig a hole in the ground for his hip. "Shoots the whole damn gang down in a damn church, tattoos the sole survivor, and he welcomes my help. Shit!"

He drew his blankets over his legs as he turned onto his side. He tossed one more confounded look over his shoulder at Hawk, beetling his thin, red brows for a long time before saying, "Mister, are you sure we never met before? Somethin' about you rakes me as familiar. . . ."

"Forget about it, Sergeant," Hawk advised, pitching his voice with subtle warning. He tossed his grounds on the fire, set his cup down, and began removing his boots. "Get a good night's rest. If you're riding with me and the Kid, you're gonna need it."

■ ■ ■ ■

"Wake up and turn me loose, you son of a bitch!"

Hawk's eyes had no sooner snapped open than the big Russian was in his hand and his head was off his saddle. Automatically, his thumb rocked the revolver's hammer back with a grating click in the dawn silence.

On the other side of the dead fire ring, Sergeant Ironside was clawing around for his Spencer rifle.

"*Yoo-whoooo!*" came another eerie chortle. "Wakey, wakey, little ones around the fire over there . . . *and cut me out of this mother-fuckin' rope!*"

Sitting up, cocked Russian extended straight out from his shoulder, Hawk shuttled his gaze toward the hitch rack fronting the church. Kid Reno slumped beneath the rack — a bedraggled silhouette in the first wash of dawn, his braided hair dangling toward the black ground.

The Kid lifted his head and bellowed, "You hear me? Cut me loose, goddamn you to blazing hell! You got no damn right to tie a man like this. Besides, I gotta *piss like a Prussian plow horse!*"

Hawk loosed a relieved sigh, and the rush

of blood in his ears faded slowly. He depressed the Russian's hammer, set the revolver down beside him, and reached for his boots.

The sergeant held his rifle across his chest and raked a weary paw down his face. "Goddamnit, Reno, you stop that consarned caterwauling or I'm gonna come over there and feed you one of my socks!"

"Get off your lard ass, old man, and cut me loose so I can piss!"

"Why, that loudmouth son of a bitch," Ironside said. "You shoulda shot him, too."

When Hawk had pulled both boots on, he got up, wrapped his cartridge belt around his waist, cinching the buckle, and donned his hat. He walked over to where Kid Reno hung from the hitch rack, yelling, cursing, and taunting.

"You got no right to tie me like this, you son of a bitch!" he bellowed, jerking against the rope wrapped taut around his red, swollen wrists that weren't quite as purple as ripe plums but damn close.

"I gotta hand it to you, Kid," Hawk said. "You got gall."

"Untie me or so help me I'll gut you and I'll hunt down your whole family — every last one of 'em — and I'll skin the boys and I'll . . ."

His eyes snapped wide as Hawk lunged for him, gritting his teeth.

"Hold on!" Reno begged.

Too late.

With his left hand, Hawk jerked the man's head back by his hair. He smashed his right fist against Reno's already badly swollen and bruised left cheekbone. When his fist had pistoned against the man's face four solid times with savage, brutal fury, the smacks sounding crisp in the still dawn air, he released the man's hair.

Reno's head sagged back down between his shoulders as, slowly, the man's lips dropped over his tobacco-stained teeth.

Hawk wiped his bloody knuckles on his pants and turned. Sergeant Ironside stood several yards behind him, grinning. The sergeant shook his head. "You certainly have your own way of doing things, don't you, Hawk?"

"Yep." Hawk straightened his hat and tramped toward the corral. "Build a fire. I'll get the wagon hitched."

19.
GETTING THE DOG
ACQUAINTED WITH ITS LEASH

When Hawk and Sergeant Ironside had eaten breakfast, Hawk led his grulla over to where Kid Reno sagged beneath the hitch rack. Already the zopilotes must have sensed the carnage inside the church, because a good dozen birds were circling the dilapidated structure about a hundred feet in the air, eagerly heckling and chortling.

Ironside had pulled the wagon up in front of the church, as well, and sat in the driver's box, the reins hanging limp in his hands. Hawk dismounted, grabbed his canteen from his saddle, opened the wagon's tailgate, then walked over to the hitch rack. Reno sat with his legs curled beneath him. His checked trousers were dark across one thigh.

He looked up at Hawk through slitted, puffy eyes and gritted teeth. "You caused me to pee myself, you son of a bitch. I ain't a well man!"

Hawk set down the canteen, then picked up the coiled lariat and, using his bowie knife, cut off a four-foot-long strip. Reno watched him. "What the hell are you doin' now?"

"What's it look like?" Hawk said as he wrapped one end of the cut rope around Reno's right ankle and the other end around his left ankle.

"Why don't you just shoot me? What you gotta torture me for?"

Hawk gave him a look.

Reno glowered and looked away.

When Hawk had tied the man's ankles, leaving two slack feet of rope between them, he cut Reno's wrists free of the hitch rack. The gunrunner screamed as his arms dropped like lead weights, and he rolled onto one side in the dirt, clamping his crossed wrists against his crotch, squirming and groaning. "Ah, Jesus, that hurts!"

"Just getting the dog acquainted with its leash." Hawk squatted beside the man, looking down at him as Reno rolled in the dirt, grunting and gritting his teeth, holding his right wrist gingerly in his swollen left hand. "Now, listen, I'm gonna make this real easy for you."

"Fuck you! I need my McCullough's! I ain't well!"

"Are you listening?"

Reno cut a miserable glance at him.

"I'm gonna ask you a question, and if you answer it truthfully, I'm going to let you ride in the wagon box. If I sense you're lying, which you're probably going to want to do though I advise very strongly against it, I'm gonna make you walk behind the wagon. For a man with the pony drip, that'll be a might uncomfortable."

Reno only stared at him through his swollen, slitted, baleful eyes.

Hawk said, "I want to know where you last saw Knife-Hand Monjosa and where you believe I'd be most likely to find him now."

Reno stared at him dully. "You're outta your mind," he said, moving his cracked, puffy lips. He stared at Hawk, and Hawk could see the man's pain-racked mind working. Slowly, Reno spread a grim, disbelieving smile. "You're lookin' for Monjosa."

"Where's the best place to look?"

"That's the craziest thing I ever heard. One man?" He glanced at Sergeant Ironside waiting in the wagon, holding the reins and staring toward Reno and Hawk. "Two men?"

"Where will I find him? I know out west, somewhere north of Yuma. I want to know where exactly."

"I don't know." Reno winced as he looked at his purple hands, which he was trying to flex. "Shit, we split up nigh on a year ago."

"Why'd you split up?"

Reno chuckled. "Oldest reason in the world."

"Money?"

"A woman."

"Okay," Hawk said. "Where will I have the best chance of finding Monjosa? Think twice before you answer. A lie will only bring more pain and a whole lot more misery. You're going with me, so the sooner we find him, the sooner you'll be a free man."

Reno's pale, hollow left cheek twitched slightly. "Free?"

"Before I meet him, but not before I'm sure I'm heading in the right direction, I'll dump you out of the wagon with one canteen and a knife. You can head any direction you want. Free as a dust devil."

Reno stared at him again for seconds before switching his gaze to the sergeant, then back again, curling his puffy upper lip. "Hell's backside. Little canyon in the La Posa mountains north of Yuma, not far from a little waterhole called Quartzsite."

Hawk gave his canteen to Reno. "There.

236

That wasn't so hard, now, was it?"

Reno shook his head as he fumbled with the canteen, glaring at Hawk. "I've known some madmen before, mister. But you take the cake."

When Reno had drunk, Hawk took the canteen, palmed his Russian, and thumbed the hammer back. He waved the gun at the wagon's open tailgate. Reno looked at it.

"You realize that's Apache country, don't you?"

Hawk nodded.

"And the country of seven brands of border snake — all of 'em bad?"

Again, Hawk nodded. "Get in the wagon, Reno. We got a long ride."

"Two weeks, at least."

"We best get started."

Chuckling darkly, Reno heaved himself to his feet. His knees shook. The rope binding his ankles allowed him to take only mincing, stumbling steps to the wagon, Hawk following six feet behind, aiming the cocked Russian at the gunrunner's back.

The Gatling gun and the rifles were all freighted up in the back, in separate crates from the ammunition. There was no way Reno could pair up any of the rifles with the ammo without making a whole lot of noise — even if he had the use of both hands.

"Yes, sir, I knowed some crazy folks in my time. Knife-Hand himself bein' one of 'em." Reno sat on the edge of the box and twisted around, lifting his legs and keeping his bemused, disbelieving gaze on Hawk. "But you, mister . . ."

"I know," Hawk said as he latched the tailgate. "I take the cake."

"In spades!"

Western Arizona was a raw, parched moonscape of gravelly flats bordered by bald, saw-toothed mountains and cut by a devil's maze of mostly dry watercourses — all of it hammered mercilessly by the giant blacksmith's hammer of a huge red sun.

Here and there mesquites, creosote, and ocotillo grew, brushing a lemon-green color across the otherwise black sand and gravel spewed across the land when the surrounding mountains blew their volcanic tops several eons past. There were saguaros and paloverdes on the long, flat stretches . . . and that hammering sun that was like a physical weight. It burned through hat crowns and scorched the skin, cracking lips, drying out nostrils, and searing eyes.

It was a long, hot trek, and Hawk confirmed Kid Reno's directions of travel to the La Posa mountains by a couple of old prospectors he ran into along one of the ancient Indian trails he and Ironside followed in the wagon, with the grulla, Ironside's army bay, and a spare horse for Reno tied to the tailgate.

Twelve days into the trip from the church teeming with Reno's dead gang, the La Posa range shone like a giant, slumbering dinosaur on the western horizon — hazel-colored under the cloudless, brassy sky.

Ironside headed the wagon toward the craggy, eroded sierra while Hawk stepped into his saddle to scout around, as they'd seen Indian sign though, as yet, no Indians. Presently, when Hawk had dismounted to climb a jog of rocky hills and knobs rising along a dry arroyo, he flinched as a bullet screeched off a granite wall two feet to his left.

The rifle's roar followed a half second later.

Hawk jerked a look into the arroyo below the scarp he was on. Smoke wafted from a greasewood shrub on the arroyo's far bank. A painted, brick-red face capped by a red bandanna peered through the greasewood's spindly branches. And then Hawk saw the Winchester's barrel jerk as the Apache levered a fresh shell into its breech.

Hawk aimed his Henry and fired — three bullets blowing up dust around the greasewood shrub, another lifting a loud whump as it tore through the bushwhacker's upper chest, sending him sprawling straight back into a paloverde tree. As Hawk seated a fresh cartridge in his Henry's breech, he glimpsed movement to his left.

He swung around too late for the Henry to be of any use. Another Indian was on him, whooping and yowling like a whipped coyote and swinging the steel-bladed, feathered ax high in his right hand.

Hawk dropped the Henry, spread his feet, and caught the brave's right wrist just before the ax would have cleaved his skull in two neat halves. Then he was falling back off his heels, the brave on top of him, whooping and screeching like a living nightmare, his sweaty, calico-shirted body hammering against Hawk's, his sour, rotten breath heavy in Hawk's nose.

Hawk hit the gravelly slope hard.

His vision dimmed and his breath left his chest in a guttural whoosh. The Indian still had a grip on the ax handle, and Hawk still had a grip on the Indian's wrist as they rolled together down the steep slope to slap onto the arroyo floor with a simultaneous grunt of more expelled air.

Hawk was still dazed from the first fall with the short, stocky brave's weight hammering on top of him. Now the brave lunged to his knees, grunting and snarling. He had Hawk's Russian in his hand. Hawk had had the same idea, and now as the brave thumbed back the Russian's hammer, Hawk jabbed his Colt .44 into the brave's guts and pulled the trigger.

"Heeeeeeeeeee!" the brave wailed so loudly that Hawk's eardrums ached.

The Russian roared, the slug slamming the rocks over Hawk's shoulder. Raising the Colt higher, Hawk drilled another round through the wailing brave's head, punching the warrior off and away from him . . . opening his view of the wash and two more braves striding toward him, crouched over rifles.

"Ah, shit," Hawk said, kicking the dead brave off his own right leg and rocking the Colt's hammer back.

The two other attackers were moving single file and spaced about ten feet apart. The first one snapped his Winchester to his shoulder, and Hawk gritted his teeth against the certain bullet.

But it was not the brave's Winchester that roared. Another rifle exploded somewhere in the scarp that Hawk and the first Indian had just vacated.

The first brave's head exploded like a ripe melon, and then the second Indian was howling and dancing around as the rifle in the scarp cracked again. There was a third shot, and the second brave, who'd dropped to one knee and was trying to scramble out of the wash, tumbled headlong into a barrel cactus, the hole in his back, just below his neck, glistening red in the afternoon sun.

Hawk lowered the Russian slightly, keeping his thumb on the hammer. A bulky, blue-clad figured came down the scarp sideways, striding and sliding, the sergeant's white teeth showing inside the scruffy red beard he'd grown since leaving his dead patrol and joining Hawk in the search for Knife-Hand.

He held the Winchester he'd gleaned from the crates in the wagon in his right hand as he leapt the last few feet to the arroyo's bottom. Jerking his head around anxiously, on the scout for more Apaches, he strode over to the dead Indian piled up against the barrel cactus. The brave's back rose and fell sharply as he breathed.

Quickly levering a fresh shell, Ironside lifted the new Winchester and drilled a finishing round through the back of the

Indian's head. He glanced at Hawk, who gained his feet, pressing a hand to the back of his neck, and watched the sergeant walk over to one of the rifles the Apaches had dropped.

A dark expression on his broad, sunburned face, the sergeant held the shiny Winchester above his head. "So new I can still smell the factory on it."

Hawk scooped his Russian out of the black gravel and holstered it, looking around cautiously. Apaches usually roamed in small packs, but there could be more reservation broncos on the prowl out here.

The thought had barely brushed across his mind before he heard a shrill bellow, and then a victorious whoop back in the direction of the wagon. The bellow belonged to Kid Reno, whom Hawk had left tied in the wagon box.

Hawk jerked his head up, then swung his glance toward Ironside, who said, "Shit, they found the wagon!"

20.
KID RENO'S RIDE

"They've been following us," Hawk grated as he scrambled up the escarpment down which he and the brave had tumbled. He heard Ironside clawing and cursing his way up behind him, the heavier, older man breathing hard with the effort.

Tension gripped Hawk's innards in an iron fist. If the Apaches had found the horses he'd tied near a spring, they'd likely hazed them off or cut their throats, which would put him and Ironside on foot, and the wagonload of guns and ammunition into the Apaches' hands for good.

Rage at Ironside for leaving the wagon nipped Hawk, as well. But, then, if the sergeant hadn't sensed the trap and come looking for him, Hawk would now be buzzard food on the floor of that arroyo. . . .

Hawk grabbed his Henry rifle from where it lay against a pipe-stem cactus and, brushing it off, ran back through the scarp's towering knobs, threading his way through the stony corridors. He'd tied the three saddle horses in a spring-fed hollow, having watered the wagon's two pullers from his hat earlier. His heart lifted like a dove's downy wings when he saw all three mounts standing where he'd left them, feed sacks hooked over their ears, contentedly switching their tails as they hunkered in the shade of a tall, gnarled mesquite.

Beyond the upthrust of chalky rock, back toward the trail where he'd left the wagon, the clatter of wagon wheels and thudding of galloping hooves dwindled quickly.

Hawk scrambled down the scarp, leapt the last several feet to the ground, landing on his heels, and ripped the grulla's reins free of the mesquite he'd tied them to. Glancing at the sergeant stumbling down the rocks, Hawk swung up into the saddle, neck-reined the horse in a tight circle, and put the spurs to him.

"Wait for me, damnit!" the sergeant bellowed. "There might be a whole war party out there!"

Hawk raced out of the gorge, around several more stony upthrusts and mesquite trees, and bounded onto the narrow trail they had been following between mountain ranges. The wagon was little larger than a matchbox as it careened along the trail, a hundred yards ahead and steadily widening the gap.

A riderless horse galloped right of the lunging wagon while a brave on a brown-and-white pinto loped along to the left, holding a Winchester in one hand and jerking quick, darting glances back over his shoulder. Spying Hawk kicking after him, he gave a bellow and jerked his head toward the wagon, apparently urging more speed from whoever was driving it.

Hawk tipped his hat low and pulled his head down as the grulla chewed up the trail. He closed on the wagon bouncing on the other side of the tan dust cloud, the riderless, war-painted Indian pony keeping pace on the right, swerving around shrubs and boulders while the outriding Apache did the same on the left.

As Hawk gained ground on the wagon, he could hear the hammering of the iron-shod wheels and what could only have been Kid Reno's wails issuing from the back pucker flap. The Indians likely hadn't realized they had a white-eyes tied in the wagon's rear until they'd started moving, or they would have killed the gunrunner by now. The way the wagon was jouncing and bouncing, the Kid was getting quite a hammering ride —

a slow death by a new form of Apache torture.

Hawk didn't give a damn about Reno. It was the guns — especially that sure-fire death-dealer, the Gatling, he didn't want the Apaches to have.

As Hawk drew within forty yards, the outriding Apache hauled his own war-painted pinto to a skidding halt, reined the horse around, and whooping and hollering and batting his mocassin-clad heels into the horse's flanks, rushed back toward Hawk.

He took his reins in his teeth as he raised his Winchester. Hawk raised his Henry and triggered a shot at nearly the same time that smoke puffed from the maw of the Apache's rifle.

The brave wasn't accustomed to the new rifle, and the slug whistled over Hawk's head.

Hawk's first round flew wide of his target, as well, but his second and third punched the brave through his naked red chest. As the grulla continued chewing up the trail, the brave hit the ground just ahead. The pinto flew past Hawk, screaming. The Apache rolled wildly, hair and limbs flying, and Hawk glanced down as the grulla's left front hoof struck the brave's head with a dull thud.

Blood sprayed and the body twisted around and then Hawk and the grulla were within twenty yards of the wagon . . . then ten . . . five. . . .

Inside, Kid Reno bellowed like a bull caught in a hawthorn thicket, the gunrunner's voice vibrating with the wagon's violent pitching and lurching.

Hawk slipped his rifle into its saddle boot as he drew even with wagon's rear, keeping the flying contraption to his left. When he was less than five feet from the hammering rear wheel, he swung his right leg over the grulla's rump and slipped that boot into the left stirrup as he slid the left one out.

Steadying himself with one hand on the saddle horn, he lunged suddenly, pushing himself away from the saddle and throwing himself through the wagon's rear pucker. He landed just inside the tailgate on his left shoulder, rolling over one of the several long rifle crates that were strewn about the bed, and rolled up against another.

"Hawk, you son of a bitch!" Reno wailed loudly.

Hawk glanced up along the wagon bed. "I know — you're not a well man."

The gunrunner's enraged, feverish eyes peered at Hawk from between two bouncing, shuddering rifle crates, his braided hair dangling over his gaunt, sun-splotched cheeks. Above and beyond Reno, the yellow-and-black calico shirt of the Apache driving the wagon shone through a crack in the front pucker flap.

Hawk slipped his Russian from his holster, steadied his arm atop one of the rifle crates, and aimed at the swatch of yellow shirt he could see through the front pucker.

Pow! Pow! Pow!

The shirt disappeared. The wagon lurched as one of the wheels hammered something more yielding than a rock in the trail.

Hawk wrenched himself around to send his gaze out the back of the wagon. In the trail beyond, he caught a glimpse of the yellow calico shirt as the Indian rolled in a roiling dust cloud before angling off the trail, piling up against the base of a tall saguaro, and growing quickly smaller as the wagon kept lumbering ahead across the rocky desert floor.

Behind the tan dust cloud, Sergeant Ironside galloped toward the wagon, hunkered down low in the saddle and whipping his bay's rump with his rein ends.

"Well, you killed the savage!" Kid Reno shouted, pulling at the braided leather strips binding him taut to an iron ring in the side of the wagon. "But this thing's a blazin' runaway now!"

Hawk was already gaining his feet, stumbling this way and that as the wagon careened along the trail, often fishtailing, always bouncing and threatening to break up against the next near boulder. He stepped over Reno's legs, pushing himself off the jumbled gun crates, and made his way toward the front.

The wagon lurched suddenly, and he twisted around and slammed his back against the front panel, the board cutting painfully into his lower back. The wagon lurched in the other direction, and Hawk used the sudden force to throw himself sideways and up through the pucker, crawling quickly over the blood-splattered seat. He was relieved to see that the reins, instead of bouncing along the ground behind the team, were coiled up in front of the dashboard, on the floor of the driver's boot.

He reached down, grabbed the reins in both hands, sat gingerly down on the seat, and set both his boots on the dashboard. Leaning back and pulling hard on the leather ribbons, he got the frantic horses stopped only after they'd galloped another hundred and fifty yards and fairly winded themselves.

With the wagon idle at last, Hawk

slouched in the seat. The ground seemed to continue to race past on both sides. The dust caught up to him from behind, filling his nostrils, making him cough.

Hooves clomped. He turned to see Sergeant Ironside ride up beside the driver's box, sparing him an anxious look. Hawk stared back. His face a mask of dust and grit, Ironside shook his head, dismounted, and ran up to inspect the silver-sweated team.

"They look all right," he said finally, letting the off-puller's hoof fall back to the ground. "Whipped and tired and hot as that sun up there . . . but all right."

Silence.

Hawk doffed his hat and ran his hands through his hair that hung in ducktails across his collar, ringing out the sweat.

Reno's voice came from the back, pitched high with jangled nerves. "What about me?"

For the third time the next day, Kid Reno barked out the wagon's front pucker flap, "Cut me loose, you sons o' bitches!"

Hawk was riding ahead of the wagon, holding his Henry across his saddlebows. He glanced back as Sergeant Ironside wagged his head and said in disgust, "I just love his personality."

"Yeah, I'm gonna miss him," Hawk said.

They were traversing a shallow canyon between high, sandstone ridges. Hawk could hear javelinas rooting around in the greasewood shrubs on the left bank.

"You're not gonna really turn this wildcat loose, are you?"

"I gave him my word," Hawk said, staring straight ahead.

From behind the sergeant, Reno shouted, "You gave me your word you'd turn me loose as soon as we got into the La Posas. Well, we made it. We're here!" The gunrunner's voice broiled up from deep in his chest, taut with exasperation. "So kindly turn me loose, goddamnit!"

"Shut up, you consarned son of a bitch!" the sergeant rasped, turning his head sideways. "You wanna bring every Apache in the whole damn range down on top of us?"

Hawk said just loudly enough to be heard above the wagon's clatter, "When I'm sure we're near where I wanna be, I'll let you go. If I find out you've sent us on a wild-goose chase, I'm gonna shoot you."

"I think you oughta shoot him, anyway, if we're not gonna take him back to the fort to hang," Ironside said. "Freein' this Mad Hatter's akin to turnin' a rabid panther loose on a herd of heifers and calves."

Reno told Ironside to do something physically impossible to himself. Ironside ground his teeth.

"I'm gonna make him promise to walk the straight and narrow from now on," Hawk said, squinting westward at the low-hanging sun. "If I find he hasn't lived up to his word, I'll hunt him down. I'll know where to find him. Men like the Kid leave a plain trail no matter how light they ride. And when I find him, I'll kill him."

"I give you my word," Reno said from the wagon box, his voice vibrating with the wagon's violent jarring. "Matter of fact, soon as you turn me loose, I'm gonna hunt me up a monastery and become a priest. No, not a priest. A monk! That's what I'm gonna be. Cool my heels in church till the end of my days.

"Say, I heard there's a monastery down by Tucson. Go ahead and cut me loose, and I'll hop on that horse you were kind enough to provide, and head on over there and introduce myself. A lost and weary lamb needin' shelter from the cold. . . ."

Ironside told the Kid to do something impossible to himself.

The Kid pitched his voice with feigned sadness. "Now, that ain't no way to talk to a man who's done vowed to give up his evil ways. Come on, Hawk — whaddaya say?"

"Shut up, Kid," Hawk and Ironside said at the same time.

After a moment, Ironside said, "Hey, Hawk. Look at that."

Hawk glanced over his shoulder. The sergeant was staring ahead and right of the sandy wash they were following through the canyon.

The right canyon was falling back as the defile spilled onto an open plain, and a quarter mile northwest a low, sand-colored bluff rose, fringed with black rock. From the other side of the bluff, tan dust climbed into the air, sifting upward toward the slowly darkening sky where the sun painted it pink.

Hawk looked around. To the left another wash opened, offering good cover. "Pull in there," he told Ironside, keeping his voice down. "I'll check it out."

He rode up out of the canyon and, a half hour later, came back to where Ironside had stopped the wagon, the grulla blowing and tossing its head after the fast ride.

"Arizona Rangers," Hawk said, swinging down from the saddle. "Three of 'em. Probably out on routine patrol, but we'd best hole up here for the night. I don't want to have to explain this wagon filled with stolen rifles and a Gatling gun. And Reno."

Ironside was sitting in the shade by the wagon's right front wheel. Kid Reno sat with his back against the other wheel, braided rawhide binding his wrists and ankles.

The sergeant doffed his blue forage hat and ran his finger around the sweatband. "Might not be a bad idea — flashing your badge and asking for a little help."

The sergeant had a point. But Hawk's mission was to kill Knife-Hand, not take him prisoner. Rangers wouldn't agree to cold-blooded murder. He didn't have to explain that to the sergeant, however. The guns offered enough of their own kind of trouble.

"They'd likely think we were gunrunners," Hawk said, leading his horse toward the shade of an arched dike. "They'd have us shackled and headed toward Yuma by sunup tomorrow."

"Hawk's right," Reno told the sergeant, smiling. "They'd probably just mistake us for gunrunners."

Hawk glanced back at Ironside, who sat staring after him, skeptically squinting one eye and snarling, "Shut up, Reno."

21.
VISITORS

Hawk, Ironside, and Kid Reno were sitting around a small coffee fire long after good dark, under a sequined black parasol of shimmering stars, when a dull voice called out of the night, "Halloo, the fire. Arizona Rangers. We're ridin' in."

Hawk had flinched at the man's first words, but he kept his hand away from his guns. He looked over at Ironside, who had started reaching for his Winchester but had stayed the move when the caller had identified himself. To the sergeant's right, Kid Reno said, "Shit," over the rim of the coffee cup he held to his mouth in his tied hands.

"We're freighters," Hawk said softly to Ironside as both men stared into the darkness beyond the fire. "Heading from Las Vegas to Yuma. Mining supplies."

"What if they look in the wagon?" Ironside said as the thud of slow-moving hooves sounded from the direction of the main canyon.

"Yeah, what if they look in the wagon?" Reno echoed, his voice taut.

Hawk glanced at the Kid's tied wrists and ankles. "Hide those bindings," he whispered.

The Kid set his cup down awkwardly, then leaned forward to draw his soogan blanket across his ankles. He picked up his cup again quickly, raising it to his chin, using it to cover the ties connecting his wrists. Hawk's innards jelled when his mind flitted across the possibility of the rangers recognizing the gunrunner. Kid Reno was notorious throughout the Southwest.

He hoped these men didn't recognize him, however. Hawk didn't want to have to choose between killing lawmen doing their jobs and fulfilling his mission to kill Knife-Hand Monjosa.

Shadows moved at the far edge of the firelight. One of the horses tied back with the wagon gave an inquiring whinny. A horse of one of the rangers responded in kind. A man's reprimanding voice hushed the beast, and there was the squawk of tack and ring of spurs as men dismounted, and then two walked forward while the third held the horses — mustached men with high-crowned hats and batwing chaps, one

257

with his thumbs hooked behind his cartridge belts with an air of feigned casualness. They both wore badges, and two pistols apiece, one about five years older than the other.

The older gent, who wore a pinto vest over a collarless pinstriped shirt, and whose face was nearly as sun-blackened as Hawk's coffeepot, spoke first. "Howdy."

Hawk nodded. "Got about a half pot of coffee here, fellas. Help yourselves."

The older ranger shook his head while the younger, surly-looking one stood sullenly regarding Hawk and his cohorts with quick flicks of his large, brown eyes. "We're gonna keep movin', ride another hour or so. I'm Ranger Bogarth. This is Dave Walters. Ted Stanley's holdin' our hosses."

He waited, eyeing Hawk and the other two men around the fire expectantly.

"Hall," Hawk said, touching his thumb to his chest. Tossing his head toward the sergeant and Kid Reno in turns, he said, "This here's Ironside and that's Ryle. Any trouble, fellas?"

Bogarth stared at Ironside, said with a grunt, "Them cavalry blues you're wearin', Sergeant?"

Ironside slid an anxious glance at Hawk, and a small tack of anger slid between Hawk's ribs. The sergeant was a career soldier, and lying to men of authority didn't come easy to him. Hawk couldn't blame him, but he sure wished the man had a little of the thespian in him.

Ironside chuckled woodenly, showing his teeth through his red beard. "Just got out. Ain't even had time to buy me new duds. Reckon it'll take me a while to get used to anything but this clown outfit."

Bogarth raked his eyes across Kid Reno, giving the gunrunner special study before sliding his gaze back to Ironside and Hawk, and saying in his low, gravelly voice that complemented his wind-beaten, sun-cured face, "What you fellas doin' this far out on the devil's dance floor?"

"Freight haulin'." Hawk sipped his coffee. "Got us a load we're trailin' down from Mesquite for Yuma. Mining supplies, mostly. Dry goods."

The younger Ranger said with a faintly challenging air, "Mind if we take a look?"

"Sure," Hawk said, not missing a beat and starting to push himself to his feet. "Come on back. I'll open —"

"That's all right," Bogarth said, instantly easing the nip of that tack between Hawk's ribs. "You fellas don't look like gunrunners to me. It's Apaches we're chasin', anyways. A dozen or so burned out a couple of prospectors just north of here, and a freighter workin' his way down from Utah was spitted over a low fire on his own wagon wheel. Burned good and slow."

Reno whistled and shook his head.

Ironside also shook his head and sipped his coffee, sliding his deferring gaze to Hawk.

"That's Apaches for you," Hawk said, settling back down on the ground and resting his arms on his knees. "We ran into a party east of here about twenty-five miles. Tried stealin' our wagon. We fought 'em off, but it was close there for a while."

Bogarth said, "East, you say?"

Hawk nodded. "We saw half a dozen or so."

"They were likely part of the cavvy that killed the Utah freighter. Probably split up when they winded us. I reckon we'll get after the others." The older ranger glanced at Walters, who continued to eye Hawk, Ironside, and Kid Reno as though there were something on his mind but he wasn't sure that now was the time or the place to express it.

"Well, I reckon we best get movin', Dave. Catch up to our other men at the cabin, and shove off again at first light."

Bogarth pinched his hat brim to Hawk's

party, touched Walters's shoulder, and headed back toward the third ranger holding the horses. Walters continued glaring at Hawk, until Hawk felt his trigger finger twitch against the side of his cooling coffee cup. Then Walters gave his chin a slight dip, turned, and tramped away, spurs chinging, chaps flapping against his thighs.

When the hoof thuds of the retreating rangers had died, Kid Reno gave a slow, relieved sigh and reached for the coffeepot. Ironside wagged his head and turned to Hawk. "What you suppose that was all about?"

Hawk hiked a shoulder. "Just rangers doin' their jobs."

"That Walters, though — he sure had the evil eye."

"Watch Reno," Hawk said. "I'm gonna go look around."

He circled the camp twice, making sure the rangers themselves weren't circling around to approach the camp from another direction, and more quietly this time. When he neither saw nor heard anything suspicious, he sat down on a low hump of gravelly ground and stared out across the star-shrouded desert.

He, too, hadn't liked the look in Ranger Walters's eye. Could be the man was just colicky. There was no way they could know of Hawk's intentions, or know what he was really freighting across the desert.

No way they could know that.

Yet a cricket of deep consternation skittered around under his shirt.

"Hawk, tell me somethin'," Sergeant Ironside said the next afternoon, as he and Hawk both rode in the wagon's driver's boot, Hawk letting the grulla trail along with the other two saddle horses.

"Let's hear it."

As he leaned forward, elbows on his knees, reins hanging slack in his hands, Ironside squinted an eye at the Rogue Lawman. "Was you gonna kill them rangers last night, if they found the rifles and the Gatling gun?"

Hawk took a drag from his cigarette and let the smoke dribble out through his nostrils.

"You was, weren't you?" Ironside prodded. "You woulda shot them lawmen just so's you could keep using the guns to bait Monjosa."

Hawk took another drag from the quirley and blew it out on the hot wind as he turned to the sergeant still squinting at him in mute astonishment. "Let me ask you somethin', Sergeant. What's worth more —

the lives of three rangers or the lives of all the folks, including soldiers, Monjosa's likely to kill in the next year if I don't snuff his candle?"

Ironside just stared at him.

A semi-crazed cackle from Kid Reno sounded in the box behind him. Hawk ignored it.

"Monjosa buried that knife hand of his in the guts of a son of a good friend of mine," Hawk said. "A good son of a good man. For that, I'm gonna kill him. And no one's gonna get in my way. No ranger. No soldier. No Apache. No one."

Hawk stared hard at the sergeant, but what he saw was "Three-Fingers" Ned Meade's kill-crazy grin just before he'd spanked Jubal's horse out from beneath the scared, baffled child, snapping his neck, leaving Hawk alone and bereft and hunting an unattainable justice.

"Why," Ironside said slowly, "you're mad, aren't you?"

"If there were a few more madmen out here, Sergeant, maybe there wouldn't be so many killers like Knife-Hand Monjosa."

Again, Kid Reno's laugh sounded above the wagon's rattle and squawk.

Hawk grinned darkly as he added, "Or Kid Reno."

Reno clipped his laugh.

"Just drive, Sergeant," Hawk said. "That's all you have to worry about."

"No it ain't," Ironside growled. "I think I gotta worry about how I'm gonna get outta this little fiasco with my hide intact, after we kill Monjosa, because I got me a creepy-crawly feelin' that you haven't given any thought to that at all. Have you?"

"One bite at a time."

The sergeant had just opened his mouth to respond when his eyes focused on something beyond Hawk and widened slightly, sharpening. "Might be time to start worryin'."

Hawk followed the sergeant's gaze to four riders sitting atop a low bluff about a hundred yards from the trail. Hawk couldn't see much of the men from this distance, but he could see that they were white men and that they were holding rifles.

There was movement ahead, and Hawk turned to watch three more men ride out from behind a jumble of large boulders and into the trail, turning their mounts to face the wagon. They were only about fifty yards ahead, and Hawk could see the hard, grim expressions on their weathered, bearded faces — the faces of seasoned desert riders.

These men, too, held rifles across their

saddlebows or snugged against their buckskin- or denim-clad thighs, barrels aimed skyward — shiny new Winchesters, their brass receivers glistening in the desert sun.

"If we got trouble, fellas," Kid Reno barked from the wagon box, "turn me the hell loose . . . as per our agreement! You ride me into Monjosa's camp, I'm a dead man."

The sergeant squinted his blue eyes into the sunlit trail ahead and bunched his sunburned cheeks fatefully. He kept the wagon moving as he said softly, "Might be a little late for that, Kid."

22.
A Helluva Son of a Bitch to Throw in With

Hawk glanced at the red and the black neckerchiefs buffeting in the hot wind from the brake handle. Knowing the ways of the Southwest, the sergeant had informed Hawk that the colored neckerchiefs were the traditional signal of contraband for sale. Hawk hoped it had been the neckerchiefs that had attracted the obvious trail wolves to him now and that they were part of Knife-Hand's band.

It was time to kill Monjosa.

Sergeant Ironside drew the wagon up to within twenty feet of the three horseback riders and hauled back on the reins with a sharp, "Whoa, there!" When the horses had settled back into their collars, the three riders toed their mounts slowly forward while the four on the bluff stayed where they were — menacing, rifle-wielding silhouettes on horseback.

"Cut me loose, Hawk," Reno urged from

the wagon box. "Give me a chance."

Hawk twisted around to look behind the wagon. Four more riders had come into the trail and were drawing their horses up to within forty yards, riding abreast and about ten yards apart. All held rifles or, in one case, a pistol with at least a ten-inch barrel — probably a Buntline Special. All four of the trailing riders wore charro slacks and jackets and palm-leaf sombreros.

"Like the sergeant said — it's too late, Reno," Hawk rasped toward the open pucker flap. "You follow my lead and keep your mouth shut, you might have a chance."

Damn little chance, Hawk thought as the three riders ahead split up to form a semicircle around the front of the wagon. But all the chance the gunrunner deserved.

The three riders regarded Hawk and Ironside coldly before the one who'd pulled his steeldust Arabian up to Ironside's side said in a heavy Spanish accent, "What you got, amigos?"

He was a tall, rangy Mexican whose ears appeared to have been hacked off with a dull knife; only grisly, knotted scars remained under the brim of his high-crowned straw-sombrero. He wore another savage scar across his mouth.

Ironside was content to let Hawk do the

speaking.

"Guns," the Rogue Lawman grunted. "Guns and ammo." He offered a savage smile. "For the right price."

"Let me see."

"No," Hawk snarled. "I don't do business with lackeys. I want to see *el capitan*."

The earless Mexican rose up in his saddle, his leathery face turning crimson with fury as he shouted hoarsely, "No one sees *el capitan* until I see what's in the wagon." He poked his chest with his middle finger and his black eyes sparked at Hawk. "I see under the tarp or we shoot both you filthy gringos and fill the wagon with lead and take what we want!"

Ironside glanced grimly at Hawk. Hawk returned the glance, then smiled at the earless Mexican, hiking a shoulder. "You wanna see? All right. Come on back and have a look."

Hawk climbed down from the wagon, glancing up at the Mexican who'd pulled his horse off the wagon's right front wheel and was aiming a carbine at Hawk from his shoulder. Hawk opened his hands and held them out away from his guns as he tramped to the wagon's rear.

The earless Mex pulled his horse around from the other side and squinted against his own dust as Hawk lowered the tailgate and threw back the pucker flaps. Glancing inside, he saw Kid Reno sitting on one of the rifle boxes to which his tied wrists were tethered by a five-foot length of rope.

Reno swallowed, looking sheepish and grim. Sweat runneled his dusty cheeks and pasted wisps of unbraided hair to his forehead. The earless Mex rode up and held the pucker flap open with one hand, aiming his rifle with the other and leaning down to stare into the shadowy cavern that smelled like Reno's sickness. When he saw Kid Reno, his brows furrowed slightly, and he made a face against the stench.

He glanced at Hawk, then back at Reno, scrutinizing the outlaw as though he couldn't quite believe his eyes, and then a look of unabashed delight washed over his face as he turned to Hawk again.

Hawk said, "Look who I found along the trail."

No-Ears looked at Reno again, then dropped the canvas flaps and backed his horse away from the tailgate, laughing. "The boss will be most happy to see his long-lost amigo. Ha! Ha! Oh, he will be quite pleased!" He reined his horse around and booted the gelding up the trail, dust wafting heavily in his wake. "Come on, gringos.

Let's get moving!"

Reno glared at Hawk again, lips pursed. Hawk crawled inside, quickly cut the man free of his ties, then crawled out again and closed the tailgate. "Let's go smoke the peace pipe with your old pal, eh, Reno?"

"If I somehow manage to get out of this, Hawk, you double-crossing bastard, I'm gonna kill you slow."

"You already tried that," Sergeant Ironside said as Hawk climbed up into the driver's box. He hoorahed the team forward, adding with a sidelong glance at Hawk, "Now it's Monjosa's turn."

Hawk blinked his eyes against the dust kicked up by the wagon's team and Monjosa's three lead riders as they barreled across the desert, branching off the trail and heading through broken country that more than once threatened to tear the wagon apart or overturn it.

Reno's agonized screams rose shrilly amid the thunder of the shifting rifle crates in the box. Two riders stayed even on each side of the wagon, with four behind, the men tilting their hat brims low against the west-falling sun.

When they'd safely crossed another in a series of rocky arroyos, Ironside turned to

270

the Rogue Lawman and yelled, "You're a helluva son of a bitch to throw in with, you know that, Hawk?"

"If you remember," Hawk said, wedging his boots up tight against the dashboard and clutching the seat with both hands, "you insisted!"

Ironside clucked, shook his head, and kept the team about fifty yards behind Monjosa's lead riders, who seemed to be leading them into a notch in the rumpled dun rise of craggy-peaked mountains growing larger and larger ahead. Soon the notch widened, then it yawned, and suddenly the wagon plunged into the shade between two steep canyon walls.

The canyon floor rose and fell, widened and narrowed, and then suddenly Hawk saw verdant green shrubs growing along its middle, in a rocky gulley snaking through the middle of the defile's floor. The air cooled slightly, and Hawk thought he detected a moistness against his sun-rawed cheeks.

Ironside lifted his head and worked his nose. "Goddamn," he yelled above the wagon's roar, "is that what it smells like?"

Sure enough, a narrow stream was rippling and flashing along the gulley, tumbling over rocks that had long ago fallen from the ever-steepening canyon walls. As the wagon continued south by southeast, the team slowing and blowing now as it tired, the greenery grew heavier and lusher. Palm trees began popping up along the widening defile, their leaves fluttering in the wind sifting down the canyon, and flashing pink in the last rays of the sun angling over the ridges.

The palms nestled in boulder-choked nooks and crannies of the canyon walls — some only a few feet tall, others reaching a good twenty or thirty feet straight up from their boles littered with the broom-colored trash of shed leaves. Roots angled out from the bases of the palms' trunks to snake into the gurgling, twinkling brook, reaching deep for the precious water.

The horses lifted their heads and shook their manes as they smelled the water. Hawk's own parched mouth watered at the prospect of dipping his face into one of those sandy back eddies or dark pools filling bowls in the steplike slabs of black volcanic rock.

The wagon followed the riders around a dogleg in the main canyon, into a broad, open horseshoe, and then suddenly the riders ahead threw up their arms and stopped their horses. Ironside hauled back on the team's reins. As the wagon chugged to a grinding, squawking halt, Hawk looked around at the adobe-brick or stone shacks and ocotillo corrals surrounding him, with here and there a small dugout shack or Apache-like jacal.

It was a rancho of sorts, with dozens of ragged-looking, heavily armed men milling about the shacks and corrals — tending horses or hay sheds or cook fires, with here and there a black-haired, tan-faced woman manning one of the several smoking iron pots suspended over the fires by iron spits.

A few children herded goats or tended brush-roofed chicken coops. A couple of dogs ran out from the hovels to scatter the chickens and goats and to bark at the newcomers, raising their hackles and tails and showing white rings around their eyes.

What caught the brunt of Hawk's attention was the large, stone, tile-roofed casa sitting on a terraced ledge on a rocky shelf, set back against the canyon's pink southern wall. The house boasted two stories, with large stone hearths abutting both ends, and arches over the ground-floor gallery. The arches were fronted by orange trees, some brown from neglect, but on the branches of the few living trees the ripe fruit fairly glowed in the fading sun rays.

The earless Mexican galloped his steel-dust Arab to the bottom of the stone steps rising to the casa above and, rising in his stirrups, shouted in Spanish, "Visitors to see you, Jefe!"

The scream echoed around the canyon for several seconds, as did the barks of the dogs and the bleating of the goats. In one of the several corrals, a horse added an anxious whinny to the reverberations.

The earless Mex rode his Arab in a tight, quick circle and was about to scream again when a gruff voice said from the direction of the corral, "Here, idiot. I'm here!"

Hawk shifted his gaze from the house to see a man separate himself from the handful of others congregated at a near corral's right front corner and walk toward the wagon. He was a stocky Mex with a trimmed black beard forming precise lines down his jaws and over his upper lip. He wore a black, floppy-brimmed hat, a coarsely woven, open-necked tunic under a dark-blue coat that Hawk recognized as the uniform of the Mexican federal police — this one with colonel's bars on the shoulders — and dusty, embroidered charro slacks that clung to his stout thighs like second skins.

A long red silk scarf was wrapped around

his neck, its pointed tail dangling nearly to his knees.

Hawk felt an unconscious prickling in his loins when his eyes drifted to the man's right hand. Or what would have been his right hand had he not been wearing a sheathed knife in its place, the soft, shiny, black scabbard extending a good foot from the bloodstained sleeve of the man's *federale* coat.

"Jefe!" the earless rider said, galloping his horse to the wagon's rear. "Come over here quickly! You will want to see this!" He grinned largely, evilly.

Wilbur "Knife-Hand" Monjosa strolled toward the front of the wagon where Hawk and Ironside waited in tense silence. The men who'd been standing with Monjosa at the corral shuffled up behind him in an interested group, hanging about ten feet back behind their knife-handed leader.

They all had their hands on their pistol grips. The men who'd guided the wagon into Monjosa's canyon-nestled rancho held their rifles and pistols on Hawk and Ironside with obvious threat and warning.

Monjosa's voice was deep and gravelly: "Who the hell are you?" He shuttled his brown eyes quickly between Ironside and Hawk. In his left hand he held a crock jug against his shoulder.

"This is Sergeant Ironside. I'm Hawk. We heard you were looking for guns."

"I am always looking for guns," Monjosa growled, his deep voice pitched thickly with drink. His eyes were rheumy, the whites owning the consistency of an undercooked egg. "But I don't usually entertain strangers, if you know what I'm saying. My canyon . . . !" He swept the jug up and around to indicate his spring-fed domain. "It is *private!* I value my privacy very much!"

He turned toward the earless rider waiting expectantly at the wagon's rear. "Fierro, why did you bring them here? You know my rules! No one comes to the canyon unless I personally okay it!"

"*¡Sí, sí, Jefe!*" Fierro said, the skin above the bridge of his nose bunching slightly. Then he grinned and glanced at the wagon. "But this you must see. I am certain you will find the unexpected visit very much worth the invasion of your privacy, Jefe!"

Monjosa glanced suspiciously at Hawk and Ironside once more, then turned and tramped heavily, bull-leggedly back to the wagon's rear. Hawk looked at Ironside, who expelled an anxious breath and set the brake. Climbing down the opposite side, Hawk walked to the back of the wagon where Fierro was backing his Arab away from the tailgate, grinning wolfishly and giving his boss plenty of room.

His mud-brown eyes sparkled like gold dust.

23.
Amigos Para la Vida

"What is this surprise, huh?" Knife-Hand Monjosa asked Fierro. "You know how I feel about surprises."

"*¡Sí, sí, Jefe,*" Fierro said from his saddle. "But I think you're gonna like this one."

Hawk looked at Monjosa. His trigger finger twitched as though stung by a mosquito. The man was within seven feet of him. He might never get this close again. Of course, if Hawk carried out his mission now, he'd be condemning himself and Ironside to certain death.

He'd wait. No one had taken his guns. As long as he had his guns, he could kill Monjosa anytime he wanted. Maybe an opportunity for killing the man and getting himself or at least Ironside out of here alive would reveal itself.

He spread his boots and hooked his thumbs behind his cartridge belt as Monjosa, scowling over his shoulder at the grinning Fierro, swept back the pucker flap. Monjosa drew a sharp breath and stepped back in awe, still keeping the stone jug propped against his shoulder.

Kid Reno sat on one of the rifle crates, grinning. He waved. "How you doin', Knife-Hand? Been a while."

"Cristo!" Monjosa whispered, as though he were watching a ghost. "Kid? Is it really you, Kid?"

Reno's grin faded to a smile. He sat with his elbows on his knees, hands laced together. His gaunt, craggy face was sweaty, and his eyes were spoked with pain lines. "It's me, all right. Your old pard, Kid Reno. Came back to say hi, see how you were doin'."

Monjosa continued staring in awe at Kid Reno, as if only half believing what his eyes were telling his brain. Slowly, he swung his head to Hawk, frowning.

Monjosa opened his mouth slowly to speak, but before he could form words, Hawk said, "The Kid's with me and Sergeant Ironside. Three-way split. What he's sittin' on are brand-new Winchester repeaters. There's a Gatling gun in there, too. Over a thousand rounds of ammunition. And there's more where all that came from. Lots more. Ironside, the Kid, and I — we got an inside connection. We four can have us a very lucrative relationship . . . if, uh . . . you and the Kid can bury the hatchet."

"Bury the hatchet?" Monjosa growled, squaring his shoulders and glaring into the wagon at the Kid. "I should bury my hand in your guts for what you did to me, you double-crossing, mealy-mouthed son of a bitch!"

"Come on, Wilbur," the Kid said, raising his hands palm out, "she was a whore, for chrissakes, and a cheap one even by Mexican standards!"

"I loved her, you bastard. I have never known a more delightful creature. And the very night I ask her to marry me, I find you two together, rutting like back-alley curs on my own kitchen table!" Monjosa paused, staring into the wagon at Reno. His tone softened slightly. "It takes cojones to come back here, Kid. Even bigger ones than I figured you for. You must think you really have a deal for me, uh?" He frowned, wrinkled his broad nostrils. "What is that smell?"

Reno's glance slid toward Hawk, then back to Monjosa, who scowled back at him skeptically, brown brows beetled. "It's a hell of a deal, Wilbur. One that'll make you forget Margaretta and any other woman.

One that'll make your head spin at all the gold we're likely to fleece them Apaches and banditos for."

Squinting one eye, Monjosa switched his glance to Hawk. Then he took a long pull from the stone jug on his shoulder and beckoned to the Kid with his menacing knife hand. "For a man with cannonball cojones, you sure cower in there like a kangaroo rat. Get out here. Let's talk about it."

Kid Reno chuckled delightedly as he tripped the latch and let the tailgate drop. "Amigos, eh, Wilbur? *Amigos para la vida.* Friends for life. We shouldn't let women get between us!"

As the gunrunner scrambled out of the wagon, Hawk felt a worm of dread turn over in his belly. The situation was beginning to angle off in a surprising direction. If Monjosa and Reno were back being friends again, that left him, Hawk, and Ironside out in the cold. He'd counted on them merely calling a truce.

The thought had no sooner oozed over Hawk's brain before Monjosa, glowering at both Hawk and Ironside, said, "Where you find these two, Kid, uh? We really need them? You know how I feel about bringing men I don't know into my canyon. Shit, I'm not running a goddamn dance hall out here."

Hawk took one step back. As he slid his hand toward his Russian, a hand reached around from behind him and snagged the big, silver-chased pistol from its cross-draw holster on his left hip. Then the stag-gripped Colt was removed, and Hawk's cartridge belts felt suddenly as light as air on his hips.

That worm turned again in his belly, just behind his belly button, and he felt a hard pressure in his temples.

At the same time, Ironside was relieved of his own Army .44, the big sergeant wheeling to scowl at the man behind him, "Hey, what's the big idea, you son of a bitch?"

Suddenly, the sergeant bent forward with a great *"Gnaw!"* of expelled air as the butt of a Winchester was driven with brutal force into his heavy paunch.

"Hey, what you talk like that for, amigo?" Knife-Hand said. "You got no right talk to my men like that. You're no guest here. You came yourself as if I invited you, but I didn't invite you, so you mind your manners, okay, you fat gringo bastard!"

"Back off," Hawk snarled, stepping toward Knife-Hand and bunching his fists at his sides. "You got no call to take our weapons."

Monjosa turned his glowering, rheumy-eyed stare at Hawk. "Hey, Kid, we really need these two? I don't think I like the way they act. I know I don't like this one's tone."

Kid Reno snarled wolfishly at Hawk and took the stone jug from Monjosa, rubbing the lip with the palm of his hand. "You know, when I think about it, Wilbur, I see no reason why we need these two at all."

Reno's eyes were glassy as cunning thoughts danced behind them, likely wondering how much he should reveal to his old partner about Hawk's mission here and how much he should keep to himself. He didn't want to do anything to imperil his precarious, two-minute-old reconciliation.

"Hell, I'm the one with all the connections," he said. "These two here — shit, they just supplied the wagon."

Hawk's pulse hammered in his temples as he cast his stony gaze at Reno. He had maybe a half minute left. He had to grab a gun or a knife and kill Monjosa. The desire was a pounding, thundering obsession. He couldn't die without having met his objective. Each mission was all he lived for. He had nothing else. Each breath he took now he took so he could kill Knife-Hand Monjosa. But he had to time it right, make his move quickly and efficiently so that he himself wasn't killed before he could accomplish his task.

He whipped around toward the man behind him, catching the man off-guard and bulling him over backward. The man hit the ground on his back, Hawk on top of him and reaching for the Schofield in the holster under the man's left arm.

"Gringo bastard!" Monjosa screamed.

Hawk rolled onto a shoulder and began to raise the Schofield in his right hand. A silver-tipped boot slammed into his wrist. The gun twirled in the air over his head.

He saw a rifle butt slam toward him. Hawk reached up with both hands, grabbing the rifle and jerking it down so hard that the man wielding it dropped to his knees with a squealed curse. Hawk thrust himself to a half crouch and hammered his right fist against the rifle-wielder's heavy, bearded jaw.

Something hard smashed against the back of his head. The world darkened as though a cloud had passed over the sun. Both his hands dropped to the ground. Hawk heard himself growling like a rabid coyote, felt spittle spraying across his lips as he tried to remain conscious and to push himself to his feet.

He had to get a gun.

"A dog, uh?" Monjosa laughed. "Growling like a dog."

Hawk lifted his head but before he could rise from his hands, another boot slammed into his right side, the toe grinding deep into his ribs. The pain was sharp and searing, barking all through him.

Ripping laughter mocked him. He whipped onto his other side, his frustrated, desperate snarls growing louder.

"Lift him up," Monjosa ordered. "Watch this, Kid. This is what I dreamt of doing to you after you fled here like a scalded javelina." His laughter roared. "And what I will do to you still if I catch you fucking any more of my *putas!*"

Brusque hands grabbed Hawk's arms from behind. He was hauled to his feet and held in iron grips. He could smell the sweat, horses, and leather on the two men flanking him, hear them grunting as they twisted his arms behind his back with so much force he thought his shoulders would pop out of their sockets.

"Hold him!" Monjosa barked, studying Hawk from beneath his shaggy brows.

The *contrabandista* lifted his right wrist and, with his left hand, slid the black leather sheath off the knife, revealing the twelve inches of polished, razor-edged steel. He tucked the sheath behind his cartridge belts as he moved slowly toward Hawk in that

285

bull-legged, heavy-footed gait.

Behind him, Reno stood holding the crock jug up against his shoulder, grinning at Hawk. Catching Hawk's eye, the gunrunner winked. All around the canyon, men and a few of the hard-looking women and half-naked children had frozen in their chores to watch the happenings near the wagon with bemused interest.

Even the corralled horses were staring toward Hawk. Monjosa's men had all moved up to the wagon, forming a ragged circle around it, watching in grim, bemused fascination.

Sergeant Ironside was on his knees, a rifle aimed at either side of his head, his hands raised to his shoulders. A desperate, miserable expression made a mask of his sweaty, dusty face.

Somewhere in one of the shacks, a baby cried.

"You come in here," Monjosa said, his chin down, eyes dark, voice rumbling up from his belly, "and think you can take advantage of my hospitality. Think you can sell me rifles, get big money?"

Hawk struggled futilely in the grip of the two men holding him, who only raised his arms higher and tighter against his back every time he moved. He watched Monjosa's knife-hand moved slowly toward him, the curled tip of the blade level with Hawk's belly.

"I show you what I do to uninvited guests," Monjosa said, stopping two feet in front of Hawk, letting a bizarre half smile pull at the corners of his mustached mouth. "Especially those that can't behave themselves. . . ."

Monjosa's smile transformed instantly into a grimace as he set his left hand on Hawk's shoulder and drew his knife-hand back, holding his arm tight against his side. *"I gut you like a pig, amigo!"*

The knife snapped forward, the blade flashing pink in the dying light. Hawk ground his teeth and squeezed his eyes shut, awaiting the last torment.

"Will-burrrrrrrrrr!"

It was a woman's yell from far away, but in the heavy silence, it penetrated the canyon like a rifle's roar. On the heels of the call, Hawk heard Monjosa give a little, surprised grunt.

He felt a wasp sting of pain just above his belly button. He opened his eyes and glanced down.

Monjosa's blade had stopped with its tip poking through Hawk's vest and his shirt. Hawk felt the blood dribble around the cold steel.

Monjosa had turned his head to look up toward the house that had turned several shades of darker pink since Hawk had first pulled into the canyon. A slender, blond-haired figure stood at the top of the broad stone steps leading up from the yard. She was a hundred yards away, so it was hard to make her out clearly, but his loins responded with an aching burn.

No. It couldn't be her.

As the blonde started down the steps, puffing a long thin cigar, Monjosa pulled the blade away from Hawk's belly and turned toward the casa. He threw up his hands, annoyed. "I'm busy here, damnit!"

Saradee Jones's musical, faintly mocking voice drifted into the canyon with a sound akin to breeze-nudged wind chimes. "Who you got there, Wilbur?"

She was dressed as she always dressed — in men's trail garb, her tan chaps flapping lightly against her delectably curved hips and denim-clad legs, her straight blond hair bouncing on her shoulders. A pearl-gripped Colt jutted from the holster thonged low on her right thigh. As she moved down the steps, her spurs rang faintly, and she removed the cigar from her teeth and blew out a long smoke plume that the light painted salmon.

Hawk's brows furrowed. Christ. Where the hell had she come from? What was she doing here? His loathing of her, and his fear, tempered by a liberal dose of uncontrollable excitement, distracted him from the fact that she had just saved him from a miserable fate.

At least, for now. . . .

"Who do I got? What do you care?" Monjosa said as Saradee came across the yard, rolling her hips and kicking her boots out with her customary expression of supreme insouciance.

She drew deep on her black cheroot and walked straight toward Hawk, who was still held by Monjosa's thugs, and Monjosa himself, who stood in front of Hawk, facing the girl with an expression on his own face like that of a peeved, sheepish schoolboy.

She stopped ten feet away, kicking out her worn brown boots with undershot heels, and tucked her thumbs behind her cartridge belt, thrusting her breasts out and smiling at Hawk with smoldering delight around the cheroot in her teeth.

"You're just in one damn fix after another," she said.

Hawk glanced at Monjosa and grunted against the pain in his wrenched arms and shoulders. "Friend of yours?"

Monjosa was scowling, cutting his eyes suspiciously between Hawk and the beautiful blond border bandita. "I was about to ask the same damn thing!"

24.
"That's One Way
to Cure the Pony Drip"

"Friend?"

Saradee flicked her eyes down across Hawk's broad chest bulging out from his hauled-back shoulders.

"I guess you could call him a friend. And to answer your question, Gideon, yeah, I guess you could call Wilbur a friend." She hiked a shoulder and stuck the cigar between her large, white teeth. "Friend, business partner, *companero* . . . Ain't that right, Wilbur?"

Monjosa stared at Hawk as he held his savage knife-hand straight down by his right thigh. "Gideon?"

"Gideon Hawk," Saradee said. "In some parts he's known as the Rogue Lawman. The folks back East just love him. I hear they can't print the yarns about his so-called exploits out here in the lawless frontier fast enough."

"Rogue Lawman . . ." Ironside grunted,

boxed in by the two Winchesters aimed at his cheeks. "I'll be goddamned."

"Uh, Wilbur," Kid Reno said, a testy cast flickering across the gunrunner's gaze, "I believe you were about to kill the son of a bitch."

"Yeah, I think you were." Saradee turned to Monjosa, shaking strands of her hair back from her face. She pitched her voice an octave lower than before as she favored Hawk with her cool, lilac blues. "You were gonna kill him, Wilbur. Gut him 'like a pig,' I believe is what I heard from the gallery up yonder."

"*Sí,*" Monjosa said, looking wary, skeptical, vaguely puzzled. "I was going to bury my knife in his guts for his insolence and general annoyance until you interrupted me. How you know this gringo, uh? How you know so much about this Rogue Lawman?"

"Hawk and me rode together down a few dusty trails."

Kid Reno scowled at the blond bandita, incredulous. "So much for him — who are you?" His eyes ran from her blue eyes to her worn, undershot boots in a brazen calculation of the girl's incredible figure.

As though she hadn't heard what the gunrunner had said, she glanced at Mon-

292

josa. "But you might have almost killed the wrong man, Wilbur. Hell, a couple months ago I heard Kid Reno roaring drunk and bragging in every cantina and shit-smelly suds hall in Arizona how he'd diddled your girl — *cuckolded* you — and rode away laughing."

Saradee grinned as she stared at Reno, letting cigar smoke trickle out her pretty suntanned nostrils. "Then he was sayin' as how he was takin' back his place as the number one gunrunner in the whole Southwest . . . and when he ran into you again, he was gonna gut you with your own knife-hand, scalp all your men, and drag 'em through Apacheria for the wives of the bronco Apaches to finish off and boil up their private parts in their stew pots."

Kid Reno staggered back, eyes blazing with exasperation. "Jesus Christ, this woman's a crazy liar!"

He glanced at Monjosa, whose glower was now on his former partner.

"Christ, Wilbur, this girl's full of lies! I don't know her from Cleopatra, but I know her kind. She lives to drive wedges between men, mess up their business deals and every kind of damn deal. She gets folks killed."

Reno swung toward Hawk, pointing. "He's the one who came here to kill ya.

Orders from some muckety-muck in the federal government. They want you dead, and they sent his crazy ass to do the dirty work. And, believe you me, he was the one to try it!"

Monjosa's face was mottled red above his neatly sculpted beard, and his eyes were glassy as he stared at Kid Reno. Sadly, he said, "This is true, Kid? You were bragging about that thing . . . uh . . . that thing with Margaretta? And you think . . . you — you green-livered, white-eyed bastard — that you were going to come back here and kill *me?*"

"No. No, Wilbur. She's lyin', for chrissakes."

"Why would she lie?"

"I don't know. Maybe you and her got a game goin' and she's afraid I'll buy too many chips. I don't know. Look at her. You can't trust a woman with tits like that. She's the one you gotta kill. Her and Hawk. They're up to no damn good, I tell ya!"

Monjosa had walked slowly over to Kid Reno, who'd backed against the aimed rifles of three of Monjosa's men. Monjosa extended his left hand. "Give me my bacanora, Dawg."

Desperation sparked in Reno's eyes. He glanced at the rifles behind him, then rolled his gaze around as if searching for a way out of this dire predicament. He let Monjosa take the jug back, and then he said, breathless, "Look, Wilbur, I spoke true. Hawk came here to kill you. Him and Ironside. They threw in together after confiscating the rifles I stole from Fort Bowie. They figured the rifles would get them into your canyon here, and they forced me to come along to show 'em the way."

Saradee said with bemusement, "You know, I can always tell when a man's lyin'."

"Oh?" Monjosa said. "How is that?"

"His eyebrows tighten up, and he sweats. Look at that son of a bitch. His brows are like a goddamn driveshaft, and he's sweatin' like a butcher carvin' meat in a hot shack on the Fourth of July!"

Reno tossed a desperate glance at Monjosa. "Wilbur, you and me were together for nearly two years. How long have you known this . . . this . . . big-bosomed, evil-eyed, caterwauling temptress?"

Saradee barked, "I don't caterwaul, you limp-dicked son of a bitch!"

Monjosa stood two feet in front of Reno, scowling, holding the savage knife-hand down against his cartridge belt. "Miss Saradee and I have known each other for a week, but some people you get to know in a day, while others, it doesn't matter how long you know them. You never really get to know them at all. *¿Comprende?*"

The *contrabandista* shook his head sadly and clucked. "What you say to folks about me — that makes me angry, Kid."

He looked at the men behind Reno. Two set down their rifles and grabbed the gunrunner from behind, jerking his arms back. Reno jerked and grunted. He glanced down at Monjosa's notorious knife, his wide eyes bright with terror.

"Oh, no! Get that goddamn blade away from me, Wilbur. She's lyin', I tell you! She might look like a schoolboy's wet dream, but damnit, I can get you half the rifles and ammunition in the Southwest. You can sell 'em north, south, east, and west. To Apaches, banditos, cattle rustlers, the *goddamn Mexican* federales. . . . We can go down to Monterrey and live like kings!"

Monjosa slid his face up close to Reno's. "You know what I did to Margaretta, Kid? I did to her what I should have done to you when I found you two humping on my kitchen table! It was only our business considerations that kept me from doing so."

"Wilbur, goddamnit, don— !"

Hawk, still being held by two of Monjosa's men, winced when he saw Monjosa's right elbow jerk toward Kid Reno.

Reno yelped. He tried to bend forward but Monjosa's men held him upright. Monjosa's arm twitched and jerked, and then the *contrabandista* bent his knees slightly and lowered his elbow as he angled the knife blade upward. He turned his head slightly, and Hawk saw a smile pull at the *contrabandista*'s mustached mouth, saw the man's tongue flick over his lips.

Bile filled Hawk, and for a moment he saw Andrew Spurlock standing there in Kid Reno's stead, the poor defenseless kid being cored like an apple.

Kid Reno gurgled and sobbed and wheezed, his chin dropping to his chest and his mouth working desperately, eyes nearly popping out of his skull as the razor-edged knife cleaved him all the way to his heart.

Blood and viscera oozed over his pants and dribbled onto the ground between him and Knife-Hand, splattering both men's boots.

Monjosa's men released Reno's arms. The gunrunner dropped to his knees, blinking up at Monjosa. He glanced around the *contrabandista* at Hawk, and then his eyes wobbled around in their sockets. He collapsed over the mound of his own blood and guts, twitched, and lay still.

Monjosa leaned down to wipe the blood from his blade on Reno's coat, then stepped back with an air of grave satisfaction.

"That's right handy," Saradee chuckled, regarding the blade. "Might have to get me one sometime."

"What about these two?" Monjosa shuttled his gaze between Ironside and Hawk and back again. "I kill them, too, now, huh?"

"It's up to you, Wilbur." Saradee dropped her cheroot on the dirt and ground it out with her boot. "Personally, I'd think it would be right handy to have a man like Hawk on your roll."

"You said he's a lawman. I kill lawmen. Everyone I see. Like flies and rats!"

"He's a rogue. Straddles the line." Saradee cut her mocking gaze at Hawk. "A fence sitter. He thinks he's more lawman than desperado, but take it from me — I know the man better than he knows himself — he's an outlaw. One of the most ruthless killers I've ever known. And I've known my share."

Hawk glared at her. His chest felt heavy, and his belly burned. His old revulsion for her hammered him. It bore the sharply filed edge of his physical desire for the crazy witch. The toxic brew made him want to kill her in the worst way possible.

Monjosa was studying Hawk, lifting one side of his mouth. "He don't like you, does he?"

Saradee spread a cool grin. "No, he don't like me, Wilbur. But he's loyal. I'll give him that."

Hawk ground his teeth as he glared at her.

She said, "What do you say you turn these fellas loose, and we all go up to the casa and powwow? I got me a feelin' — knowin' Hawk like I do — that we could have us a lucrative partnership, make a shitload of money off the bronco Injuns in this neck of the desert, then fog the trail for Monterrey. Like the Kid said, we might could live like kings down there."

Monjosa wiped his forehead with his right coat sleeve just up from his knife, leaving a broad smear of Kid Reno's blood. "I don't know. How do I know I can trust them?"

"I'll vouch for Hawk," Saradee said. "And you trust me — don't you, Wilbur?"

She threw an arm around the *contrabandista*'s neck and planted a sweltering kiss on his lips. She stepped into him, groaning softly and mashing her breasts against his chest. After a time, she pulled her head away from his, licking her lips and feeding him her soft, womanly gaze.

"Don't you, Wilbur?"

Monjosa grinned at her. "It couldn't hurt to go up and talk about it, I suppose. I'll look at the guns in the morning, and we can . . . how you say? . . . haggle." Still staring at Saradee, who stood with her arm around his neck, he barked, "Release them! But keep a gun on them until I say otherwise! To the casa. Someone, grab a goat!"

As the men behind Hawk released his arms, he groaned as his shoulders rolled painfully back into place. He stood hunched, trying to work some feeling back into his badly wrenched limbs. A few feet away, Ironside knelt where the other men had left him on his knees, staring up at Hawk skeptically.

"Someone needs to tend our horses," he told Monjosa.

"What? You expect me to do it?" Monjosa looked at several of his men standing around the wagon, peering inside as though to get a look at the guns. "Philipe! Raoul! Tend their horses. Leave the wagon where it is."

He glanced at Hawk and Ironside. He still had a dark, suspicious look, but he growled as he used his knife-hand to carefully scratch the back of his neck, "You'll be joining us for supper in my casa. It is a humble sanctuary, but I like it. Saradee's men are there, enjoying my wine and my *putas*."

"You're a most gracious host, Wilbur," Saradee told him, giving him a peck on his pockmarked cheek.

Monjosa chuckled and goosed her.

She chuckled back at him, and then he turned to the casa and stuck out his elbow. Saradee hooked her arm through it, and they headed for the stairs rising whitely to the darkening house. The girl glanced over her shoulder at Hawk and winked.

Hawk didn't know what her game was. At the moment, he didn't care. It was enough to still be alive, to have Reno dead, and to have another shot at Monjosa.

Ironside must have been thinking of Reno, as well. "That's one way to cure the pony drip," he muttered, glancing back at the dead gunrunner.

"We best get us a weapon," he added as they followed Knife-Hand and Saradee up the steps. "I got us a feelin' we're gonna need to shoot our way out of here, Hawk."

Hawk looked over his shoulder. Two of Monjosa's men were following him and Ironside, staying about five steps behind, casually aiming rifles at their backs. Several more men were moving up the steps behind them. All were armed for bear.

Hawk felt the lightness of his empty holsters.

He turned his head forward, absently glancing at Saradee's perfectly formed rump swaying beneath her wide shell belt.

"What gave you that impression?"

25.
KNIFE-HAND'S
HUMBLE SANCTUARY

"Jesus, Joseph, and Mary," Sergeant Ironside said as he and Hawk gained the top of the steps and stood looking up at Monjosa's casa, which was completely in shade now that the sun had sunk behind the western ridges.

It wasn't that the house was so grand. Likely built long ago by some don who ran a rancho in the canyon, it was a two-story barrack with a large gallery off the bottom floor and a wooden-railed balcony running along the second. What was impressive about the place was the large number of men sitting at tables carelessly arranged around the gallery as well as on the balcony — as hatchet-faced, devil-eyed, and as well armed a gathering of border snakes as Hawk had ever seen in one place.

They were drinking and smoking and laughing, some loudly. There appeared to be white men, black men, half-breeds,

Mexicans, and even some full-blood Apaches, two of whom were playing poker with a couple of white men and a black at a table at the gallery's far right end. The poker players, including Apaches, were smoking cigars.

A handful of bronco Apaches dressed in deerskins and red bandannas slumped on the gallery's floor and along the stone steps leading up to it, swilling from wooden cups and pitchers and laughing drunkenly. One was passed out and leaning against a ristra-trimmed adobe pillar, a Winchester repeater resting across his naked thigh.

At the far left end of the gallery, a couple of *rurales* — Mexican rural policemen far north of their stomping grounds — sat on a couch with a couple of young, gaudily dressed *putas*.

Mandolin chords emanated from inside the casa's broad open doors and open windows, as did the low hum of conversation, with the occasional roar of male or female laughter. The air was rife with the smell of many different types of liquor, tobacco, wood smoke, and the fresh-cut-hay smell of marijuana.

Hawk felt the worm in his belly twitch its tail as he stared up at the house — an obvious perdition teeming with lobos of every stripe. Each one deadlier than the next.

His right hand began to stray automatically toward his cross-draw holster, but he checked the movement. Both his holsters held only air.

A rifle barrel was shoved against Hawk's lower back. The leather-clad Mexican behind him grinned a crooked-toothed grin. "Go on and enjoy yourselves, gringos. Not everyone gets to join Knife-Hand's party!"

He glanced at the rifle-wielding Mex beside him, and both men laughed with menace.

Hawk glanced at Ironside, then crossed the cracked flagstone gallery, the intoxicating, revolting amalgam of smells growing stronger and the din growing louder until Hawk moved inside. It was like entering a Juarez cantina on a busy Saturday night — so loud that Hawk couldn't hear his spurs ching on the flagstones or what Ironside had said to him though the sergeant's mouth had moved and he'd been scowling at Hawk.

The bottom floor of the barrack was one big, smoky room half filled with more desperadoes of the same type as outside. Wall flares had been lit, and the massive hearths on each side of the building, likely a shadowy ruin of its former self, were adance with sparking flames. Tables of every shape

305

were arranged about the quarters, with an elaborate mahogany bar and mirrored back bar against the back wall and fronting a broad stairs curving down from the second story.

As Hawk and Ironside followed Monjosa and Saradee, Monjosa tripped over something. He stopped suddenly, incredulous, and looked down.

At his feet was a corpse — a fresh one judging by the texture of the blood pooled on the flagstones. The dead man, who lay curled on his side as though he were only sleeping, wore a bull-hide charro jacket and bandoliers crossed on his chest. A low-crowned leather sombrero dangled from a chin thong down his back. His arms were crossed over the bloody knife wound in his chest.

Monjosa lifted his head, shouting shrilly in Spanish, "What I tell you hombres about roughhousing in the casa?"

Only a few men turned toward him, frowning befuddledly. A Mexican in a brightly striped serape continued strumming his mandolin back near the bar, a girl standing on a chair behind him and wrapping her arms around his neck, her cheek pressed against the back of his head.

Monjosa looked around, scowling, then

made a chopping motion with his knife arm, as if to exclaim, "What's the use?"

Shaking his head, he gave the dead man a kick, then continued to a long, wooden table with high-backed chairs against a plastered stone wall supported by adobe pillars and that at one time had probably displayed a weathly don's game trophies, maybe a Spanish tapestry and an antique shield or spear of a long-dead conquistador. Now it wore nothing but bullet pocks and long cracks and dried blood stains.

The table, ten feet long, with ten or twelve chairs around it, was the only table in the large room unoccupied, so it must have been Monjosa's traditional perch, left alone by those who knew what was good for them. The bearded *contrabandista* tramped to the head of the table, made a show of pulling out a chair for Saradee, then indicated the chairs to his left for Hawk and Ironside.

Apparently the men who'd followed Hawk and Ironside up the stairs weren't invited. They shouldered their rifles and headed into the smoke clouds to the left, where, amid a clot of men and black-haired women, female groans rose like those of a she-cat in heat, while men whistled, yowled, and stomped the floor.

Hawk didn't like giving his back to any

room, much less one filled with as many cutthroats as this one was, but he had little choice. Glancing around, his gaze caught on Saradee's gang whom Hawk had met at Sweetwater — the sullen-faced Indian girl, April, the oily-eyed gunfighter, Melvin Hansen, and the rat-faced, derby-hatted Seymore Lindley, and about seven others playing stud poker a dozen yards away.

April was ladling a clear liquid into her wooden cup from a pail on the table and smoking a brown-paper cigarette. Melvin Hansen, looking toward Saradee, caught Hawk's eye. He hardened his own and stretched his lips back from the cheroot in his teeth. Then he turned away to toss some coins on the table.

Again, Hawk's hand brushed the holster where he usually kept his Colt as he sank into his chair across from Saradee, to Monjosa's left. Ironside was still on his feet, looking around like a rabbit that had been tossed into a lion's cage. He jerked when a pistol popped at the back of the room.

Hawk swung his head around as the pistol popped a second time.

A big, blond Americano with an eye patch stood at the top of the stairs, holding a *puta* behind him, extending a silver-chased .44 with his other hand. Smoke licked from the pistol's maw as another man, standing about five steps down the stairs, screamed suddenly in Spanish and, clutching his chest, dropped to his knees.

He screamed again and fired his own pistol into the steps between his knees. His own forehead caught the ricochet, and his chin jerked sharply up. He gave a mewling screech before twisting around and tumbling down the stairs, then piling up with a cracking thump at the bottom.

There was barely a letup in the din, and the killing seemed to warrant only a couple of looks from the main drinking hall. A few men laughed, another whooped, and the festivities continued, complete with mandolin strains. The woman sleeping against the mandolin player didn't even lift her head.

Monjosa had twisted around in his chair to view the killing. Scowling, he turned toward Hawk with an expression like that of a father of incorrigible boys.

Throwing up his knife-hand and his real hand in a show of defeat, he reached for the jug already on the table, keeping the jug he'd been carrying on his shoulder close to his chest, as though afraid someone might try to swipe it from him.

"As you can see, Señor Hawk," Monjosa said, just loudly enough to be heard above the din, "despite my precautions, I have been overrun by bad dogs."

Monjosa laughed through his teeth and plucked several cigars from his coat pocket. He extended the hand holding the cigars to Saradee, who leaned forward and took one with a girlish grin of delight. Monjosa leaned forward to extend that hand to Hawk and Ironside, and when each had taken a cigar, Monjosa leaned over to light Saradee's.

Hawk and Ironside lit their own cigars.

Hawk kept glancing cautiously over his shoulder. His back was crawling with dread. He'd given up on the possibility of making it out of here alive, but he had to get his hands on a gun and kill Monjosa before he himself was turned out with the snakes.

Too bad about Ironside. The sergeant was a good man, but he shouldn't have insisted on coming. It wasn't his game.

When Monjosa had his own cigar going, he plucked the cork from the fresh jug with his teeth and tipped the jug to his lips. Two streams of clear liquid ran down the corners of his mouth. Monjosa's eyes acquired a new sheen of drunkenness as he lowered the jug, smacking his lips, and slid it across the table to Saradee.

The girl hooked a finger through the

handle and lifted the jug as easily as any man. Her throat worked. Hawk saw a trickle of the bacanora dribble down from the corner of her rich, ripe mouth. It traced a line down her chin and neck. As it headed for her deep, alluring cleavage beneath the silver cross hanging around her neck by a rawhide thong, Hawk glanced away.

Saradee grinned at him, blue eyes sparking amusingly. She slid the jug across the table to him. "Firewater," she said, poking her cigar between her lips and favoring the Rogue Lawman with a lusty sidelong glance as she drew on it. "Try it. It'll loosen you up a little."

Hawk lifted the jug. Firewater was a good word for the Mexican whiskey that must have been nearly a hundred proof alcohol. Tasting like coal oil modestly flavored with corn squeezings and a liberal dose of strychnine, it burned off a good layer of Hawk's esophagus and sizzled down into his chest before hitting his belly like the molten head of a sledgehammer.

At the same time, cool fingers slithered up over his brain, caressing the tension knots. He cleared his throat and slid the jug to Ironside, who was regarding Monjosa through a slitted eye.

When Ironside had taken a drink and

sleeved the excess panther juice from his brushy mustache, Monjosa crossed his arms on the table — a bizarre arrangement, given the knife hand running down out of his bloodstained, blue sleeve.

"Now, then, Señor Hawk — let us now get down to the beans and tortillas, uh? Tell me why I shouldn't kill you and confiscate your wagon?" He smiled, flicking his eyes quickly to Saradee, who merely blew cigar smoke at the high ceiling on which painted angels had long since faded behind smoke soot.

Hawk thought fast while keeping his eyes emotionless. If his fib wasn't convincing, he might very well be the next man to die here in Knife-Hand's humble sanctuary.

He drew deep on the cigar, then sat back in his chair, ignoring the danger behind him, and hiked a boot on a knee. "You blow my lamp, that'll be all the gold you'll mine from a rich vein." He lifted the hand with the cigar in it to indicate the room. "And it looks like you have enough customers to make several wagonloads feasible. Especially if you're supplying *rurales* like the ones on your gallery, in addition to the Apaches and anyone else with shooting on the brain."

"How you have such a steady supply?"

"None of your business."

Monjosa wrinkled a pockmarked cheek with incredulous anger.

"What Hawk means is," Ironside growled, taking another pull from the jug, obviously warming to the *contrabandista*'s firewater, "we got connections at Bowie. Especially since I'm the quartermaster sergeant in charge of all shipments of all guns and ammo between Forts Bowie, Chihuahua, and Apache, and I know the timetables of all the freight lines including those of the railroad that ships everything into the territory from El Paso. When I don't want guns to make it to me, I inform my men, and they see that they don't. We have our own private depot, my associates and me, and we hold everything there and sort of . . . uh . . . watch the market."

Ironside grinned wolfishly around his cigar. He gestured at the crock jug in the middle of the table. "That's damn good javelina piss. Mind if I have another pull?"

Hawk glanced at Ironside, impressed. He'd have never have been able to come up with a story as convincing as the quartermaster sergeant's. He looked at Monjosa, wondering if the *contrabandista* was equally impressed.

Monjosa stared dully at Ironside from beneath his bushy brows. After a time, he pooched out his lips and nodded, letting a slight grin quirk his mouth corners. "Ahhh. I see why guns have been in such short supply lately. Someone has been stockpiling them." The smile grew, dimpling Monjosa's sweaty, sooty cheeks. "Now I know who."

Ironside grunted a self-satisfied laugh and helped himself to another pull from the jug. Hawk was so relieved, he decided to have another pull himself.

"Hey, quit hoggin' that stuff," Saradee chided him.

Hawk slid the jug across the table to her, and she hiked it to her shoulder.

"Okay," Monjosa growled at Hawk. "How much for the wagonload?"

"I don't know — that's seven cases of rifles, ten rifles a case — and a brass-canistered Gatling gun. How 'bout we say two thousand dollars?" He'd pulled the number out of the air, but a glance at Ironside told him it wasn't out of line.

Saradee lowered the jug and turned to Monjosa, her eyes cool and faintly bemused. "I told you you boys would come to a lucrative understanding."

"Hokay," Monjosa said, the corners of his mouth pulled down. "I will pay you tomorrow. Then you go back and you bring me three. . . ." He held up three dirty, blood-

314

splattered fingers. "Three wagonloads of Winchesters. And I want a Gatling in each one. Hokay?"

Ironside seemed to be enjoying the drama. Likely the bacanora was helping. He hiked a shoulder and raised his hands. "Three wagons, three times the risk. The price will go up two hundred dollars a wagon. But it can be done."

"It can be done, but only if I send an escort of my own wolves. Not that I don't trust you, but . . . well, I don't trust anyone." Monjosa looked at Saradee's breasts and leaned toward them slightly. "Not even friends of those with pretty *chiconas*. Or, maybe I should say . . . especially not friends of those with pretty *chiconas*?"

"Slow down, amigo," Saradee said, hiking a boot onto her chair and resting an elbow on her knee. "It's early yet. You fall down there, you might not get back up again, uh?"

She laughed. And then Monjosa did, as well.

26.
FORBIDDEN FRUIT

The bacanora flowed freely, and Hawk couldn't keep himself from indulging.

The raw Mexican liquor lost its sting after the first few gulps, and then it went down like nectar, swathing Hawk in warm gauze. It did not dull the knife edge of danger he sensed around him in every man and every woman, however.

His senses grew more and more acute. He heard the tinkle of a whore's bracelet from across the room and detected the movement of every hand toward a gun or jutting knife handle. Amid the smell of burning mesquite, sweat, leather, horses, marijuana, and fragrant perfume, he sniffed the spicy, cloying aroma of opium.

The smell grew stronger as the night wore on, and he saw its effect in bloodshot eyes, dreamy smiles, and the lovemaking, if you could call it that, occurring on tabletops and on the stairs angling down from the second story at the back of the room, men bucking against women and grunting while the speculators cheered and the women screeched like love-fevered panthers, their tan Mexican legs flapping like wings.

Now that the business conference was finished, Monjosa called more men over to the table until it was possible for Hawk to slip away, drifting through the crowd. The room swiveled about him as though between him and it lay a smoky filter. Several times female hands grabbed him, tried to pull him down. He jerked away and kept moving though the liquor and, likely, the room's intoxicating vapors made it hard to resist the carnal delights being waved at him.

Fights broke out.

Guns barked outside as well as inside.

There were the clash of knife blades, shrill screams, shrieks, groans, and thundering guffaws. At one point Hawk saw Ironside disappear up the curved stairs, a waifish little whore pulling him along behind her, the sergeant leaning forward to lift the girl's flowered silk skirts above her knees.

Hawk leaned against a cracked plaster wall and ran a hand down his face. Well, there went his partner. The sergeant would be no help if and when Hawk needed it. Hawk would lay low tonight. He was in no condition to start anything. He'd find Ironside in the morning and, before all the revelers stirred from their deep, drugged slumbers, he'd see about assassinating Monjosa and hightailing it with the wagon and the guns.

A big half-breed Apache moved from left to right in front of Hawk, revealing the glowering, oily-eyed face of Melvin Hansen. The gunslick had lost his hat, and a wing of black hair hung in his eyes, near a smudge of purple rouge. Staggering from drink, guns bristling on his hips and from a shoulder holster, and leaning on a red-haired *puta* who seemed in little better condition than Hansen, he moved up in front of Hawk.

He wagged an admonishing finger and glanced over his shoulder toward where Saradee was sitting on a chair back, playing dice at a round table with Monjosa and several others who appeared more interested in the blond desperado than the game.

"Hawk, you lay off, hear?" Hansen drawled. "I got my brand on that wildcat."

"Wildcats are hard to brand," Hawk grunted. "Tonight, she appears Monjosa's trophy."

Hansen glanced again at Saradee, who was smoking another of the *contrabandista*'s good cigars.

"She's playin' the son of a bitch." Hansen

dropped his chin, grinning, his head wobbling on his shoulders. "Not unlike yourself."

"I didn't think she was after that knifehand of his in marriage."

Again, Hansen wagged his finger in Hawk's face. "Keep away from her . . . or I'll gun you down like a tin can off a fence post. Understand?"

Without hesitation, Hawk said he did. Then, when Hansen wheeled, him and the *puta* entangling feet and nearly falling, Hawk reached forward and grabbed a pistol out of one of the man's holsters. He shoved the Colt down in his vest pocket, doubting that anyone in his inebriated state would notice a couple inches of exposed walnut handle, and leaned casually back against the wall.

Hansen and the girl disappeared in the chaotic crowd and wafting, webbing smoke.

Hawk decided to head outside for some fresh air and to get away from the crowd. He seemed to have the run of the place. He'd just started toward the front doors thrown open to the cool, starry night when he suddenly felt a tug on the right side of his vest. He looked in that direction.

Saradee stood a foot away from him. In her hand was the gun Hawk had swiped from Hansen. She jammed the barrel against his ribs, a smoldering smile on her long, full lips. Her breasts swelled.

Hawk's ears warmed. "Now what?"

She waved the gun. "Outside."

Hawk continued through the crowd. None of the loud, liquor-swilling revelers saw the gun Saradee kept shoved up against Hawk's ribs as they walked together, as close as lovers, through the arched front doors.

On the gallery, flares cast sparks into the night. Dark shapes slumped here and there in the shadows, some sitting over card games, others humping like dogs in the shrubs at the edge of the light.

Hawk glanced at Saradee. She jerked her head to the far end of the gallery, and Hawk headed that way. She prodded him out to a small shack surrounded by dead, spindly pepper trees and flanked by an empty stock pen, about sixty yards from the howling casa. An old peon hovel.

"Inside."

Hawk pushed open the unlatched wooden door. Light from the main house spilled over the brush-roofed, earthen-floored shack, showing a simple cot against the far wall, a niche in one wall for a shrine, a saddle on the floor with a saddle blanket and bridle. A rifle leaned against the wall beside the shrine.

Saradee followed Hawk inside and kicked the door closed behind her. For a few seconds, the shack was dark. Then a match flared.

Saradee touched the flame to a candle. She waved out the match, flipped Hansen's gun in the air, caught it by the barrel, and held it out to Hawk. He took it, frowning at her.

She stared at him. Her face was expressionless, but her blue eyes sparked with feral want. She spread her boots a little farther than shoulder-width apart and began unbuttoning her blouse with trembling fingers.

Hawk's temples throbbed. The shack pitched around him. Before he realized what he was doing, he was kicking out of his boots and fairly ripping off his own vest and his shirt.

Lust seared his loins. His brows hooded his flaring green eyes. Dust shone above his lip, glowing molten gold in the candlelight.

How had he ever thought he'd be able to resist her?

When he'd shucked out of his balbriggans and tossed them against the wall, he looked across the room to see Saradee standing against the wall beside the door. She'd propped a plank against the door, locking it. She was naked, regarding him almost warily as she fingered her silver crucifix, holding it up near her neck. She held her other hand down low against the wall.

Her full, cherry-tipped breasts rose and fell heavily.

She smiled at him wistfully, challengingly.

Hawk tramped across the room. She turned away from him suddenly, dropping her chin. Her hair fell down her shoulder to hide the side of her face.

He placed his left hand on her hip, his shaft jutting against her belly, aching with need. With his trembling right hand, he slid her hair back away from her smooth, fine-boned cheek, hooked his fingers beneath her chin, and turned her face toward his.

At first she resisted. Then suddenly she faced him of her own accord, her jaws hard, cheeks flushed, lilac eyes spitting sparks of raw passion.

She dropped her hand down between them, squeezed him. She wrapped her other arm around his neck and kissed him hungrily. He groaned as he ran his hands down her slender back to her flaring hips, spreading his fingers across the ripe globe of her rump.

After a time, he swung her up into his arms. She laughed from deep in her belly

— it was more of a primal yelp or a wail —
as he tossed her onto the cot and mounted
her, grunting.

Later, Hawk pulled his head away from her
breasts and, rising to a sitting position,
dropped his feet to the floor.

His head throbbed dully from the poison
he'd been consuming — both the liquid and
the female kind. He didn't know how long
he and the irresistible blond desperado had
been here, but he was bathed in sweat, and
he felt as though he'd been dragged a mile
through rocks and sage.

His spent loins ached pleasantly.

Outside, the revelry continued — occasional muffled pistol shots, shouts,
screams. Sometimes boots thumped the
ground near the shack, staggering footsteps
that dwindled quickly into the distance.

Hawk glanced over his shoulder at Saradee. She lay propped on an elbow, as
naked as before, her breasts sloping toward
the wool blanket beneath her. She wore an
oblique expression. Strands of her sweat-
damp hair were pasted to her cheeks.

She arched a brow. "Just like old times,
eh, lover?"

Hawk was too spent to protest. Too
flogged to even feel regret for not having

resisted her. If he had it to do over again, he'd likely do it over again.

"What you got going with Knife-Hand?"

She studied him for a moment, as though measuring his intentions. Finally, she hiked a shoulder slightly and said in her catlike purr, "Opium."

"That's what you hauled back from California?"

"*Sí, señor.* Five barrels. Worth two thousand dollars a barrel most places. Here it's worth twice that."

"Congratulations." Hawk lowered his head and ran his hands through his mussed, black hair.

"It would have been a nice deal."

Hawk glanced at her again.

One corner of her pink mouth rose. She kept her catlike blue eyes on Hawk's back as she absently cupped a breast, chafed from Hawk's nuzzling, in her right hand. "The problem with being beautiful and running with wolves is that often a certain wolf gets his fangs into you and doesn't want to let go."

"Monjosa?"

"I'm afraid the man won't settle for a broken heart."

Hawk kept his eyes on her as she moved a finger around on her large aureole. "If I don't stay, he'll try to shoot me. And that will be the end of what could have been a beautiful business arrangement."

"We all have problems." Hawk stood and began dressing.

"You have problems, lover? Tell Saradee. Maybe I can make them right for you?"

Hawk sat down to pull his balbriggans onto his aching body. "I've got to find a way to kill that son of a bitch."

Outside, a man's drunk-thick voice rose: "Sar-a-deeee?"

Hawk lifted his head, pricking his ears. Shambling footsteps grew louder — Monjosa heading toward Saradee's shack.

"Shit, I thought he'd be passed out by now!" she hissed.

"Stay where you are." Hawk quickly pulled his black denims on, then his shirt.

Outside, above the loudening boot scuffs and faint spur chings, Monjosa's voice rose once more: "Saradee — you turn in early tonight, *amiga?* But we have much to celebrate."

He pounded on the door, angrily. "Let me in, you blond bitch, or I break this door down!"

Hawk had stomped into his boots, removing his spurs and dropping them into his vest pockets. Now he pulled his shell belt on, buckled it, and slipped Hansen's Colt from the holster. He glanced at Saradee lying naked on the cot as he sidled up to the door.

Her eyes, so cool before, were pinched with fear. Hawk had never seen fear in the woman's eyes before, and whether it was spawned by the coupling or the liquor, it made him feel a tenderness toward her.

But Monjosa's savage hand would put the fear into the most fearless Mexican wolf.

Hawk rocked the Colt's hammer back and, as he pressed his back to the wall, held the gun above his head.

"Just a minute, killer," Saradee said, staying where she was, head resting against the heel of her hand. "I had a headache and retired early, but hell — let's share a bottle!"

27.
AMBUSCADE

Hawk kicked the plank away from the door. The metal and leather latch clicked. He shifted his weight from foot to foot, squeezing the butt of the Colt in his hand.

The door bolted open and banged against the wall. The bulky figure of Monjosa, wearing a leather hat and what appeared a purple boa around his neck, shuffled into the shack.

"Why you turn in so early, mi . . . ?" Knife-Hand's voice trailed off. He stopped halfway between the open door and the cot on which Saradee lay smiling and nervously flexing her bare, pink feet.

Monjosa gave a raspy, lusty wheeze, and doffed his hat. "Ah, you wait for me, huh, my blond bandita?"

Hawk slammed the barrel of the pistol across the back of Monjosa's head. Knife-Hand groaned and, as his knees buckled, he reached upward with his hands. Hawk wheeled to the open door, extending the cocked Colt out in front of him as he stared out.

No one else was near. Saradee's visitor had come alone. Sixty yards away, beyond low shrubs, rocks, and the dead orange trees, shadows moved in the casa's windows and laughter rose and fell like the roar of ocean waves.

Hawk stepped back, closed the door, then turned back to where Monjosa was down on his hands and knees. The *contrabandista* pressed his hands to his head as he blubbered and stretched his lips back from his teeth, grunting and groaning miserably.

Saradee was off the cot and scrambling around, picking up her strewn clothes and dressing.

"What now, lover? I got a feeling my humble little digs have become a filled powder keg, and the fuse is lit."

Hawk holstered the Colt and grabbed Saradee's coiled riata hanging from her saddle horn. "I'm getting out of here, and he's coming with me."

"Why bring him? Kill the son of a bitch. That's what you came here for, wasn't it?"

Hawk cut a four-foot length off the riata's end. "I'll kill him after I've gotten some leverage out of him. He's the king of this castle. His friends and associates will likely think twice before risking his smelly but valuable hide to get to us." If it were only him here, he'd kill Monjosa now. But he wanted to get the sergeant and Saradee out alive first, since he had a chance at doing so. Especially the sergeant. With Monjosa dead, they'd likely die for sure.

"Christ. Just tie that hand of his up good. You're not going without me." Saradee was buttoning her shirt, her legs still bare, as she watched Hawk trussing the grunting, groaning Monjosa's hands behind his back. "I don't know how many times I've dreamt of that damn blade being driven into my guts since I've been here. How'd you like to have someone nuzzling your neck and pressing a blade tip against your belly button?"

"What about your gang?"

"They've bought chips into Monjosa's game. He's their leader now. If I stay, and he's not here, things'll likely get too hot for me. April's been wanting to slit my throat and take my place with Melvin for weeks now."

"You have something to gag him with?"

She looked around, then tossed her panties to Hawk. "Here."

Hawk glanced at her ironically. "Thanks."

Hawk kicked Monjosa onto his side, the

bloody knife-hand tied snug against the other one behind his back. Monjosa gritted his teeth and blinked his eyes, fighting to remain conscious.

Hawk wadded the girl's lacy panties and shoved them into Knife-Hand's mouth. Ripping his own bandanna from around his neck, he wound it around Monjosa's face, threading it through his mouth.

The man's eyes snapped wide in sudden realization and horror. Hawk kicked him belly down once more, and tied the bandanna tight to the back of the killer's head. He looked at the knife angling down across the man's buttocks. It wasn't in its sheath, with blood crusted on it, but was out of commission for now. If Hawk had time, he'd remove the grisly contraption from the killer's arm, but he had to get him out of here pronto.

Hawk leaned down to snarl into the man's ear. "You make any noise, any sudden moves, and I'll give you a taste of what a blade feels like. Understand?"

Monjosa grunted and arched his back, enraged.

Hawk slammed his head down against the earthen floor. "I asked you a question."

Under his hand, he could feel Monjosa try to nod.

He looked at Saradee. She was stomping into her second boot as she buckled her cartridge belt. Her tapered cheeks were pink with anxiety, but her eyes were cool. "Saddle some horses?"

"Unless we want to walk out of this canyon."

He stood and pulled Knife-Hand to his feet. The man had returned to his senses. In fact, he almost looked sober. His liquid brown eyes rolled around in their sockets. They held on Hawk, glaring.

"We're heading for the corral," he grunted. "Nice and slow, no tricky moves." He glanced at Saradee and tossed his head toward the door. "Lead the way. If you see any trouble, whistle."

The blond bandita had checked to make sure her guns were loaded. Spinning the cylinder of one, she dropped it into its holster, blew out the candle, grabbed her rifle, and opened the door. Hawk held Monjosa back as she looked around.

Beyond her, the casa loomed, shadows still moving behind the windows. A figure slumped against the wall facing the shack, the man's sombrero-clad head tipped over his knees.

"Wait." Saradee pushed past Hawk as he moved back into the shack. She slipped

331

around him again, this time shouldering her saddlebags. "I'm not leaving my gear. Come on."

As she moved out, swinging left, Hawk pushed Monjosa out with his pistol barrel, and they followed Saradee through the dead trees and the spindly shrubs, around the front of the shack. They moved slowly so as not to appear suspicious, for there was no way to be completely out of view of the casa where Hawk, glancing over his shoulder, saw silhouettes milling around the gallery, and the small pinpricks of lit cigarettes and cigars.

"This way," Saradee whispered when they were several yards away from the shack and moving down the slight grade toward the barn and corrals nestled at the base of the canyon's southeast wall.

Starlight shone on the barn's tile roof and on the back of the horses milling in the corral, not far from a large windmill rising against the sky.

Thirty yards from the corral, Saradee stopped suddenly, then swerved behind what appeared a crumbling brick springhouse. Hawk shoved Monjosa toward her, then held his gun to the man's right ear as he turned to Saradee. "What is it?"

She was leaning slightly out from the

springhouse, saddle on her shoulder, rifle in her hand, peering toward the corral. Hawk followed her gaze. A pinprick of umber light smoldered in front of the corral gate. Hawk's eyes made out the figure of a man standing there, leaning against the corral slats, holding a rifle on his shoulder and pulling a quirley down from his mouth. Gray smoke billowed in the darkness around his head.

Stock guard.

Saradee turned to Hawk and whispered, "What should we do?"

Hawk flicked his gaze across her chest. "You're better built than I am."

She gave a caustic chuff, then turned back toward the guard whom she studied for a few seconds before looking at Hawk over her shoulder. "Keep him quiet. I'm going to circle around, come up on him from the other direction. I'll distract him while you come up behind him and put him to sleep."

Hawk cast an anxious glance toward the casa. More figures seemed to be moving around in front of it. Or maybe he could just see more from this angle. Tension pricked the hair under his collar, and his heart beat insistently.

He turned back to Saradee. "Hurry up."

She glanced once more at the corral

guard, then ran off, circling wide, staying as far as she could from the horses, several of whom were staring toward the springhouse and working their noses. When Hawk saw her materialize on the other side of the lean-to shelter at the corral's rear, rifle in her hand, saddle on her shoulder, he turned to Monjosa, whom he'd shoved down onto his knees behind him.

Knife-Hand's eyes met Hawk's. They widened with exasperation. He'd just begun to grunt behind the gag, when Hawk smashed the Colt's barrel across the top of the man's head. It wasn't a hard blow — he'd tried to glance it, as Monjosa would be no insurance for him dead — but Monjosa crumpled at the base of the springhouse, out cold.

Hawk touched a finger to the man's bristly neck, sticky with alcohol sweat, felt a fluttering pulse.

He turned to the corral. Saradee was moving up to the guard, who jerked with a start and turned toward her, lowering his rifle. Saradee stopped and laughed, dropping her saddle and throwing her head back on her shoulders, thrusting out her breasts.

Hawk heard her ask for tobacco. He bolted forward and, running on the balls of his feet, headed to the front of the corral.

The horses snorted, and the guard began to turn away from Saradee. She laughed and wrapped her free arm around his neck, stepping in close to him. A second later, Hawk pushed up behind the man and laid him out cold at the base of the gate.

"What took you so long?"

"I thought I killed your man."

"My man." Saradee cursed.

Hawk holstered the Colt as he cast a glance toward the casa looming at the top of the rise. The men and women outside were vague shadows from this distance, and he doubted any of them were looking this way. Even if some were, they were likely too drunk and distracted to become suspicious.

Hawk pulled Saradee's saddle off her shoulder. "I'll get our horses. Keep an eye on Monjosa."

Saradee headed back to the springhouse, ignoring the now-milling horses. As Hawk went into the corral, he looked again toward the casa.

He'd like to get Sergeant Ironside out of there, but he wouldn't know where to start looking for him. Besides, there was no time. It looked like the sergeant was on his own. But Hawk and Saradee taking off with Monjosa should be enough distraction for the sergeant to slip safely away and hightail it back to Bowie.

Hawk found his own gear piled with other gear in a corner, then roped and saddled his grulla, Saradee's buckskin, and a third mount for Monjosa. He led the horses as quietly as possible out the gate and into the yard. He closed the gate and turned to see Saradee moving toward him, nudging Monjosa, who was awake again but shamble-footed, along ahead of her with her rifle maw.

From somewhere rose the faint ching of a boot spur. Hawk looked toward the casa then turned left. The wagon sat just beyond the windmill, which was between him and the wagon. It was a vague shadow from this distance, facing away from him.

Tension pinched his short hairs.

"Hurry," he rasped out to Saradee heading toward him, stopping occasionally to poke Monjosa ahead with her rifle barrel. She poked him too hard, and he stumbled, dropped to his knees, his groans muffled by the gag.

Hawk hurried over to him, jerked him up by his coat, careful to stay clear of that razor-edged knife angling down across the man's ass. He shoved him against the third horse, a coyote dun, and the horse nickered and sidestepped away from him. Hawk cut

336

the man's hands free and, while Saradee kept her rifle snugged against the man's head, tied his hands in front of him.

Finished, he stepped back away from the bloody knife. "Get up there. I've got the reins in my hand, you son of a bitch. You try to get away, you're finished. *¿Comprende?*"

His chest rising and falling heavily, breathing loudly through his nose, Monjosa reached up and hooked his tied hands around the dun's saddle horn. At the same time, Hawk took the slack out of the reins, holding the horse close to him.

As Saradee stepped into her own saddle, Hawk led the dun around to the grulla's left side, and there was the high whine of a slug screaming off a rock followed by the racketing crash of a near rifle. The dun jumped and nearly tore its reins from Hawk's hand.

He'd been about to toe his stirrup, but now, holding both the dun's and the grulla's reins, he looked toward the casa. Inky, man-shaped silhouettes were spilling down the hill from the house, a couple stumbling down the steps.

Melvin Hansen's voice, pitched with sneering and thick from drink, said, "Where in the hell you two think you're goin'?"

Hansen was moving directly toward Hawk and Saradee, aiming a pistol while half a dozen other men flanked him on both sides. A low murmur rose from the casa, and the mandolin, which Hawk had heard intermittently all night, had fallen silent.

Starlight winked dully off Hansen's revolver and off those that the other men had drawn behind him. Hawk's gut tightened.

"Melvin, you son of a bitch," Saradee growled.

"What the hell kinda double cross is this?" Monjosa was jerking wildly around on the dun's back and grunting and groaning hysterically behind the gag in his mouth.

"Kill her!" A girl's shrill cry rose behind Hansen, and Hawk shuttled his gaze to see a slender figure with flared hips and long black hair extend a pistol from her shoulder and aim it at Saradee. April's voice resounded around the now-silent yard, *"They got Monjosa!"*

Starlight flashed off the Colt in Saradee's fist. The hammer clicked, and the gun roared as Saradee screamed, "Don't *ever* aim a gun at me, bitch!"

April grunted and fired her own pistol into the dust at her feet as her knees buckled. At the same time, Hansen jerked his revolver up, but before he could snap off a shot, something flashed brightly in the left periphery of Hawk's vision and a near-deafening roar filled his ears — the thundering rataplan of a Gatling gun being cranked hard and fast.

Blam-Blam-Blam-Blam-Blam-Blam-Blam!

Hawk dropped to a knee as the .45-caliber rounds hammered into the yard in front of him, blowing up dirt and gravel and plunking into bodies, evoking shrieks and screams and howled curses. Melvin Hansen tossed his gun into the air, and went spinning, throwing up his arms. As he turned away from Hawk, he bought two more rounds in his back that thrust him off his feet and several yards back in the direction of the casa.

A handful of others around Hansen were cut down in that first blast, spinning and flying and yowling, several slugs ricocheting off drawn pistols with angry whines.

There was a pause in the Gatling's thunder.

Through the smokelike dust Hawk saw several men scurrying for cover. Then, as Hawk turned toward the wagon fifty yards off to his left, beyond Saradee's pitching, screaming buckskin, a bright red light flickered at the wagon's rear. The thunder resumed, sending the scurrying Monjosa riders and a couple more of Saradee's gang twisting and turning and crumpling in bullet-riddled heaps.

One man in a steeple-crowned sombrero and flashing spurs almost made it to a jumble of shrubs and rocks at the bottom of the casa's hill, but before he could dive for sanctuary his sharp miserable yelp rose beneath the machine gun's thunderous caterwauling, and he threw his arms up and pitched forward, his tall frame disappearing against the velvet black of the ground.

A screech rose from the wagon as the Gatling's canister swung toward the steps leading down from the casa, and down which several men ran, yelling.

Blam-Blam-Blam-Blam-Blam-Blam-Blam!

As the gun fell silent once more, the men on the steps were left in groaning heaps, some rolling and thumping toward the yard below.

Saradee checked the pitching buckskin down and jerked her head toward the dark wagon, holding her cocked Colt uncertainly above her shoulder. "What in Christ . . . ?"

Hawk swung up onto the grulla's back. "Ironside."

As if in response, the big sergeant's gravelly voice shouted, "This here train's leavin' the station, Hawk!" A loud guffaw and then the raspy "Whoo-whoo!" of a train whistle imitated by a giddy, inebriated cavalry sergeant.

Jerking Monjosa's dun along behind him, Hawk ground his spurs into the grulla's flanks as another bellow rose from the wagon and the heavy freighter bolted forward, rattling and clattering loudly in the dense silence that had fallen in the wake of the Gatling's deadly belching.

He passed Saradee, who was still getting her buckskin back on its leash and staring uncertainly toward the wagon.

"What're you waitin' for?" Hawk yelled as he passed her.

He cast a glance toward the casa to see what looked like a small army of dark stick figures scurrying around in front of the lit windows behind them, and to hear the exasperated shouting and screaming. "The yard's about to be swarming with every man in that house, and I'm guessing they're a mite mad — seein' as how we busted up their party an' all."

"It was a damn good one for a while, too," Saradee said, managing to put some lasciviousness in her voice as she galloped after him.

"Don't flatter yourself, woman."

28.
CARRION CRY

Hawk and Saradee followed the wagon through the canyon, watching their back trail that remained eerily empty and quiet.

After fifteen minutes of hard riding, though the trail was wide and easy to follow with the vibrant starlight and a bright powder-horn moon, Hawk galloped up beside Sergeant Ironside, who was hoorahing the team as though the devil's hounds were nipping at his rear wheels.

"No use blowing out the team," he yelled above the hammering of the crates in the box. "If riders come, we'll polish 'em off with your Gatling gun."

Ironside nodded and checked the team down to a walk. "I reckon you got a point." He lifted a crock jug from the seat beside him. Starlight flashed off his teeth and drunk-shiny eyes. "Drink?"

Hawk kept the grulla even with the driver's box, pulling Monjosa's mount along behind him. The *contrabandista* rode slope-shouldered in frustrated defeat, his hands tied taut to the horn.

As they clomped along, Hawk said, "How in the hell did you get the mules out of the corral without that stock guard spotting you?"

"Ha!" Ironside threw back a sloppy drink then set the jug down beside him again. "He *did* see me. Fact, he *helped* me. I reckon I sorta shamed him — said no hombre worth his beans would leave good equipment out in the weather like that. That wagon and them guns needed to be in a shed. So, he helped me lead the mules over, and I was just done hitching 'em up to the wagon when I heard you smash the poor son of a bitch's head for him."

Hawk looked at him, his upper lip curled.

Ironside chuckled and shrugged as he leaned forward, elbows on his knees. "I told you I was gettin' these guns back to Bowie."

Hawk gave a snort and glanced back at Monjosa. To Ironside, he said, "Pull 'em down for a minute. I want to get him inside the wagon. We'll likely run into lookouts farther down canyon, and I don't want him out in the open."

Monjosa said nothing as Hawk and Ironside wrestled him up into the wagon, taking the late Kid Reno's place among the rifle crates and the Gatling gun that Ironside had unpacked, put together, and mounted on its wood-and-steel tripod. The murdering *contrabandista* didn't say anything in words, that was.

The man's cold, black eyes said plenty.

Finding that the man had loosened one band of rope around his wrists, Hawk retied him — tethering his knife-hand behind and to one of his ankles, and his other wrist to a heavy rifle crate that he couldn't pull more than a few feet around the box. Saradee's gag and Hawk's neckerchief were still knotted tightly around his head.

When Hawk had jumped out of the wagon and put up the tailgate, Ironside continued down the snaking canyon trail, along the stream glistening silver in the moonlight. Hawk stepped into his saddle and turned the horse to look once more along their back trail.

Saradee rode her buckskin up close and gave him a smoky smile.

Her voice was raspy. "This remind you of Mexico?"

"What?"

"This? Shooting and running, all hell breaking loose . . . and the other." She smiled.

"Damn," Hawk said. "I can't remember yesterday, and you expect me to remember Mexico?"

"That's all right, lover," Saradee said, reining her fidgety buckskin around, pointing him down canyon. "We'll have plenty of Mexicos, and I'll bet you'll remember one or two of 'em."

She winked and spurred the buckskin, lunging off after the wagon in a spray of rocks and dust.

Twenty minutes later, riding ahead of the wagon with Saradee now riding behind and keeping an eye on their back trail, Hawk spied movement ahead. He threw up a hand. As Ironside slowed the wagon, Hawk booted the grulla slowly ahead, holding his Henry rifle out along the horse's right wither.

A silhouette took man shape on the left track of the two-track trail, growing slowly as Hawk approached. A massive saguaro stood beside him. He held a rifle across his chest, feet spread a little more than shoulder width apart. Another man stood atop a flat-topped boulder to his right, aiming his own rifle at Hawk from his shoulder.

"*¿Quien va alli?*" said the man on the rock. *Who's there?*

Hawk sensed their tension. They'd likely heard the Gatling's distant hiccupping but had orders to leave the canyon's mouth under no circumstances.

Hawk whipped the Henry up suddenly. The rifle crashed twice — ripping, echoing barks. As the man atop the boulder slumped, grunting, he loosed a wild shot past the wagon, causing the mules to jerk and lunge and Ironside to curse. As the man rolled forward off the boulder, the guard in the trail was punched back into the shrubs where he fell into a cat's-claw mesquite with a crackling thump.

There was a low, liquid sob. Then silence.

Hawk levered a fresh shell into the Henry, and the spent cartridge it replaced made a faint ping as it hit the ground around the grulla's hooves. He shuttled his gaze left and right of the trail.

Spying no more movement, he said, "All right."

"I don't think so." Saradee's voice, clear in the silent night, rose from behind the wagon. "We got riders coming from the casa."

Hawk turned the grulla and heard the rataplan of several horses moving toward him fast. Ironside looked at him.

"Wanna make that cannon sing once

346

more, Sergeant?"

"Be glad to."

Ironside set the wagon's brake, wound the ribbons around it, then scurried back into the box. Hawk heard Monjosa groan sharply as though he'd been stepped on. Ironside chuckled, and there was the squawk of a dry swivel as he adjusted the Gatling gun on its tripod.

Monjosa groaned again, this time in heated protest. Hawk toed the grulla to the back of the wagon. Saradee sat her buckskin to the far side, staring along their back trail.

They waited. The horse thuds grew louder.

They were in a good spot, around a slight bend in the trail. Their pursuers wouldn't see them until it was too late.

Hawk looked at Ironside standing crouched behind the Gatling gun's brass canister, poking his head out the rear flap. Sweat glistened on the sergeant's ruddy, bearded face. He stretched his lips back from his teeth, and they, too, glistened in the star- and moonlight.

Hawk looked ahead as the riders stormed around a jumble of boulders and greasewood and low mesquites, and then the Gatling gun set the night alive with its belching roars.

Ironside whooped and hollered. The .45

slugs whistled and plunked through flesh.

Men yelled. Horses screamed. Smoke wafted.

And when it was all over only one of the dozen or so fallen men moved in the trail, and Ironside finished him with a short, raucous burst.

Two horses fled back the way they'd come, neighing and trailing their reins, one also trailing its rider who'd gotten a boot caught in a stirrup but who flopped silently along the ground, probably dead before he'd left his saddle.

Hawk, Saradee, and Ironside waited, but no other riders came from the direction of Monjosa's casa.

Aside from occasional calls of owls and coyotes, the night was grave quiet. Deciding that no more pursuers were likely, the group at the casa now being so drunk they couldn't see or think straight, and a leaderless pack of curly wolves soon to be in search of other packs and other quarries, Hawk and his *companeros* continued up the trail, soon leaving the canyon mouth for the open desert beyond.

They were heading back the way they'd come when, at ten o'clock the next morning, they stopped amid boulders in a broad, black-graveled basin to rest the animals. Ironside climbed heavily, tenderly down from the driver's box, looking rumpled, peaked, and gaunt in the wake of the long, hard night and a gallon or so of Mexican panther juice.

He looked at Hawk and jerked his thumb toward the wagon's rear. "What about your friend back there?"

Hawk hadn't forgotten about Monjosa. He had orders to kill the man, but there was little need to hurry. Monjosa wasn't going anywhere. Besides, it was never easy to shoot an unarmed man trussed up like a Fourth of July pig.

But then, Knife-Hand was never really unarmed.

Hawk glanced at Saradee. She curled her lip at him.

He rode the grulla over to the back of the wagon and flipped the flap of the pucker back. Monjosa lay inside, in the same ridiculous position Hawk had left him in, looking ragged and sweaty, eyes bright as a trapped bobcat's. Hawk reached in and untied the neckerchief from around the *contrabandista*'s head, then pulled Saradee's panties from the man's mouth.

Monjosa coughed and sucked air and when he found his tongue, he said raspily,

349

pathetically, "Don't kill me."

Saradee, who'd ridden up behind Hawk to peer over his shoulder into the wagon, laughed. "Finish the bastard. I'm gonna ride over to them cottonwoods, see if there's any water."

Hawk didn't look at her gigging the buckskin off through the brush and rocks toward two distant cottonwoods. He kept his eyes on Monjosa.

"Know who sent me?" Hawk slipped Melvin Hansen's Colt from his holster and aimed the gun at Monjosa's face.

The *contrabandista* winced. Fear sparked in his mud-brown eyes.

"The father of a young soldier you gutted."

Monjosa shook his head slightly. "Don't. Please, I beg you. Don't kill me. You're a lawman, no?"

"I'm a lawman," Hawk said. "I'm a father, too. We fathers love our sons. Take it right personal when they're taken from us by privy rats like you."

A hand tapped his knee. He looked down to see Ironside standing beside the grulla, looking up at him, faint beseeching in the sergeant's eyes. "He ain't armed, Hawk. It ain't right to kill him. Let me haul him back to Bowie. He'll stand trial there, and they'll hang him, sure."

Hawk looked at Monjosa. The man hunkered there against the wagon floor like a frightened animal. His eyes were shiny and damp, and his thinning, brown hair hung over his eyes. He was breathing hard and his throat was working as though he couldn't swallow fast enough.

Hawk was torn. His orders were to kill the man. On the other hand, why release him from his torment? Hanging him might be a more fitting way to kick him off.

Hawk opened the wagon's tailgate, then stepped off the grulla into the box, tossing his reins to Ironside. Monjosa jerked back away from Hawk, snapping his eyes wide.

"I'm not gonna kill you." Hawk fished a folding knife from his pocket. "Not yet, anyway."

He cut the ropes binding the *contrabandista* like a frog caught in a cat's cradle, then tied the man's knife-hand behind his back. He kicked him out over the tailgate, and Monjosa hit the ground with a wail and a thump.

Hawk jumped down from the wagon and, grabbing his prisoner by the collar, half dragged and half led him into the brush beside the trail. He gave the man a shove, and Monjosa stumbled and fell between a rock and cholla cactus. He twisted around and rose onto an elbow.

The fear was gone from his eyes, replaced with raw fury, his upper lip curled in a sneer.

"I kill you for that, you bastard," he said softly.

"Take a piss and get back in the wagon. You try to run, I'll back-shoot you."

Hawk stepped back and reached into his shirt pocket for his makings sack. As Monjosa climbed to his feet and the sergeant went about tending his coffee fire, grumbling against the throbbing in his head, Hawk troughed a brown paper between his fingers and sprinkled a line of chopped tobacco along the fold. Ten feet away, muttering angrily, Monjosa heaved himself to his feet one-handed.

Suddenly, as Hawk was about to pull the drawstring on his makings sack closed with his teeth, Monjosa wheeled. The *contrabandista* bolted toward him, snarling and shouting, *"I empty your belly for you, pig!"*

He dropped the knife-hand he'd somehow freed from his back and began to swing it up in an underhanded throwing motion, gritting his teeth. Hawk stumbled back in surprise and, dropping his makings sack and the half-built quirley, threw his hands forward, palms down.

The knife whipped toward his belly in a blur of sun-reflected steel. Hawk caught it three inches in front of the buckle on his cartridge belt, wrapping both his hands around Monjosa's false wrist, just behind the razor-edged blade.

Monjosa grunted and shuffled his boots toward Hawk, his face stretched bizarrely. Wrapping his hands firmly around his attacker's stout, wooden wrist, Hawk stepped into him and managed to get the blade tilted upward, away from his own belly.

Monjosa snarled and cursed. Spittle frothed on his mustached lips, and his nostrils flared. He was as strong as a bulldog. Hawk couldn't shove the knife away from him, but, his strength working against Monjosa's, the knife rose straight up between them, the savagely curved tip moving toward their grimacing faces that were now about seven inches apart.

Behind Hawk, boots thumped. Ironside shouted, "Monjosa!" and there was the ratcheting click of a cocking gun hammer.

"At ease, Sergeant," Hawk ordered through gritted teeth, his shoulders and arms bulging as he wrestled his opponent, who was nearly as tall, broad, and powerful as Hawk himself.

The rising tip angled toward Hawk's chin.

Then Monjosa's. Then back again. It closed to within an inch of Hawk's neck.

Hawk gave a fierce groan as, summoning all his strength to his shoulders, arms, and hands, he got the blade angled away from him and toward Monjosa. His and Monjosa's combined thrust buried the tip of the knife in the underside of his opponent's bristled chin.

Monjosa's eyes widened, terror-glazed. "Ahhh!" he cried, as blood dribbled slowly down from the slit in his chin and down the quivering steel blade — thick as warm molasses and red as a desert sunset.

The slit grew wider as the blade climbed up deeper into Monjosa's neck.

"Tickles, don't it?" Hawk growled, grinning as he watched the blade and the flowing blood.

"*¡La Madre Maria, me pardona!*" Monjosa wailed, begging for mercy.

The cry was clipped as, feeling his opponent's strength wane, Hawk gave one more savage thrust, driving the knife blade up through Monjosa's open mouth and high into his skull. The man's eyes crossed, quivered in their sockets, and acquired an opaque death glaze.

Blood formed at their corners as the blade passed just behind them on its way to the man's brain, and began to slowly run down the side of his face.

Blood flowed down the blade and across Hawk's hands and arms. Monjosa quivered violently, blood gushing from his lips now, as well.

Hawk released the knife handle. Monjosa staggered backward, threw out his arms, and fell on his back. He kicked a little more, flapped his arms, and lay still.

Hawk stared down at the man. So did Ironside, who slowly lowered his pistol.

A voice sounded behind both men: "Hold it, Hawk. Sergeant."

Hawk felt his shoulders twitch with a start. Ironside jerked, as well, and started to turn toward the desert south of the wagon, but the vaguely familiar voice froze him.

"Nope. Don't turn around. Stay right there, just like that. Only I'd like you both to toss them shootin' irons into the brush. Nice and easy. Just so you know, you got seven Arizona Rangers holdin' cocked Winchesters on you."

Hawk stood statue still for a moment. He glanced at Ironside, who'd turned a shade lighter than he'd been before, then, using his thumb and index finger, Hawk slid his Colt from its holster and gave it an underhanded toss into the brush. Ironside gave his own army-issue pistol the same toss.

"Raise those hands," the voice behind them ordered. "Raise 'em high and turn around slow."

Raising their hands shoulder high, Hawk and Ironside turned to see the Indian-dark Ranger Bogarth aiming a Winchester at him and the sergeant from behind a broad saguaro. To both sides of Bogarth, a half dozen more rifles poked out over rocks or boulders or from the small-leafed branches of mesquite shrubs.

Bogarth stepped out from behind the saguaro, aiming his cocked Winchester out from his right side. He had a weed stem stuck between his teeth. His blue eyes nestling deep in dark, deeply lined sockets owned an affability that sharply contrasted the Winchester he kept aimed at Hawk's belly.

As he came forward, by ones and twos the other men — all dressed in dusty trail garb and all wearing Arizona Ranger stars — moved out from their own covers, keeping their Winchesters and, in one case, a Sharps carbine — leveled on Hawk and Ironside. Hawk recognized the other Ranger, the hard-eyed, younger Stanley, who'd sauntered with Bogarth into his, Ironside's, and Kid Reno's camp a few nights back.

"Ain't it a small, damn territory?" Hawk said.

Bogarth regarded him with grim bemusement. "Nah, I reckon it ain't all that small, Hawk. We was expecting you out here, matter of fact."

Ironside said, "Expectin' him?"

"Yeah, we was expectin' him." Stanley smiled coldly as he and the others formed a ragged semi-circle around Hawk and Ironside from about ten feet away.

Hawk narrowed an icy eye. "The only way you could have been *expectin'* me was if you were tipped off I'd be heading here."

Bogarth and the other rangers stared at him. Their ragged hat brims shaded their faces. The warm wind jostled their neckerchiefs and string ties and duster flaps. It lifted a dust devil behind them — rolled it high and dropped it.

Hawk laughed. "Spurlock."

Bogarth only blinked.

"Well," Hawk said, his smile belying the fact that he felt as though he'd been kneed in the groin, "does Gavin want me dead outright, or you supposed to take me in and hang me in front of a crowd?"

Still, Bogarth said nothing. He and the other men, sun-seared and wind-burned lawmen of the desert sands, looked hard and grim. One or two looked vaguely troubled. Mostly, they just looked gloomy.

"Step away, Sergeant," Bogarth said.

Ironside studied him from beneath wary, sun-bleached brows. "What're you gonna do?"

"Step away, Sergeant," Bogarth repeated in the same low, even voice as before.

Ironside glanced at Hawk skeptically. He sighed. "Ah, shit."

Hawk kept his eyes on Bogarth. "It's all right, Sergeant. This cat's been on my back awhile now. Time to get it off."

But he hadn't expected to be double-crossed by the man he respected more than anyone, Gavin Spurlock. He could have done without that grim bit of news.

Ironside walked toward Bogarth, throwing his hands up with beseeching. "Come on, fellas. You're lawmen."

"Step aside, Sergeant," Hawk growled. He was eager for the end now. It couldn't come fast enough.

Ironside continued toward Bogarth. "You can't execute —"

He stopped suddenly as, from the direction of the wagon, a familiar squawk sounded. Bells clanged in Hawk's ears. He turned and saw Saradee's blond, hatted head jutting above the Gatling's brass canister from the end of which the six deadly tubes bristled.

She aimed the gun to Hawk's left. He threw an arm toward the wagon and shouted, "Saradee, *no!*"

The girl's white teeth flashed as she turned the crank.

Smoke and flames burst from the Gatling's maw.

Hawk squeezed his eyes closed and did not open them again until the long, hammering burst from the belching machine gun had died and drifted off into echoes, and the powder smoke wafted, rife with the smell of hot brass and rotten eggs.

He heard the squawk again and opened his eyes.

Saradee swung the back of the gun down so that the maw was raised skyward. Her lilac eyes were dark with grim purpose as she stared back at him and climbed down from the wagon's rear.

Hawk swung his head around, his gut clenched by a giant, invisible fist. Bogarth and the other rangers and Ironside lay twisted and torn, blood glistening in the desert sun.

None of the men moved. They looked as though they'd been flung off a high cliff.

Saradee closed the tailgate and then disappeared around the wagon to return a minute later, leading her buckskin. She tied the horse to the back of the wagon, then, slapping her hands on her thighs, blowing up dust around her, glanced at Hawk. She slid blowing locks of hair from her face.

"We can sell this load in Mexico."

Hawk stared at the dead men.

He felt sick and raw. He felt as though his knees would buckle at any moment, and that his howling torment would suck him into space.

"You didn't think I'd let them badge toters kill you now, did you, lover?"

Hawk's heart was a sledge blow in his ears. His chest heaved. His voice was thin and taut with exasperation. "You should have let them do their jobs, goddamnit. Oh, goddamnit!"

His knees buckled, and he dropped, clenching his fists at his sides.

Saradee frowned at him. "Nah." She smiled. "We got a special bond, you and me."

Hawk swiveled his head toward her. She smiled at him and glanced at the wagon. "Stop lookin' so glum. Hop aboard. We'll stomp with our tails up in Monterrey."

Hawk heard one of the dead men evacuate his bowels.

He said nothing. Tears burned in his eyes. They began to roll down his cheeks.

Saradee made a sour expression. "Had a feelin'." She climbed onto the driver's seat, released the break, and looked back at him. "You got your mind made up?"

Still, Hawk said nothing. He could find no thoughts, no words beneath the roaring in his ears and the searing agony in his soul.

Saradee sighed. "See you around, lover."

She shook the reins over the team and lurched away.

Hawk turned once more to the rangers. He knelt there for a long time, clenching his fists at his sides, sobbing through gritted teeth, not hearing the wagon's rattling fade to silence.

Before him, the powder smoke thinned on the breeze.

In the distance, a raptor sounded the carrion cry.

ABOUT THE AUTHOR

Peter Brandvold was born and raised in North Dakota. Currently a full-time RVer, he writes Westerns under his own name as well as his pen name Frank Leslie as he travels around the West. Send him an e-mail at peterbrandvold@gmail.com.

The employees of Thorndike Press hope you have enjoyed this Large Print book. All our Thorndike, Wheeler, and Kennebec Large Print titles are designed for easy reading, and all our books are made to last. Other Thorndike Press Large Print books are available at your library, through selected bookstores, or directly from us.

For information about titles, please call:
  (800) 223-1244

or visit our Web site at:
  http://gale.cengage.com/thorndike

To share your comments, please write:
  Publisher
  Thorndike Press
  295 Kennedy Memorial Drive
  Waterville, ME 04901